BAD ANALYSIS

BY
COLIN KNIGHT

Also by Colin Knight

Some People Deserve To Die

Public Service

For my wife, children, family and friends: Thanks

"Racism is man's gravest threat to man -
the maximum of hatred for a minimum of reason."

Abraham J. Heschel

One

November 2012, London, England

ANTHONY MITTON-WELLS FLIPPED open the silver cover of the cheap prepaid Alcate 2010G cell phone, scrolled to contacts and pressed enter. One entry, ten numbers, no name, illuminated white on black. Mitton-Wells pressed enter again and waited as an icon spiraled. The preloaded ten-digit number corresponded to a phone in the jacket pocket of Morris Marshall, the leader of the English Defense League. Simon Spencer, the Assistant Deputy Director of MI5 for Domestic Extremism, had provided the phones: One openly given to Mitton-Wells, the other secretly planted in Marshall's pocket.

On Fern Street in Bedford, England, Marshall, in need of a break from the monotony of his pawnshop, dodged left, right and criss-crossed the street then stopped to search for the men who followed him. Unable to detect the men, Marshall smiled and turned to continue his walk. A woman blocked his way. Alert eyes, out of sync with the ear and nose piercings, Doc Martin boots, ripped jeans and worn camouflage jacket, projected calm confidence. Her voice matched her eyes:

"Mr. Marshall, your childish antics to lose your surveillance are placing you in danger. More to the point, you are endangering the lives of the officers assigned to protect you. We don't give a damn about you or your life, but we have a job to do and we don't need you fooling around because you are bored. Now get back to your shop and stay there."

Marshall, a foot taller than the undercover police protection officer, bit back a caustic remark as he realized his spontaneous decision to have fun with his 24-hour protection team had not been a good idea. For three weeks, Marshall, as leader of the racist right wing English Defense League, had been under constant police protection to counter threats against his life from Muslim extremists. At first, Marshall had reveled in the media attention and notoriety that police protection attracted. Now, the reality that 24-hour protection also meant 24-hour observation and surveillance left Marshall frustrated and hemmed in.

As Marshall slunk between elderly people with worn shopping bags and single moms with cheap strollers the left pocket of his black windbreaker vibrated. Instinctively, he reached in and grasped a buzzing object. Protection and surveillance had heightened Marshall's tendency to paranoia and he stared at the unfamiliar cell phone until curiosity overcame suspicion. Marshall thumbed open the silver cover and placed the phone to his ear.

"Mr. Marshall, good afternoon. I hope I haven't called at an inconvenient time?"

Marshall, surprised by the refined voice, held the phone at arm's length.

"Are you there Mr. Marshall?"

Marshall swiveled his head. About fifty feet away, the tough police protection woman watched.

"Mr. Marshall I understand your reluctance to acknowledge an unknown caller on an unknown phone, however, I have a proposition to make that requires both privacy and anonymity. I can hear background noise, so I assume you are listening."

Marshall was not naive. He had used thousands of disposable cell phones to organize and coordinate EDL protest marches and other less public EDL activities. He also knew that cell phone conversations were easy to record and intercept. What he did not know was how someone had put a phone in his pocket. Marshall remained silent and turned his back on his watcher.

"Mr. Marshall, first and most importantly, I want to assure you that I fully support the objectives, motives and tactics of the English Defense League. I, and my associates, have followed the development and growth of your organization since its foundation in 2009. Indeed Mr. Marshall, we have provided you and your organization with many anonymous financial contributions and have worked behind the scenes to encourage positive media coverage of EDL events."

A snort escaped Marshall's mouth at the mention of the anonymous money. Seeking privacy, he ducked in the doorway of a disused shop and continued to listen.

"Mr. Marshall, since November 2011, you have received twelve individual contributions of exactly fifteen thousand pounds. Each contribution, delivered to your pawnshop on Fern street, comprised small denomination bills. I imagine you are skeptical about my claims, which is why each package included an Algis rune, drawn on a plain white sheet of paper. I assume you recall the money Mr. Marshall?"

Marshall did recall the money. Without the money, the EDL would have failed. He also remembered the Algis rune, a vertical line branching at the top in to three smaller lines. In pre-Christian Europe, the rune had meanings related to hunting, honor, nobility and protection. More recently, in the 1930s and 40s, the rune was called the "life rune," from the German lebenrune, and was used as a symbol of the SS's Lebensborn project. To white supremacists, it signified the future of the white race. Marshall had also known that one day, the EDL's anonymous benefactor would call and he 'acknowledged' the question with another un-attributable snort.

"Very good Mr. Marshall; this call was to establish my credibility. Another indicator of my authenticity will arrive in five days. This time the symbol on the paper will be the Tyr rune, the Norse god of war and battle. Please keep the phone available and charged. I will call you again after the fifteenth to discuss my proposal."

The line went dead. Marshall slipped the phone back in his pocket. Today was the tenth. In five days, he would receive fifteen thousand pounds for the cause. Well, thought Marshall, ten thousand for the cause and five thousand for his remuneration. Smiling at the prospect of how many EDL members he could mobilize with ten thousand pounds, Marshall set off with purpose back to his shop.

~

Mitton-Wells closed the phone with a disdainful snap. Marshall was a thug. One of the white lower classes fit only as a supplicant. He felt dirty. Simon had offered to make contact with the EDL leader, but Mitton-Wells had insisted, claiming that no matter how unpleasant contact with Marshall might be he, Mitton-Wells, had to lead from the front.

In truth, Mitton-Wells did not want his friend and fellow conspirator Simon to have direct contact with the EDL. Many times Simon had explained to Mitton-Wells how and why terrorists used compartmentalized intelligence and unlinked cells to protect and manage an operation. However, while Simon emphasized the objective of a clandestine cell structure was to organize a group of people to resist penetration by an opposing organization, Mitton-Wells had been more interested in how the methodology facilitated and supported manipulation, deceit and control.

Compartmentalization that had made a great impression on Mitton-Wells, especially Simon's explanation of how so-called suicide bombers did not know they were committing suicide. According to Simon, the bomber was in reality killed by another person who detonated the bomb when the person carrying the bomb got into position.

Mitton-Wells did not intend to blow up his friend Simon, but he expected that after October 6th their friendship would never be the same.

Two

November 2012, Ottawa, Canada

REALISTIC DIRECTORS OF NATIONAL INTELLIGENCE agencies accept it is impossible to prevent a well-planned terrorist attack. Craig Wilson, a Senior Analyst in Canada's Integrated Terrorism Assessment Centre, agreed. He agreed not because the terrorists were smarter or had more resources than the intelligence agencies, but because Wilson knew the truth. Weak intelligence, personality conflicts, distorted jurisdictions, miscommunication and misaligned resources certainly contributed to successful terrorist attacks but for Wilson the greatest contributor to successful attacks was bad analysis.

Wilson had witnessed bad analysis many times. An eager junior analyst, often a recent university graduate, would forget the basics of critical thinking, connect dots with rigid lines, ignore outlying data, and 'fit' complex and multi-dimensional information into shallow textbook conclusions.

Effusive with his or her accomplishment, the analyst would then promote, repeat and defend their analytical conclusion and become convinced of its correctness. Meanwhile, the slightly higher ups, the midlevel decision makes, who realized the limitations of the newbie, would nod knowingly, ignore the analysis and carry on.

Tepid analysis and loose management created foundational problems that generated deeper systemic problems: first, due to lazy and condescending management, the new analyst developed analytical conclusions with neither rigorous challenge nor experienced guidance. Second, and more damaging, the junior analyst, miffed by the dismissal of his work, would make damned sure the analysis and conclusion were entered into the organizations data base in every conceivable format and with as many key search engine words highlighted in the subject line. The higher ups might ignore the intelligence analysis this time, but it would live forever in the system until the day they realized how brilliant the analysis had actually been.

This 'bad analysis' existing forever in an electronic storage and retrieval system was the real long-term systemic problem. Months, or years later, that original piece of shallow, unchallenged analysis by the newbie analyst would, in part or in whole, creep into other analytical documents and gain by default a measure of undeserved legitimacy and accuracy. An incorrectly identified location, a misspelled name, an incorrect association, a prejudiced interpretation, a wrong translation, all and any of these critical foundational information nodes could compromise the analysis of intelligence data and unintentionally mislead or misdirect the progress of a terrorist investigation.

The threat of bad analysis haunted Wilson and it was the reason why, in late 2004, Wilson joined the then newly created Canadian Integrated Threat Assessment Centre. Renamed the Integrated Terrorism Assessment Centre in June 2011, in an attempt to give the centre a new look and focus, ITAC's role was to conduct integrated analysis of the intent and capability of terrorists to carry out attacks.

Other people's bad analysis frightened Wilson, but the possibility of his own terrified him.

Three

November 2012, London, England

THE CELL PHONE WAS LIGHT and unassuming in Mitton-Wells' hand. He turned the phone over and wondered at the power such a small device could convey. He imagined for a moment the Prime Minister approving a pre-emptive missile strike against some far off Taliban or Al-Qaeda training facility, or perhaps the President of the United States authorizing an attack on Osama Bin Laden. Excited by the image of destruction, Mitton-Wells called the head of the EDL.

"Mr. Marshall, good morning. I see you received my contribution yesterday?"

Marshall, taking the caller literally, jerked his head left and right in search of a person or a camera. Somewhat assured he was alone in the rear of the pawnshop Marshall whispered a soft yes.

"Excellent Mr. Marshall, you speak at last. A little trust will go a long way."

Marshall, suspicion rather than trust tightening his face, spoke tersely.

"Who the fuck you are and what do you want?"

"I would expect Mr. Marshall, that one hundred and thirty-five thousand pounds tax free and non-accountable would purchase a little civility and respect. If you wish to continue receiving my largess, I suggest you keep a civil tongue in your head."

Marshall, appreciative of the others advantage, stifled a profane retort and said.

"You had a proposition?"

"Indeed we do Mr. Marshall. In the near future, I will identify to you one or more EDL members. I will ask you to direct these members to follow the instructions given to them via cell phones provided to them. You are to explain the need for secrecy and obedience."

"Obedience to who?"

Mitton-Wells ignored Marshall and continued.

"You will also explain to them that their actions will make a vital contribution to a larger plan that will rid England of Muslims and other undesirable foreigners. Under no circumstance are they to contact you for any reason and you will explain they will be an isolated cell for security and safety reasons."

More used to giving than receiving orders, Marshall stiffened and clenched the phone. Choking back a desire to tell the caller to fuck off, Marshall adopted an irreverent mocking tone.

"What's this great plan then Mr. Money bags? Are you going to kill them all eh?"

Letting need trump distaste; Mitton-Wells ignored the mockery.

"The plan Mr. Marshall is to make your dreams come true. We shall rid England of all foreigners, especially Muslims. We will purify England and return England to its glory. Our task is to provide jobs, security and health for Englishmen first and Englishmen last. We will rule ourselves Mr. Marshall. You and the EDL have begun the work. Now you need help. Help that only money, position and influence can provide. You are the soldiers and you have fought many battles well and bravely. Now it is time for war

Mr. Marshall, a war that will return England to the English: Forever!"

Marshall's body tensed. His head came up, chest expanded and chin jutted forward as he caught the fever of the oratory.

"Tell me more."

"We want you to accelerate your membership drive Mr. Marshall. We will need many more thousands of honest English men and women ready and willing to march, demonstrate and demand action from the government. We will need many for other activities that I am sure I do not need to spell out for you. Twelve months Mr. Marshall and the time will be ripe. Twelve months, you, and the EDL will rise as the saviors of England. You Mr. Marshall will lead England back to its rightful place and order in the world."

Agitated, Marshall paced. Sweat leaked on palm and forehead. Moisture collected in his eyes. Hope stretched his face and one word expressed his thought.

"How?"

"Two ways Mr. Marshall: Money and action. Beginning next month my contributions will increase to two hundred thousand pounds a month. Enough money, Mr. Marshall for you to recruit, plan, prepare and act."

Marshall's eyes glinted with mischievous intent.

"OK. What about the action, what do you mean?"

"Over the next twelve months you will use the money to organise more protests, more confrontation, and recruit more EDL members. Then an event will occur to move Englishmen off their seats and out of their homes to demand an end to the Muslim and foreign occupation of England. You and the EDL will need to be ready to do their part Mr. Marshall."

Expectancy buffeted the phone static as both men paused to consider the point of no return. Marshall, a risk taker by nature, said.

"If I don't do what you want?"

Based on the personality profile provided by Simon, Mitton-Wells was unsurprised by Marshall's challenge. The file portrayed Marshall as deceitful, dishonest and narcissistic. Drawing of the MI5 summary of how to handle Marshall, Mitton-Wells made things clear.

"Then I and my associates will have misjudged you Mr. Marshall. We will of course expect you to account for the hundreds of thousands of pounds - either in money or in a more permanent way. Do you understand?"

Marshall's jaw muscles quivered and ground his teeth as he digested the threat. A smirk relaxed his jaw and his free hand formed the shape of a gun pointed at the cell phone. Marshall did not intend to follow orders from some unknown maniac and in step with his personality provided the desired meek response to Mitton-Wells.

"Yes, I understand."

Four

April 2013, Ottawa, Canada

BEFORE JOINING ITAC IN 2004, Wilson worked for ten years at the Canadian Security Intelligence Service. There, like many junior analysts, Wilson had accepted without question the mantra that CSIS was the holy grail of Canadian intelligence capabilities and capacity. However, the horror of the September 11 terrorist attacks in the US revealed, with devastating consequences, the fallacy of reliance on exclusive intelligence analysis by a single federal or national 'intelligence' agency.

Guided by the US intelligence failure, ITAC's mandate and focus to pursue and create 'integrated' intelligence analysis was the light that drew Wilson. For Wilson, integrated meant cooperation with other intelligence entities; consideration of other opinions, information and analysis; constructive challenges to developed conclusions and above all a conviction that better integration produced better analysis. Despite evidence that integrated analysis had contributed to the prevention of many terrorist acts, Wilson still believed bad analysis remained a constant threat.

~

Nine years later, in April 2013, Wilson sat in the ITAC boardroom and waited for the welcome speech to begin. Back in 2004, when Wilson joined ITAC, there had been no welcome speech. Instead, like the other fifteen founding members, he began with a desk, a tiny office, a list of suspected terrorists and a list of threats to 'look in to'. There had also been no board-room.

Wilson studied the faces of the latest ITAC recruits as they listened with interest to David Priest, the Director of ITAC, emphasize the importance of ITAC and its role to assure the safety and security of Canada and its institutions. The attentive expressions and relaxed body language of the recruits should have encouraged Wilson. However, the recruits', one thumbing a iPhone, one drawing a face on a coffee cup and another stifling a yawn, conveyed an assured smugness they were joining a club in which they already knew the rules, expectations and rewards. As preferred candidates of Director Priest, they were right.

Unimpressed, Wilson wondered what had gone wrong with ITAC. Sure thought Wilson, in the early days, departments had resisted the creation of ITAC because they feared an erosion or under-minding of their authority or sphere of operations and had been reluctant to provide people to staff the facility.

By 2008, ITAC had established its credentials and had begun to attract capable analysts and management. Then, in May 2011, David Priest became the new Director of ITAC. He replaced Valerie Bertrand, who after running ITAC with apparent success for four years, suddenly announced she was done with intelli-gence and accepted a lateral move to the Department of Canadian Heritage.

Priest's first act as Director had been to announce the renaming of ITAC from the Integrated Threat Assessment Centre to the Integrated Terrorism Assessment Centre. During the following six months, Priest ruthlessly replaced all 'Bertrand era' senior and middle management staff with people of his own. They in turn replaced many Senior Analysts with people from their own departments. Within twelve months, by spring 2012, almost eighty percent of ITAC personnel were new. Priest, a twenty-five year career bureaucrat, had assembled ITAC in his own image: a bureaucratic edifice devoted to the aggrandizement of its chief bureaucrat, David Priest.

Priest's welcome speech and the six new recruits underlined Priest's creation: The speech emphasized the safety of Canada and its institutions rather than Canada and its citizens; the recruits, all known quantities from either Priest's past or the past of his own management appointments, were recruited without competition or announcement: jobs for the boys thought Wilson.

Wilson chastised himself. That wasn't fair. Even though connected to Priest, and or his new management team, the new recruits and those brought in during the past twelve months, were professional, educated and for the most part committed to the task. Indeed several new analysts had shown their analytical skills in 2011 and 2012 when ITAC correctly pieced together signals intercepts and intelligence from informants, along with a smattering of apparently unrelated purchases, to stop a bombing attack on military recruiting stations in the US and Canada.

More recently, the Western Europe Division, which Wilson himself used to lead as a Senior Analyst, had been right about a plan to blow up cargo planes. ITAC had convinced the US and UK intelligence services that the October 2010 bomb plot that hid explosives inside printer cartridges destined for Chicago synagogues had not originated in Yemen as originally thought, but had actually come from an Al-Qaeda offshoot in Syria. An important terrorist connection the public had not been told about and one for which the implications had yet to play out in Washington and London as both countries struggled to focus their Syrian policies.

Wilson had to admit that even though Priest's new order might lean toward the bureaucratic, they had achieved concrete results and he wondered why he had mixed feelings. Was it because he had lost his Western European files or because he mistrusted bureaucracy and believed without constant vigilance even the best intentioned bureaucracy would become like all bureaucracies, self-serving.

Perhaps he didn't like wholesale change. Maybe he worried that policy wonks didn't truly grasp the life and death dimension of their work. Maybe he was a grumpy bastard who liked to work his own way.

~

That Wilson remained an ITAC employee was indicative of the new order. Priest viewed terrorism through an international prism, which allowed the management and senior or favored analysts' abundant international travel. Paradoxically, it also meant Wilson had a job.

Wilson often recalled the day Director Priest had sent for him to explain his reassignment from his Western European terrorism file to a more 'challenging and growing file': Domestic terrorism.

Reassigning him had been a clever move by Priest. No one said Priest wasn't smart. Wilson had been with ITAC since the early days and had established himself as a solid analyst, held in high regard by other Canadian government departments and the departments of the other Five Eyes intelligence community members. By 'offering' Wilson a reassignment to a less visible file, Priest had avoided any unwanted attention and still removed Wilson from the international scene. Especially the plumb Western European file, which Priest assigned to one of his long-time adherents, Roger Cook.

Reassignment had sent Wilson a clear message: you are not wanted. At first, Wilson had been tempted to jump ship and leave ITAC to the bureaucrats until Wilson did what he does best: analysis. He analyzed the current state and likely trends concerning domestic terrorism in North America, Western Europe and the Middle East.

Unsurprisingly, from Wilson's perspective, interest and concern about domestic terrorism was on the rise. Events in Boston, Madrid, Norway, and the UK had pushed homegrown-domestic terrorism, or radicalization as the UK called it, high on the security and intelligence services agenda.

Priest, with his eye tightly pressed up against his international telescope, had misjudged the situation. Wilson might be out of the 'sexy' international terrorist files, but he was far from being stuck at home with the forgetful grandparents.

Five

April 2013, London, England

MITTON-WELLS PEELED A ten-pound note from his gold billfold and passed it through the gap in the clear Perspex that separated him from the taxi driver. A heavily accented "Thanks Guvnor" bounced off Mitton-Wells' back as he stepped out of the cab and up the stone steps of White's gentleman's club.

Mitton-Wells liked the sound of 'Guvnor' delivered by a white Englishman in local cockney slang. Yesterday, distracted with a phone call, he had gotten into a cab for the short ride from his office on Dartmouth Street to White's and had not noticed until too late the cab driver's turban. 'Thanks Guvnor' was much better than an Indian or Pakistani 'whank you wery much sir'.

Originally founded in 1693 at 4 Chesterfield Street, White's gentleman's club moved to thirty-seven St. James Street in 1778. For three hundred and twenty years, White's has provided a congenial refuge for members of the English ruling class and a home for the best of English conservatism. Dukes, Barons, Earls, Viscounts, Princes and kings ate, drank and made merry within the exclusive walls of the club.

British Prime Minister, the Rt. Hon. David Cameron, a member since 1993 before resigning in 2008 in protest at the club's refusal to admit women, continues to visit the club as a guest. Prince Charles is a member and held his bachelor party at the club before he married Lady Diana in 1981. White's, a traditional gentleman's club, retains a "no women" policy, although in 1991 a visit by Queen Elizabeth required an exception to the archaic rule.

Anthony Mitton-Wells joined White's in 1998. His family had graced the club since 1718; five years after Queen Anne bestowed the title of the Duke of Exeter on the Mitton-Wells family. For Mitton-Wells White's was England, or England as he thought it should be; tradition, status, order, honor, and above all, English. Members wore suits not sweaters or T-shirts. Conversation was private, discreet, and never about business. Members did not 'network' and were always gracious to staff.

~

Seated at his favourite table by the window overlooking the bustling street, Mitton-Wells admired Simon Spencer's confident stride to join him. Simon had aged well thought Mitton-Wells. A full sandy hair mop, blue eyes, clear skin, better than most British teeth, though a little crooked on the left and stained tea-yellow. Simon, a life-long and accomplished tennis player was tall and upright with an open angular face, and a slim wiry figure. Sporting a smart Saville Row suit and tie, Simon slumped uncharacteristically into the chair opposite Mitton-Wells. Perspiration rested on flushed cheeks and a hand swept back his thick hair.

"Christ I'm thirsty," said Simon.

"Good day to you to Simon. What's wrong?"

"I'm sorry Anthony. It's those bloody Americans. They are in a tiff because they lost two Muslim brothers from the North Caucasus who had been running around Boston gathering bomb making materials. Now the brothers have disappeared and the Americans are asking us if we have any intelligence or information that might help them. I ask you Anthony, how the hell can the Americans let two men run around making bombs then lose them?"

Mitton-Wells, concerned for his friend, signaled a waiter to fetch chilled water.

"What do the Americans expect you to do Simon?"

Un-slumping, Simon became serious.

"We have our own cadre of ex-Soviet Muslims in the UK. As far as we know, they have never shown any intent to blow anything up. Actually, as I told the Americans, our eastern European Muslims are too busy with identity theft and credit card fraud to get involved in terrorism. Anyhow, the Americans wanted a rush job on any information we might have that could help locate the brothers."

"Did you have anything for them?"

"Unfortunately not, I wish we did. The Boston Marathon is on Monday. Tens of thousands of people will participate and hundreds of thousands will watch the run. The risk is enormous."

Thoughtful, Simon said, "It's too bad we don't have a couple of ready-made Muslim bombers available ourselves. It would save us a lot of work and risk."

"We've been over this before Simon. We don't just need Muslim bombers; we need the right kind of Muslim, the right target and the right time."

"Yes, I know and I agree. However, reducing the risk is always desirable. There is little point in creating a new order if one left to rot in prison."

Mitton-Wells regarded his friend and conspirator with affection and nostalgia. They had met in 1979 at the University of Oxford. They had both been twenty-one. Simon was working through a Bachelor Degree in Classical Studies while he had focused on a degree in history and economics. An easy friendship began with their first handshake as they greeted each other as newly accepted members of the Oxford University Chess Club.

Intellectual compatibility, social status, and similar heritage strengthened their friendship during their Oxford years and now, more than thirty years later, Mitton-Wells winced inside as the prospect of betraying his friend dew closer. Shaking the thought from his mind Mitton-Wells got down to business.

"Simon, have you found the EDL members we need?"

Simon drained his glass of chilled water, pushed an ice cube into a cheek pouch, and said.

"Yes I have. In fact, I have identified a perfect group of malcontents for our purposes. However, I still don't understand why you insist Manchester is a better target than London."

Mitton-Wells suppressed his irritation and resigned himself to repeat a conversation held several times before.

"Manchester has almost three million people."

"London has more than eight million."

"In Manchester, nine percent are Muslim, fifteen percent foreign born, and ten percent Asian. In short Simon, there are a lot of people to blame in Manchester."

"London has a similar demographic Anthony and many more foreigners."

"London is paranoid and highly security conscious Simon. You of all people know that. Manchester might be England's second largest city, but they are not on the same level when it comes to security. We don't want to risk coming to the attention of some over-zealous security minded employee."

"But I know London better Anthony. I have more contacts and more assets I can…"

"Actually, your extensive knowledge of London and your contacts works against you. Too many people know you and that increases the potential for someone to make a connection. Beside, London is an established terrorist target. I want to do the unexpected, or at least the less expected. In addition, there is precedent. You no doubt recall the plan by six Muslims to bomb an English Defense League rally in Dewsbury last year. Well, Dewsbury is just 28 miles from Manchester."

Water and ice clunked and gurgled as Simon re-filled his glass and took a long gulp before responding to Mitton-Wells.

"Well, I have identified the people we need, but it will be more difficult to coordinate things in Manchester than London."

"False modesty does not become you Simon. As the Assistant Deputy Director of MI5 for Domestic Extremism, I am confident you will manage."

"OK, then tell me why soccer and why Manchester United? Why not Lords Cricket ground or the city centre or…?"

"First, Manchester United's stadium holds more than 74,000 people. It is the largest capacity stadium in England outside the national stadium in London. More important, the stadium is used twice a week and is guaranteed to be full at every game."

"Second, and most importantly, Manchester United games are broadcast live throughout the world to hundreds of millions of fans. Media coverage and impact will be instant and global."

"Third, soccer is sacrosanct in UK. Who cares about the death of a few politicians or cricket players? Hit the people where it hurts most."

"Forth and most relevant, soccer fans have a strong core of right-wing anti-immigrant supporters. They are the working class thugs we need to galvanize in to action. When they witness the slaughter they will be filled with hate and violence."

A condescending superior grin distorted Mitton-Wells' face as he imparted his last reason.

"Last of all Simon, I detest soccer. It is a crude game played by vulgar people for an equally vulgar and crude audience."

Silence hung as Simon swilled ice in his glass until Mitton-Wells prodded Simon.

"Now, tell me about these malcontents you have identified for our cause."

"There are three as requested, all live in Manchester and they fit our needs perfectly. Their names are Brad Short, Darren Blackley and Steve Mackenna. Short is stupid, greedy, deceitful and dishonest. Blackley is smart, organized and desperate for some meaning in his life. Mackenna is a violent, frightening opportunist."

"Well, I must say Simon, they are an unsavory bunch. How do you propose we use them?"

"Short is a good candidate to keep an eye on the Muslim at work. Blackley could be the minder while the Muslim is not at work and ensure the Muslim does what we need him to do. Mackenna, while a bit unpredictable, would help kidnap the wife and kid and keep them hidden until were done. He will also be able to convince the Muslim that his family's life depends on his cooperation. I've brought copies of the MI5 files on each of them for you to look at."

"Excellent Simon, now what about the Muslim?"

"No problem there, Manchester has a huge Muslim community and MI5 has files on more than four hundred of them. I reviewed all the files and whittled the list down to three. I prefer Aalim Hussein. Why don't you review the files and we can decide later?"

"Yes I will, but tell me why do you prefer this Aalim character?"

"First, there is no complication of a second wife or multiple children. One wife and one kid are easier to kidnap and keep. More importantly, Aalim Hussein traveled to Egypt in 2008 to visit relatives. He was followed of course and intelligence reports indicate he attended a Mosque controlled by the Muslim Brotherhood. There is no direct evidence he contacted anyone or received any training or funding, but the mere record of his visit will add credibility to his guilt. He also meets the other criteria concerning age, education and appearance."

When Spencer stopped speaking Mitton-Wells picked up and studied the lunch menu. Instead of reading what he already knew by heart he thought about Spencer and the information he had provided. He wanted time to think. Efficient, reliable and perceptive were qualities Simon had in spades. Mitton-Wells had watched these qualities propel his friend steadily through the ranks of Britain's venerable MI5 organization. Spencer, originally recruited by MI5 in 1981 during his last undergraduate year at Oxford University had several years ago, risen to become the Assistant Director of MI5 for Domestic Extremism. Mitton-Wells placed the menu on the table and responded to Simon's expectant expression.

"Thank you Simon. You have done excellent work. I will study the files over the weekend and I am sure I will confirm your recommendations. Now, shall we have lunch?"

"Yes indeed. I am famished, Scotch woodcock and Angel Oysters?"

Six

April 2013, Ottawa, Canada

WILSON SHIFTED IN HIS SEAT as Priest concluded his welcoming remarks. A confident smile assured the gathered disciples of their importance as Priest said he looked forward to working with each one of them. When Priest moved to shake hands with each recruit, Wilson exited the small boardroom and hurried to the sanctity of his office.

Wilson valued his office, not as a status symbol or a retreat from responsibilities, but as a place to organize, evaluate and stretch his mind without concern for who might watch or listen.

Wilson was old fashioned and low tech. White boards, flip charts and chalk boards were Wilson's preferred tools to organize, evaluate and extrapolate information. With thick black markers, Wilson scrawled, in abbreviated and sometimes irreverent alphanumerical symbols, random thoughts on the appropriate board until a synaptic connection caused Wilson to either link the random thoughts with dotted or bold orange lines, or group them with dotted or bold brown lines. Black, orange and brown were Wilson's developmental analysis colors. Red indicated initial conclusions, yellow revised conclusions and green the 'final conclusion' 'at a point in time'.

Wilson always provided analytical conclusions 'at a point in time' arguing information concerning terrorist threats was never static, never complete, and always contextual. In Wilson's experience, a terrorist needed to be convicted and incarcerated, or dead before making a final conclusion concerning his or her intentions.

Until either of those situations, existed, all analytical conclusions could only be valued and used with the understanding and appreciation of the 'point in time' principle.

Supporters, mostly veteran analysts and a few younger converts, referred to it with affection as Wilson's way. Detractors, such as Priest, Cook and many recent ITAC recruits, mocked and called it Wilson's way 'out'.

Wilson's analytical tools may have been low tech and old fashioned, but his coffee system was definitely high tech and ultra-modern. In the corner of his office, atop a sleek stainless steel mini-fridge, a $799 Nespresso Delonghi Latissima Red Passion coffee machine waited in 'energy save mode' for the caress of Wilson's index finger.

Director Priest's welcome speech, scheduled for seven thirty am, so Priest could finish by eight and catch his ten am flight to Washington to attend a Conference on Central American Security had prevented Wilson's morning coffee routine. The conference didn't start until nine am the following day, but Wilson had checked the NBA schedule and confirmed the Toronto Raptors would play the Washington Wizards that night, hence Director Priest's early departure.

Glad to be away from the welcome ritual Wilson stood pilgrim-like before his coffee machine and contemplated his options; espresso, long or cappuccino. Nespresso offered sixteen varieties of coffee concoctions contained in individual plastic and aluminum capsules. Discounting the three decaffeinated options, which Wilson never drank, and the seven he had tried but hadn't enjoyed, Wilson had six to choose from; three 'espressos', one 'origine' and two 'lungos'.

His finger hovered and rotated clockwise over the capsules as craving toyed within him. Decision made, Wilson selected a 'lungo', placed the capsule in the machine and pushed the start button. Fifteen seconds later steam lifted the aroma of a Vilvato Lungo coffee to Wilson's eager nostrils. Hot frothed milk hissed, gurgled and dripped from the high-pressure steamer to sit cloud-like atop the dark brew.

~

Coffee had come late to Wilson's palate. Born in Manchester, England to working class parents and raised on strong sweet tea, coffee had first passed Wilson's lips when, at twenty-four, he lived in Southern Italy and worked as a product-marketing analyst for an American multi-national.

Patient until the last drop of foamed milk left the hot steel spout, Wilson reached for his long anticipated morning coffee. A firm knock on his office door halted the cup's travel from machine to lips. The door opened and Roger Cook, the new Assistant Director responsible for ITAC's Western European intelligence analysis section, entered unbidden.

"Ah Craig, here you are. How was your vacation in England? How are things on the domestic terrorism front?"

Wilson un-paused his coffee cup and used the time to taste, swallow and collect his thoughts. Roger Cook did not give a fig about his vacation to England or the state of domestic terrorism. He wanted Wilson's evaluation on the latest intelligence conclusions the British had provided about British Muslim nationals who had traveled to Nigeria and disappeared.

The file was not new, and Wilson had an opinion. In late 2011, multi-colored arrows and circles had busied several of Wilson's boards and flip charts as he de-constructed the original British intelligence conclusions about British Muslim nationals in Nigeria. Now it seemed new intelligence had surfaced.

Wilson had no problem sharing his opinions with Cook. The problem was Wilson thought Cook was lazy: smart but lazy. Wilson knew Cook had not read all the documentation the British had sent and he had not read ITAC's own internal reports, the ones Wilson had prepared two years earlier. One had to read all the intelligence and supporting data to understand and evaluate the opinions, which is what Wilson always did. Cook wanted a short cut, a definitive answer that he could memorize and produce with confidence and without the need for deep subject knowledge. Cook wanted a bureaucratic answer. Wilson, who didn't play head games, pre-empted Cook and said.

"I reviewed the latest intelligence you sent me on the five British Muslims who disappeared in Nigeria. The British have concluded that the disappearances indicate the Muslims are being given Nigerian identities to enable them to infiltrate other West African nations to radicalize disenfranchised and minority Muslims against western allies and UN agencies. The British conclusion is compelling, but I read the intelligence differently."

Cook grimaced, confirming Wilson's view that Cook wanted the easy answer: agreement with the British. Unable to disengage because Wilson had raised a flag, Cook reluctantly indicated for Wilson to explain.

"I agree with the likely explanation for the disappearances is that the Muslims have indeed been provided with Nigerian identities to give them legitimacy with other African nationals. I also accept the Muslims, as Nigerian citizens, are destined to cross into neighboring West African countries. What I have reservations about is the intention, objective and action these individuals will undertake."

Cook, unable to walk away now Wilson had opened the door to an alternative analytical conclusion, perched himself on a corner of Wilson's small fridge.

"Alright Craig, what do you think these Muslims will do?"

Froth, light and airy, discoloured Wilson's lips and teeth as he pulled the cup from his mouth to answer Cook's question.

"I believe, based on the intelligence data that they intend to attack UNOWA."

Cook, without shame, said.

"UNOWA?"

Cook's ignorance of UNOWA affirmed Wilson's view of Cook's laziness, and with irritation, Wilson enlightened his superior.

"As you know, the UN Office for West Africa, UNOWA, has operated in West Africa since 2001 and has made significant progress on many core UN social, economic and political fronts. In addition, UNOWA has earned legitimacy in Western Africa and among Western allies. UNOWA may be small, but it has been effective. Especially concerning elections and stability in West Africa, which from a radical Muslim perspective, is counterproductive to instilling anti-western, pro-Islamic sentiment among the people."

"Exactly Wilson," said Cook, "that's why the British conclude the intention of the Muslims is radicalization to undermine…"

Wilson held his hand up and said.

"Radicalization takes too long Roger. The intent is to destroy the instrument of Western success and set the region back as much as possible. Crippling UNOWA, probably by killing the majority of UN staff, would significantly contribute to the destabilization of the region."

"Come on Wilson, that's just guess work."

"Not really. There is one clue in the intelligence data to support my conclusion."

Cook, a raised eyebrow and a tight smirk, nodded for Wilson to continue.

"None of the missing five individuals have ever attended a mosque or school identified by intelligence agencies for teaching radicalization methodology."

Cook's eyebrows narrowed and a frown replaced his smirk as he eased off the small fridge and challenged Wilson.

"You mean these five Muslims didn't attend a mosque? I don't believe that Wilson."

Wilson sighed at Cook's quick reaction and thought it typical of how Cook did not really listen. Exasperated, Wilson spelled it out for Cook.

"I didn't say they never attended a mosque Roger. I said there is no intelligence linking them to a mosque or school that trains young Muslims to radicalize disenfranchised, poor, uneducated people. Yes, they are Muslims, yes, they attended mosques, and yes, they are most certainly radicalized. And that's the point and the difference Roger."

Not waiting for Roger to articulate his puzzled expression Wilson continued.

"They are themselves radicalized Muslims, but not Muslims trained to radicalize others. They are not going to Nigeria to commence a long-term strategic radicalization program. Their objective is to destabilize the established organization and retard the progress. British intelligence, which I understand originated from leads from British domestic MI5 anti-terrorism efforts, also suggests, but down plays for some reason, that the five men are seeking explosives and possibly chemical weapons. I believe more emphasis should be given to the possibility of the men obtaining explosives to conduct an attack on UNOWA."

Roger huffed, sighed and squirmed until he acknowledged Wilson's conclusion might have some merit. Then he said.

"Don't take this the wrong way Wilson, but if you can work this out, why didn't the British?"

Wilson regarded his new superior and fought what had recently become an increasingly frequent internal battle. Roger was OK. He had reasonable analytical skills, decent perception and managed people well, yet he continued to miss the point. Setting these discouraging thoughts aside, Wilson responded to Roger's question with another.

"The question isn't why the British didn't reach the same conclusion Roger. I am certain they did. The question is why the British analysis is weighted more toward radicalization activities rather than the possibility of a direct attack on Western interests such as UNOWA?"

"You can't be serious Wilson. Are you suggesting one of our key intelligence allies is holding back intelligence analysis...?"

Wilson placed his cup on his desk.

"Why don't you listen Roger? I did not say the British withheld analysis. I think the analysis is weak or the intelligence about the explosives and chemical weapons is not very strong. Look, in 2011, Boko Haram undertook suicide bombings of police buildings and the UN office in Abuja, the capital of Nigeria. If the British have intelligence from within the UK that British Muslims have traveled to Nigeria to purchase explosives I'm surprised the UK analysis does not make a stronger link to the threat and activities of Boko Haram. If the intelligence is correct, the use of explosives by Boko Haram makes sense. Otherwise, we need to consider that the explosives, and don't forget the mention of chemical weapons, are being obtained by radicalized British Muslims for another reason."

Wilson waited for Cook to ask the obvious questions: had the British done this before? What should we do? Do we confront the British? With no questions forthcoming Wilson hoped Cook might ask the right questions: Why would British intelligence supply incomplete intelligence analysis? What stake did the British have in the region related to UNOWA? Had the other Five Eyes community members, New Zealand, Australia and especially the US, received the same incomplete analysis as Canada? A faint beep from the coffee machine as it switched to 'sleep mode' broke the silence between Cook and Wilson.

"Roger, you and Priest have been very clear that European related intelligence is not my responsibility anymore, but I'm telling you that you might want to ask some follow up questions on the UK report."

Instead of asking questions, obvious or otherwise, Cook moved to the door, smiled and said.

"Wilson, you certainly have a knack for drawing conclusions from information that isn't there. If I follow your logic, the absence of intelligence reports to indicate the British Muslims received specific training to radicalize others means they are not actually capable of radicalizing others. An absence of intelligence can't be used to make a point Craig."

Wilson sighed inwardly. Before Priest took over Wilson had introduced and led an internal ITAC debate about the tensions in the intelligence community over Intuitive versus Structured analysis techniques. The tension wasn't new. A debate among intelligence entities had waxed and waned for many years, especially in the context of the American failure to predict the attack on Pearl Harbour in 1941, and more recently in 2003 when the US and others misjudged Iraq's weapons of mass destruction.

Wilson subscribed to the view that understanding complex transnational issues, such as terrorism, needed alternative analytical approaches that included more than rote organizational processes or a set of analytical tools for analysts to use.

What was needed to compliment, not replace such tools, was an ability and willingness to see what wasn't there and draw 'fact-less' conclusions from which reverse extrapolation could be used to focus analytical efforts, data collection and non-linear validation.

In other words, intuitive deduction based on what is not apparent, or what is missing. Valerie Bertrand, the previous Director of ITAC, had been supportive of Wilson and encouraged him to stretch and challenge the analytical norms that existed in ITAC. That changed when Priest replaced Bertrand and Roger Cook, an appointee of Priest, could not or would not try to stretch. Cook, half way in to the corridor, paused and said.

"Thank you Wilson. Your views are interesting as always. If I get a sense of similar views from anyone else, I will mention your ideas and listen to what others say. I'll get back to you if I need more."

Wilson did not speak. Cook would not be getting back to him.

~

Wilson retrieved his cup from the table and held his lips to the double walled stainless steel camping mug he used to prolong the heat of his coffee. His wife Jane had given him the mug twenty-two years earlier during their first canoe camping trip together. Wilson drained the mug. Disparate thoughts about British intelligence, incomplete analysis, Muslims, Africa and bombs bounced between his ears in need of a synoptic connection. None came. Instead, Wilson's eyes drew his mind to the contents of the two white boards hanging on the wall in front of his desk.

His desk, an unattractive Government issued utilitarian model with drawers that stuck, squatted two feet away from the blue gray wall. Between the desk and the wall well-worn synthetic one-foot, square carpet tiles illustrated Wilson's endless pacing as he populated the white boards with his multi-coloured notes and analytical process. Today though, only six words and one colour occupied the boards. Flights, London, Manchester, Attractions, Threats, Risk. The words, written in black, remained from an analysis Wilson had done before he and his family had taken a two-week visit to England to meet Wilson's family for the first time.

While Wilson had heeded all official Canadian, UK and EU travel warnings he would only act on his own threat risk analysis. By the time he and his family had boarded their Air Canada flight from Ottawa to

Heathrow on Sunday, March 3rd, Wilson had committed his 'point in time' threat risk assessment to memory and ensured he and his family steered clear of any potential danger areas.

To keep his threat analysis as current as possible Wilson had arranged to meet his long-term UK intelligence contact and friend Chris Thornton for lunch in London. Wilson did not tell his wife Jane anything about his threat risk analysis or that he intended to meet with Thornton and indeed keep in touch with him during their vacation.

Wilson had made the mistake of informing Jane about the threat and risk assessment he had done for their family trip to Cancun, Mexico in 2010. Wilson had merely reviewed reports about the fourteen assaults and three deaths involving Canadians in Mexico in 2009 and concluded, through analysis, the chance of falling victim to assault or murder in Mexico was, despite media hype, actually lower than the global average. Jane had not really listened to the positive analytical conclusion and had told Wilson all she could think about during their vacation was the chance of being involved in some incident or other.

After Mexico, Jane told Wilson he worried too much. However, Wilson did not 'worry'. Worry was neither productive nor effective. Wilson analyzed and prepared.

Seven

May 2013, London, England

ASIDE FROM TERSE AND INFREQUENT calls to verify money, demand recruitment numbers, and praise him for the ten-fold increase in EDL activities, Marshall heard little from the unknown EDL supporter and benefactor. In fact, Marshall had begun to suspect his benefactor might be a demented eccentric who would one day forget what he had started. Because the money might end any time, Marshall had skimmed from the donations and built himself a nest egg of over one hundred thousand pounds. Just in case. Marshall was counting his money when a cell phone vibration interrupted his math. The phone was on the table between stacks of ten and twenty pound notes. His hand reached and hovered over the phone, reluctant. The vibrations stopped. Seconds later the vibrations resumed. Marshall picked up the phone.

"Yes."

"Mr. Marshall, May Day. A good time for making summer get-a-way plans eh?"

Startled by reference to a get-a-way plan and the pile of money on the table Marshall spluttered and coughed.

"Yes I suppose so. I stopped believing in the East-er Bunny a long time ago."

"I see. Well Mr. Marshall the time has come for more direct action. I have the names of three EDL members. All belong to the Wythenshaw Division. You are to contact them today and explain what we need from them. Moreover, Mr. Marshall, be certain they understand the vital nature of their role in the forthcoming changes. Also, make sure they understand the importance of obedience. The three we need are Darren Blackley, Brad Short and Steve McKenna."

Marshall fumbled for pen and wrote the names on front of ten-pound note.

"Look. Whoever you are, I'm not certain I know any of these people, but we don't exactly attract the brightest members of the Aryan race. If you need people to do something big or complicated I can't vouch for them. I don't want you putting it on me if they fuck up whatever it is you want them for, I…"

"Mr. Marshall, you can be assured that you will not be held responsible for any shortcomings these men may have. We have done our homework. They have the, how should I put it, the strengths and weaknesses we need. All we need from you, and all they need from you, is an assurance from their leader they are engaged in vital and secret activities sanctioned and supported by the EDL and yourself. We will take care of the motivation, management and direction of the men. Now please contact them today. Time is of the essence my good man."

Marshall placed the phone back amongst his nest egg. He recognized manipulation, coercion and control. He had employed them all habitually for years and he knew he was on the receiving end, big time. Of the three names he had scratched on the ten-pound note one brought a smile to his face. The other two he did not recognize. With over a hundred thousand members,

Marshall did not try to remember them all. Instead, he had a system. Marshall entered the names into his personal database and clicked on each name. No notes or recognizable words accompanied the basic tombstone data for each name. Marshall used letters and numbers and only he knew what they represented. He entered each name and the corresponding code appeared:

Darren Blackley: CMGYTNY(MC)YNO

Brad Short:CMGYTFVY2YWANNNJ

Steve Mackenna:DRSFYTEVY5NNNYF+

Deciphering his code Marshall sat back and tried to recall Blackley and Short. Nothing came to mind. They were two basic EDL members with nothing special or particularly interesting. Unimpressed by Blackley and Short, he wondered how two seemingly bland nobodies could be part of the plans the man on the cell phone had boasted about. No way these two losers could kick rag head Muslims and the rest of them out of England. Marshall chuckled at the thought and said aloud to no one "What a fucking joke."

Marshall's mocking chuckle and expletive changed to a cruel smirk as he interpreted the code for Steve Mackenna. Marshall already knew Mackenna. He didn't really need to consult the code, but being a smug and self-important man, he enjoyed 'reading' a code he had created and one he believed only he understood.

Mackenna and Marshall had first crossed paths on May 25, 2009. Both men were one of five-hundred protesters who marched and rioted in Luton town centre in protest against Al-Muhajiroun Muslim extremists who had disrupted a homecoming parade of British soldiers returning home from a tour of duty in the Helmand province in Afghanistan.

Mackenna, dressed in his trademark business suit, trendy overcoat and carrying an umbrella despite the good weather, had been hard to miss. Mackenna had impressed Marshall as he led a mob of protesters to Bury Park, an area of Luton where many of the town's Asian population live, to inflict brutal beatings on any non-whites that came within range of his fists and boots.

Marshall soon recruited Mackenna into his fledgling EDL organization and used Mackenna to spice up protest marches with extreme violence, sow anti-immigrant sentiments, and participate in a variety of illegal moneymaking activities. Despite Mackenna's usefulness, he came with a price: Mackenna was unpredictable most of the time, but when he had access to drugs, Mackenna became uncontrollable.

Unattractive crease lines formed between Marshall's eyebrows and hairline and his lower lip pushed out as he sucked the upper lip. Concentrate as he could he could find no logic to link the two twats, Blackley and Short, with the maniac Mackenna. What the hell, thought Marshall, was his benefactor planning.

Eight

April 2013, Ottawa, Canada

WITH ROGER COOK GONE, Wilson stared at his white board. Flights, London, Manchester, Attractions, Threats, Risk. The words brought pleasant memories of his recent holiday to England and smothered thoughts of Cook's myopic views about Muslim terrorists in Nigeria.

Wilson had been nervous about visiting his homeland, not for himself, but for his Canadian wife and children, for whom England was a new destination. Wilson and his family had traveled before of course. To the US, Mexico, and various Caribbean resorts, but England was not the Caribbean! Their decision to travel during March school break, when Ottawa was cold and miserable, made sense for Caribbean destinations, but England in March to swap one cold and miserable location for another had made little sense to anyone. Yet they had been fortunate with the weather. Aside from some light snow on the three hundred meter peak of Halligan's Craig in the Lake District of Northern England, and a few blustery rain swept half-days, the weather had been warm and sunny.

One huge bonus of travel to England in March had been the scarcity of tourists. Every attraction they visited, the London Eye, the Tower of London, Madame Tussuads, Horse Guards, Buckingham Palace, the

Royal Albert Museum and many others had been devoid of line-ups. It was the same in Manchester at the War Museum, and in York at the world famous Viking settlement and York Cathedral. Another benefit of off-season travel, but one that he did not share with his wife Jane, was the risk assessment for a terrorist event in the UK.

~

JTAC, the UK Joint Terrorism Analysis Centre, and the MI5 Security Service were responsible for setting the UK threat level. In March 2013, the official threat level had been 'Moderate' for threats from Northern Ireland and 'Substantial' for threats from international terrorism.

UK threat levels, Wilson knew, had remained un-changed since October 2012 largely due to two events: in early 2012, five Muslims unsuccessfully plotted to bomb an English Defense League rally in Dewsbury and in June 2012, police arrested two men on suspicion of involvement in a bomb plot aimed at the London 2012 Summer Olympic Games.

While these two events were serious, Wilson's own assessment of the risk had been much lower due in part to current Signals Intelligence reporting, which Wilson had unfettered access to, that had reported nothing of note concerning the UK or Europe.

More importantly, Wilson had consulted with his long-time friend and fellow terrorism analyst Chris Thornton who represented MI5 in the UK's JTAC. Wilson and Thornton's history stretched back more than fifteen years. In 1998, Wilson had been an interna-tional intelligence analyst with the Canadian Security Intelligence Service and Thornton had been with MI6, the UK agency that supplies Her Majesty's Government with foreign intelligence.

Wilson and Thornton had met in Washington during a meeting of the Five Eyes intelligence sharing community, a decades old multilateral agreement to share signals intelligence. Member countries include Canada, the United Kingdom, the United States, New Zealand and Australia. Face-to-face meeting were frequent and secret.

Wilson and Thornton, both schooled in intelligence gathering techniques and analysis, and then both junior analysts in attendance to primarily 'fetch and carry', had initially circled each other and made clumsy efforts to glean information tidbits from each other. Intelligence people do not become 'fast friends' with anyone and several more Five Eyes meetings, in Australia and the UK, passed before Wilson and Thornton discovered their mutual interest and fixation with the problem and challenge of 'bad analysis'. Later, as their professional and personal relationship developed, they became advocates of complimenting the established Structured Analysis techniques with Intuitive Analysis. Neither was surprised by the other's move to their respective countries joint intelligence assessment centers.

Wilson, before leaving for England, had contacted Thornton to get his unofficial assessment of the terrorist threat level in the UK. As expected, they reached the same conclusion: The threat level was low. The exchange had led to lunch plans and on an unseasonably bright and warm day in mid-March, the two friends met at the Prospect of Whitby public house on Wapping Wall in East London.

~

The Prospect of Whitby, originally called the Devil's Tavern, due to its clientele of smugglers and thieves, had stood since the reign of Henry VIII in 1520 and claimed to be the oldest riverside tavern in England. Unfortunately, five hundred years of experience had produced neither exemplary service, outstanding food nor a distinctive ambiance and it existed as a 'run of the mill' pub that survived in large part because of its river views and old world decor.

The pub was five miles, or a thirty-minute Tube ride, from the UK Joint Terrorism Analysis Centre, located at Thames House on Milbank Street and just far enough and discreet enough for two intelligence analysts to meet unobserved and unheard.

Wilson arrived at the Prospect of Whitby at 12:30 pm, thirty minutes before the appointed time. Wilson and Thornton had used the pub for more than ten years. Except for newer music choices on the ancient duke box, and the addition of over-priced exotic sounding cocktails to the drinks menu, little had changed since Wilson's last visit in 2010. Back in 2010, Wilson had been in London to attend an anti-terrorism conference about how to engage critical infrastructure owners and operators to create a culture of security vigilance and awareness.

Wilson seated himself at a small table for two deep in the pub's interior: a wall behind and to the left, a limited view of the main bar, and directly below a large base-heavy speaker that hung on the wall above his head, all helped obscure Wilson and make it difficult for anyone to eavesdrop. Wilson wasn't a spy, but he couldn't help himself sometimes. Thornton arrived fifteen minutes before their planned one o'clock rendezvous.

~

Chris Thornton, short and wiry, with light brown hair, slopped shoulders and a clean open face that projected a calm serenity, plonked himself down in the chair opposite Wilson and whispered with feigned drama.

"You do realize Craig that sitting alone in a dark corner draws attention. Better to hide in a crowd in plain view."

Wilson leaned in toward Chris and whispered back.

"I'm not hiding Chris, which is why you found me."

Both men laughed and exchanged firm handshakes. They had greeted each other this way for years and Wilson's wife Jane, and Thornton's wife Kathryn, had both rolled their eyes with disbelief when they had learned of their husbands clandestine fantasies.

Thornton sat, wriggled his arms out of his coat, draped the coat over the chair back, and pulled his chair and body in to the table.

"What did you do with Jane and the kids Craig?" said Thornton.

"They have gone to the Kings Place Festival. It's some kind of family-focused play based on the Wimpy Kid show with quizzes, drawing contests and a puppet version of 'Alice in Wonderland'. I managed to beg off and said I preferred a long stroll by the Thames."

"Did Jane believe you?"

Fingering a worn and stained beer mat, Wilson rolled his shoulders and said.

"Maybe, probably not, but she's knows me well enough to believe whatever I'm up to its likely harmless."

"What about Kathryn, Joe and Molly? How are they doing Chris?

Wilson and Thornton caught up with the pedestrian aspects of each other lives and exchanged light banter until they got down to the business of terrorists and risk assessments.

Wilson and Thornton reaffirmed their analysis that the actual threat level in the UK was low. They had long shared the view that maintaining a threat level at 'substantial' for six months was counterproductive: Joe Public was a fickle beast with a short attention span. After six months 'substantial' would become the norm and essentially meaningless. The next level was 'severe'. How was the public supposed to act in response to a change from 'substantial' to 'severe'?

~

The espresso longu Wilson began when Roger Cook had entered his office had long since transferred from his stainless steel cup into his eager mouth and he stared at the empty vessel in his hand. He hadn't moved from in front of the white boards and as his eyes fell away from the boards and the memories of England and his friend Thornton one of Wilson's subconscious synaptic connections bubbled an additional memory to his conscious mind.

During his meeting with Thornton at the Prospect of Whitby, a skinhead, adorned with vulgar tattoos, a Swastika and a Union Jack briefly poked his head into the area where he and Thornton sat. The man had peered in as though searching for someone. Gaunt and menacing, the denim and leather clad figure had lingered a moment and Thornton, alerted by Wilson's stare, had turned to face the man. When Chris turned, the man left.

Wilson had noted how Chris' back and neck tensed when he had turned and how Chris had grimaced and commented on how the man seemed familiar.

"Probably all those mug shots of neo-Nazi right wing thugs you look at Chris. They all look the same after a while. Although I wouldn't expect this pub would hold much attraction for right-wing skin heads."

"Yes, your right Craig, more likely an EDL member keeping any eye on me."

Wilson had wondered what Chris had meant by his comment, but when he had asked his friend, Chris shrugged and said he had been joking. Wilson knew all about the EDL. The English Defense League was a vicious right wing organization dedicated to the removal of all non-whites or non-English people from England. One rarely joked about the EDL.

As Wilson passed the eraser across the white board, he wondered about his friend's offhand comment. Had the EDL really been watching his friend? And if so why?

Nine

July 2013, Ottawa, Canada

SINCE APRIL 15, THE Boston Marathon terrorist bombing had monopolized the attention and resources of the North American and allied security and intelligence communities. The US had engaged international intelligence partners, especially the Five Eyes, in search of information related to the two bombers, Dzhokhar and Tamerlan Tsarnaev. While the media, transient and fickle, had moved on, intelligence and security agencies excavated the minutia of the Tsarnaev's lives in search of other terrorists.

One week later, Operation Smooth, a Canadian and international intelligence agency collaboration, which had been investigating two other would be terrorists since August 2012, reached its climax. On Monday April 23, 2013, police arrested two men, Raed Jaser, 35, of Toronto and Chiheb Esseghaier, 30, of Montreal and charged them with plotting to derail a Canadian passenger train.

By mid-July, while the Canadian public, afraid of their vulnerability and the reality of global jihadism, tried to enjoy their short summer, Canadian intelligence and security agencies continued to eviscerate the lives of their homegrown domestic terrorists.

Wilson, as ITAC's senior analyst for domestic terrorism, had the responsibility to synthesize the intelligence information and data collected by Canadian government departments and agencies and international intelligence partners.

Wilson, reclined on his worn faux leather tilt, swivel and roll chair, crossed the heels of his feet on the edge of his dull grey metal desk and closed his eyes and opened his mind.

In the eight weeks since the arrest of Jaser and Esseghaier, hundreds of pieces of additional information arrived to support the thousands already gathered by Operation Smooth. Reports and analysis had poured into ITAC from Canadian agencies and departments. Major entities such as the Canadian Security Intelligence Service, the Communications Security Establishment, and the Royal Canadian Mounted Police provided ongoing reports and analysis of newly discovered information and evidence.

Lesser known, or less directly engaged entities, such as the Financial Transaction and Reporting Analysis Centre, Citizenship and Immigration Canada and the Department of Foreign Affairs, supplied information concerning money, travel and documents. Foreign partners, INTERPOL, the United Nations Terrorism Centre and the Five Eyes intelligence community supplied external data, views, opinions and highlighted potential international links and connections.

Wilson was under pressure. Director Priest expected Wilson's analytical conclusion in thirty minutes. Not only that, Priest expected a certain conclusion. Wilson uncrossed and crossed his legs and reflected on his original tasking from Director Priest.

"Craig, the arrest of Jaser and Esseghaier has been a great success for ITAC and the government, but as you and I both know the job is only half done. We still need to find out all we

*can about Jaser and Esseghaier and confirm there is no residual
threat from their plan to blow up the train. I want you to do
ITAC's follow-up on Operation Smooth and make sure these
men acted alone. Do you understand?"*

Wilson had understood; he must reach a predeter-
mined conclusion about the two terrorists and endorse
Priest's assertion there would be no future terrorist
threats connected to Jaser and Esseghaier.

Wilson had not been concerned with the first part
of Priest's directive. He had absorbed the information
from Operation Smooth in the days following the arrest
of Jaser and Esseghaier. Since then, Wilson had dissect-
ed and incorporated the information and intelligence
collecting efforts of Canadian and international partners
into his system.

Wilson had organized, evaluated and extrapolated.
He had fully populated his white boards, flip charts and
chalkboards with his black, orange, brown, red and
yellow analytical rainbow. Only green, the herald of a
conclusion was absent.

As the moment of his report to Priest approached,
one thing did concern Wilson: Canada had a four-point
strategy to counter domestic and international terrorism: Prevent, Detect, Deny and Respond. ITAC's
function within the strategy was to detect the activities
of individuals or organizations who may pose a threat.
Based on this role, Wilson provided analytical conclusions 'at a point in time' on the basis, that information
about terrorist threats was never static.

In Wilson's experience the threat posed by a terrorist, and by extension the detect aspect of ITAC's
role, ended when the terrorist was captured. ITAC, as
part of Operation Smooth, had already filled its detec-
tion role concerning Jaser and Esseghaier. Moreover,
ITAC had been right.

Now Director Priest wanted Wilson to provide an analytical prediction about the threat posed by any associations or legacies Jaser and Esseghaier might have had.

"I want to tell the National Security Advisor and the Government that Jaser and Esseghaier were an isolated case and there is no legacy threat to Canada from their activities."

Wilson had tried to counter Priest's directive by pointing out that such a determination was not appropriate until the investigative and prosecution processes were completed.

Wilson was concerned that Priest's intention to pre-empt prosecution's outcome would expose ITAC, and more importantly Canadians, to unnecessary risk.

"Don't worry about that Wilson. You do the analysis and provide me with the right conclusion. You don't seem to appreciate the broader intelligence community environment in Canada."

Wilson did though, and that was the problem. Priest was being the career bureaucrat he was: more concerned with scoring points with ministers and senior bureaucrats than adhering to the core principals of ITAC and the protection of Canadians first.

Wilson sighed, withdrew his feet from the desk and eased himself from recline to stand. He reached for his green marker and wrote his conclusion. Priest would not like it, but Wilson was not about to commit himself to an untenable and indefensible position so that Priest could rush to proclaim the threat was over. Wilson had no doubt that if, or more likely, when the investigative and prosecutorial process ended, and new evidence surfaced, his predictive analysis would be considered premature. Wilson had no illusions Priest would be quick to point the finger and might well be driving the bus under which Wilson would find himself.

Wilson typed up his brief two-sentence conclusion on a plain document and placed it in a beige folder with red 'Secret' letters across the front and back. Wilson's appointment was in three minutes at five forty-five pm. With folder tucked under his arm, Wilson exited his sanctuary and headed to Director Priest's top floor office.

A large open concept area lay between Wilson's office and the elevator that led from the second floor to the fifth floor where Priest's office commanded a panoramic view of Ottawa's Green Belt area. About fifteen cubicles occupied the open area, each adorned with pictures, posters, books, clothing and personal knickknacks that spoke to the personalities and habits of each cubicle's occupant.

The cubicles were empty. Unless there was an emergency, Friday afternoon in high summer was not a time to be in the office. The exodus had begun around 4pm when junior analysts, living for the day, disappeared quietly and without fanfare. Support staff and clerks followed and by 5pm, dust had begun to settle on abandoned keyboards.

Priest's door stood open and Wilson paused to peer in to the office. Inside, Priest and Cook hunched together over an array of papers and files arranged on Priest's desk. Excited but unintelligible words bounced up off the desk and tumbled toward Wilson. Wilson, certain Priest had forgotten their appointment, or had his attention drawn by a different shiny object, stifled a cough and turned to leave. On the half-turn Priest's high-pitched voice ended Wilson's escape.

"Ah Craig come in."

Priest and Cook's eager eyes and active body language signaled enthusiasm and Wilson, unsure if he had come to the right meeting, faltered until Priest said.

"Craig, you have your summary of Operation Smooth?"

Reassured, Wilson handed Priest the folder and ran through the words in his mind as Priest read them.

"While incarcerated and unable to communicate, and based on information available as at July 31 2013, Messrs Jaser and Esseghaier present no physical or discernible threat to Canadian domestic or international interests. However, the possibility of the existence of undiscovered accomplices, or nascent sympathizers, cannot be determined or discounted."

Priest read the terse conclusion and Wilson braced for the expected rebuke and confrontation. Instead, Priest surprised Wilson and said.

"Excellent Wilson, exactly what we need. What do you think Roger?" said Priest as he passed the paper to Cook.

While Cook, a deliberate reader, worked his way through the two short sentences, Wilson stretched his eyes to capture a few phrases from the documents strewn across, and upside down, on Priest's desk.

"Yes, agreed Cook, quality analysis as always. Thank you Wilson."

Priest handed the paper back to Wilson.

"Please have this formalized in a briefing note Wilson. I think we can close the file on this for now eh?"

Wilson backed out of Priest's office and watched as Priest and Cook drew together around the documents on the desk, Wilson and train terrorists dismissed and forgotten.

Past the deserted cubicles and safe inside his sanctuary, Wilson exhaled a pent up gasp of irritated frustration and chastised himself for not predicting the outcome of his tasking by Director Priest. Two months Wilson had worked to meet the illogical demands of

Priest to produce a premature and predictive conclusion. He should have known. Two months was too long for Priest to maintain his interest and attention on one issue.

The documents Wilson had briefly observed on Priest's desk showed Priest had indeed moved on to another shiny object: An invitation for ITAC to present their views on intelligence gathering and priorities to the Cabinet Committee on National Security. Priest, a career bureaucrat, would not allow an analysis of an actual terrorist event distract him from spending weeks of time and resources to produce a presentation for ministers.

Wilson hoped that Jaser and Esseghaier did not have unidentified accomplices and that Priest's decision to 'close the file' would not endanger more lives.

Ten

May 2013, Manchester, England

DARREN BLACKLEY SAT, DRANK, smoked, brooded and waited. It had been three days since Marshall, the head of the EDL called to tell Darren he would be part of a master plan to rid England of foreigners. Everything, said Marshall, was secret and someone would contact Darren on a cell phone that would be provided to him.

"You must do everything and anything they tell you. Don't ask questions and don't fuck up. Also, you must never to contact me."

Bullshit thought Darren to the stale air of his squalid one room flat in rough end of Wythenshaw on the outskirts of Manchester. Someone was messing with him. Yet, Darren, purposeless and broke, wanted the call to be true and had, despite instructions, tried to contact Marshall to verify the call. No one responded.

Tired, out of cigarettes and angry, Darren reached for his coat. A faint old fashioned 'bring' stopped Darren mid sleeve and he followed the sound to his gym bag. Puzzled, Darren opened the bag. Inside, a silver cell phone vibrated as it rang. The phone wasn't his. The ring stopped, then rang again. This time, thinking of the call three days ago from Marshall, Darren answered and his life changed forever.

"Darren Blackley?"

"Yeah, who is it?"

"My name isn't important. You received your instructions from Mr. Marshall?"

"What, yeah, but I don't know…"

"Darren. Please stop talking and listen. You are an intelligent and talented man Darren. We know you had a difficult start to life with your father."

"What the fuck do you know about my dad? Who the hell are you?"

"We know he was a drunk. That he beat you, your mother and your sisters. We also know he 'disappeared' without a trace."

"Yeah, so what, everyone knows he was a piss head and left one day on a binge and never came back. What you trying to say?"

"I'm not saying anything Darren. I am merely pointing out that we know a little about your background. More importantly though, we know how you feel about foreigners, especially Muslims. We know you are an EDL member and you have participated in many marches and protests."

"You think I'm some kind of Muppet or somethin'. You don't know nothin' about me. What do you want?"

"What I want Darren is to give you an opportunity to make things right. To punish those who hurt you. To get back at the ones who ruined your life. We know how you feel about certain persons and why you joined the EDL. We are also disappointed with the lack of success and believe more needs to be done. The longer we wait the stronger the Muslims and foreigners get. The more of them there are. Action is needed Darren, action to force the foreigners out of England.

That's what we have for you Darren. We can offer you a chance to be part of something that will move every Englishmen and women to act. A chance to be one of the few who begin the movement to rid England of the Paki's and rag-heads and all the rest of them you hate Darren. You Darren will be a key part of the plan. No longer will you march, shout, and beat up the odd Muslim. With your help Darren we can destroy them all."

Darren, his face a spasm of hope and disbelief, said.

"Nah man, I don't believe you. What the fuck do you take me for? When I find out who you are I'll..."

The threat did not bother the caller who interrupted calmly and said.

"Darren, I understand you are reluctant to believe what I have told you and that you need proof."

"Yeah, you are dammed right I need proof before I..."

"The proof will come soon Darren. I promise you. Now take some time and think about what I have said. I will call you again in a few days. Keep the phone with you at all times. Do you understand?"

"Yes," said Darren hooked and hopeful.

~

Hate defined Darren Blackley. Calculated and rationalized hate. In October 1993, his father William Blackley, an electrical engineer for twenty-seven years with the Italian company Ferranti, lost his job when the company contracted and took jobs back to Italy for Italians. Without work, and with few prospects in a depressed northern town, William Blackley turned to drink for support and solace. He wasn't the only one. Alcohol, already a staple of Oldham's working class community, tempted hundreds of unemployed men and women who soon spent more time in pubs and bookmakers than at home or the employment center.

The late 1980's and early 1990's had seen a global depression and almost six years elapsed before engineering jobs returned to Oldham. By then Blackley senior had drank himself to alcoholism. A violent alcoholism that fostered fear and hate, destroyed the Blackley family, and laid the foundation for Darren's warped and destructive development.

Initially his father used open-handed slaps to the legs, arms and face. During the first abusive year his mother, home because the kids were school age, absorbed the majority of the slaps. When welfare money replaced his dad's unemployment allowance, his mom found cleaning work and escaped the house as often as the kids did. Left alone, William Blackley drank and pitied himself even more. With less frequent opportunities to lash out his violence grew more physical and the slaps changed to punches, kicks, pushing and toward the end, belts and any object that came to hand. Darren, who looked older and more robust than he actually was, soon drew the attention of his father who had grown tired of beating his mother who had declined into a state of passive and indifferent resistance that didn't satisfy his dad's need to instill fear. Darren was afraid though. He cowered, pleaded, ran, and hid and unintentionally fed his father's need to dominate and hurt. His sisters, spared direct physical abuse, suffered verbal assaults as their father demeaned their worth and battered their self-esteem.

Nurtured by physical violence and psychological pain, hate thrived inside Darren Blackley. He hated his father for the beatings, the abuse and the fear. He hated his mother because she was weak and helpless. He hated his sister's because he never hit them. He hated the world for what it had done to him and he hated everyone else who, complicit through indifference, stood by and watched.

On Christmas Eve 1999, the Blackley family ceased to exist. Darren's mother, finally done with passive indifference, packed her bags while his father drank in the local pub, and took the two youngest children, Ann and Debra, to live with her sister in Newcastle on the East coast. Susan, the oldest sister, who was seventeen and a year younger than Darren was, moved in with Billy Davies, a divorced local man twice her age, who dealt in stolen goods and marijuana.

Darren, alone, waited for his father to come home. While he waited, hatred brewed. Darren, paced, clenched fists acting like pendulum weights on his arms as they swung back and forth with purpose. Then he sat, then stood, and then paced some more. Impatient and angry arms collided with old and faded furniture until hemmed in and claustrophobic Darren seized a chair and smashed it against the cracked mirror that hung above the fireplace. Empowered by his action Darren flung, stomped and hurled furniture and fixtures around the living room until little but kindling and broken glass littered the floor. Darren assaulted the kitchen next. He smashed and broke as objects flew into walls and doors. As the manic rage engulfed Darren, his father, William Blackley, inebriated, stumbled into what was left of his home.

Through his alcoholic haze, the sixth sense of a serial abuser recognized the madness and power in his son's eyes. His time was up. At five forty-five on Christmas Eve 1999, William Blackley and his son switched roles. Abuser became abused. Victim became predator. Six years of hate unleashed itself as Darren hammered merciless blows on his father's alcohol ravaged body. Knuckles cut heedlessly on teeth. Nails tore as fingers ripped hair and clothes. Boots cracked bone, bruised muscle and burst veins. Blood and saliva sprayed, tears flowed and words garbled as facial features mangled and coalesced.

William Blackley survived the beating. For four days, he lived amongst the ruins of the living room and kitchen. Unable to climb the stairs he defecated and urinated where he lay, knelt or stood. Neglected and ignored, William Blackley withered and died alone in his own excrement, with neither compassion nor charity. Darren contemplated his dead father with detached disdain born from hate. Without feelings, he bundled his father's shrunken corpse into an oversized black plastic bag used by builders for home renovation debris and propped the bag in the corner of the hallway next to the trashcan. Two days later, with thanks from a tired garbage collector, Darren heaved the bag into the city garbage truck and watched the compression jaws crush his father's remains and mix them with the city's trash.

Weeks passed before anyone asked about Darren's father and no one questioned Darren's story that his father went out drinking and never came back. Even Darren's sister, who by then had succumbed to the deprivations and dependencies associated with the drugs supplied by Billy Davies, simply shrugged and said good riddance. Eventually, William Blakeley faded from community memory and Darren continued playing soccer and took occasional legal and illegal jobs to pay the rent.

The hate forced on Darren by his father should have been enough for any person, and soccer should have been Darren's escape, but hate wanted more with Darren. Like many boys, Darren kicked a ball the first week he could walk. By five, he could dribble, chip, bob and weave. Through his teen years, to escape the horror of home, Darren attended every available soccer practice at school or with local teams until exhausted, he crept home and hoped to avoid his father's drunken abuse.

Darren's hard work combined well with a natural talent, and as expected by many, the local professional soccer team, Oldham Athletic took notice and recruited Darren for their junior farm team. What Darren might have lacked in skill he made up for with brute determination. While professional soccer could only accommodate so much raw aggression with discipline and training, many expected Darren Blackley would one day wear an Oldham first team shirt.

However, in 1997, two years before Darren killed his father, the self-preservationist actions of a frightened brown-skinned man who refused Darren safety and refuge, ended Darren's professional soccer dreams and planted a seed that would twist Darren's hate into a repugnant, seething racism.

Eleven

May 2013, Manchester, England

BRAD SHORT WAS A BASTARD. Not an illegitimate bastard because his birth certificate named a father, but a vernacular bastard, as in 'a right bastard'. Nice on the outside, mean on the inside, and marked by a deliberate deceptiveness where he pretended one set of feelings and acted under the influence and interest of another. His god was money, easy money. When Darren Blackley asked Brad if he was interested in an easy job that paid well and had a little unexpected bonus Short had been eager for the details.

"Like whot then?"

Blackley sipped the froth of his second pint of Boddingtons Bitter as he contemplated Brad Short. He did not like Short. He was a simpleton. A nasty little shit who really would sell his own sister if he had one. The Boddingtons, smooth and cool, slid down his throat satisfying a thirst that had grown all day since he had gotten an early morning text message demanding a progress report on his efforts to contact Brad and recruit him for the job.

Short rolled a wet toothpick between grey teeth and cracked lips then turned it sideways in his mouth and sucked until the two points stretched over his sallow cheeks. Short expanded his cheeks parted his lips and teeth and with his tongue pushed the tooth pick back to resume a left to right roll. A dirty habit for a dirty man thought Blackley as he masked disdain with a long swallow.

"No night work, just straight days, Wednesday to Sunday."

The toothpick stopped mid roll, parked in the gap between Short's two upper front teeth.

"Wednesday to Sunday? Nah, man, that's bobbins. I'm not working the weekend."

"Don't worry Brad. The weekend work is only until end of May when the soccer season ends. During the summer it's Monday to Friday 8 to 4."

"What's the job got to do with the soccer season?"

"The job is at Manchester United's stadium."

"Whoa. Man United. What the fuck, you hate Man U! What you got to do with Man U then eh?"

"Don't bother your head about how much I hate Man U. Do you want a cushy job that pays a shit load of money or not. I can get someone else."

'Alright, alright, keep ya shirt on. What the fuck do you want me to do then?"

"Janitor."

"Janitor; like cleaning and shit?"

"Yes, you know sweep, mop, empty the bins and clean the loos."

"Nah man. That's mingin. I'm not cleaning other peoples' shit. Fuck that. I don't need money that bad."

Typical thought Blackley. Any hint of actual work and Short ran for the hills. Blackley recalled how he and Short had first met in January 2010. Both men had been new recruits to the EDL and were attending their first meeting at the EDL Division in Wythenshaw, a small town eight miles from Manchester proper. Even then, Short had dodged the request from the EDL Division leader for help in making placards for an upcoming protest by claiming he had carpel tunnel syndrome in both wrists because of a congenital predisposition disorder.

At the time, Blackley had been surprised Short could pronounce the words syndrome, congenital and predisposition and doubted very much if he knew what the words actually meant. Fortunately for Short the EDL Division leader, who himself displayed a vocabulary light on multisyllabic words, simply nodded as though congenital predispositions were an everyday discussion among EDL members.

"You'll get good coin Brad."

"Oh yeah, how's that then? Hey, you don't want me to steal something do you, you sneaky bastard? Is that what this is about? You want me to take something that will hurt Man U?"

Blackley hadn't thought about that. What a good idea. Maybe he could take advantage of the bigger plan and use Short for his own purposes.

"Maybe you could do a little something for me while you are inside Man U, but that's not what I am really after Brad. This is much, much bigger. We are gonna get rid of all the foreigners Brad. We have a plan to get rid of the rag-heads, Pakis, jungle bunnies, and all the other trash that have ruined England and taken all the jobs. It's gonna be a fucking war Brad. I mean it. This is the big one. No more just marching and waving banners. "

Brad, toothpick racing side to side, soon caught the racist fever, leaned in and asked.

"Whot you blathering about man? What the fuck does cleaning the loos at Man U. got to do with getting all the rag heads out of England?"

"Never mind that. You will get five hundred quid a week. All you have to do is to work hard, keep out of trouble and no goin off about blacks, rag heads, Pakis and the rest of them."

"You're kidding me. I hate them all. If I could, I would just kill the lot of them you know that and… "

"You don't have to love them for Christ's sake. Just pretend you have no problem with them that's all."

"Why Darren, what's it all about? What the fuck are you up to?"

"Look Brad, this is a big, and I mean a real big EDL plan. I can't tell you all of it right now. You know, for security reasons. The less you know, the better it is."

Darren did not know the whole plan either, but this little shit Brad didn't need to know that. In fact, Darren had no idea what the plan was. All he had so far was the phone calls from Marshall and another person. Since then, money and instructions had arrived in plain envelopes. Recruiting Brad was his first assignment and Darren didn't want to mess it up.

"So, do you want the job or not? It's easy money."

Twelve

August 2013, Ottawa, Canada

JULY AND AUGUST, HIGH summer, is the dead season in Canadian bureaucratic circles. With Parliament closed for summer recess, federal government employees' intent on summer vacation and BBQ season in full swing, many bureaucrats procrastinate, obfuscate and gossip. An exception is the security and intelligence related public service, particularly CSIS, CSE and ITAC. Summer means large crowds, numerous sporting and entertainment events, swollen commuter hubs and the potential for decreased vigilance by front-line security personnel. All of which can combine to induce terrorists to act.

Mitch Donaldson, one of the few surviving analysts from the pre-Priest era and working on the European desk under Roger Cook, sat across from Wilson and sipped a Lungo coffee from a white Ikea cup that Wilson kept in his office for friends.

"You're a snob Craig. You know that don't you?"

Wilson, fresh froth wet on his lips, smiled and said.

"Hey, it's only 68 cents a cup. That's almost a dollar less than Tim Horton's and two fifty less than Starbucks."

"68 cents a cup from a $700 machine doesn't seem like such a good deal."

"Three cups a day, four when you come by, is $2.72 a day. That saves me almost $4 a day at Tim's and about $10 at Starbucks. This machine paid for itself within six months. I can hardly be a snob if I pay half what other people pay for their coffee can I. Anyway, what does Roger have you working on?"

Mitch reached for a raisin tea biscuit, which was his contribution to their mid-afternoon coffee ritual, and shared his news.

"Roger and Director Priest are going to Geneva next week to attend a cyber-security conference and Roger wants me to provide a threat risk assessment on their travel itinerary and risks to the conference."

Wilson smiled at Mitch.

"You won't pull me in with that one Mitch. Even they are not that silly. What are you really working on?"

"You are no fun anymore Craig. Actually, Roger tasked me to assess the latest intelligence on threats to the G20 meeting in St. Petersburg in September. There is concern that Islamists from Russia's Northern Caucasus are intent on staging an attack and Cook and Priest want constant updates so they can keep the NSA advised. What about you Craig, what's going on the domestic front?"

Wilson nodded to the white board behind him and gestured to the list on the left side.

> Freemen on the Land - Oil pipe lines Alberta
> Initiative de Résistance Internationaliste (IRI) 2010 - Recruitment Centre - 2010
> Right wing loner - Utoya, Norway, July 22, 2011.
> Canadian terrorists - 2013 - gas plant in Algeria

John Nuttall, and Amanda Korody, "self-radicalized" Canadians bomb BC Canada Day 2013.

"I've been reviewing these and using them as part of ITAC's contribution to the draft version of the Federal Governments annual report, The Intelligence Assessment, 2013 Domestic Threat Environment in Canada."

Mitch eyed his friend with open skepticism.

"That's not all is it Craig? I heard you have been nosing around Intel reports on European rail networks. If Roger finds out, he will be pissed."

With his contribution to the report completed by early August, and with Nuttall and Korody under arrest, Wilson had indeed scanned the latest intelligence reports on European terrorist threats. Despite losing his European files the previous year when Priest had given the files to Cook, Wilson maintained his interest and concern for European wellbeing. He supposed it was in part due to his English heritage and an affinity for the 'old world'.

"Well of course I have. You know I can't rely on Cook to make connections. Anyhow, I found an August 4, Five Eyes report from the US with intelligence about an Al-Qaeda plot to attack Europe's high-speed rail network. The report indicated a plan to bomb trains, tunnels and destroys tracks and electrical cabling. The information came from the US National Security Agency which intercepted a phone conversation in July between the Al-Qaeda leader, Ayman al-Zawahiri and operatives from the group's network."

Mitch waited.

"Alright, so I sent a request to the NSA for a review of their intelligence for any link between the two

Canadians, Jaser and Esseghaier, who had plotted to bomb the Via Rail train last year. That's all and it's well within my scope of domestic terrorism."

"No argument from me Craig. I am glad you are the one on the domestic files to be honest with you. Imagine if Jaser and Esseghaier had planned to bomb the Toronto subway or the Sky Dome. Just imagine the casualties."

Wilson sighed and said.

"That's the problem Mitch, I can and do imagine."

Thirteen

June 2013, London, England

HIGH DEFINITION FULL COLOUR CHAOS played across the fifty-inch wall mounted Samsung TV that dominated the nine hundred square foot room Mitton-Wells called his den. On screen, a CNN Special Investigation interspersed footage of the Boston Marathon bombing with dialog between establishment experts, who portrayed Islam as a religion of violence, and moderate Muslim apologists, who maintained that fanatical extremists had hijacked and distorted a peaceful religion.

Mitton-Wells sighed with self-righteous content as he imagined how the Boston bombing was a divine sign in support of his own mission to destroy the Islamic threat in England. A soft chime interrupted Mitton-Wells' warped delusion and signaled the arrival of his friend and co-conspirator Simon Spencer.

"Simon, come in. I was worried you wouldn't be able to make it tonight."

Disheveled and tired, Simon tossed his coat on an armchair, ran fingers through his hair, and nodded to accept an invitation from Mitton-Wells to have a drink.

"I didn't think I would either Anthony. In fact, I can't stay long. The fallout from the machete attack on that poor soldier in May still has everyone on edge. MI6, MI5, Special Branch, the National Crime Agency, as well as MI and even NID are all reviewing intelligence leads for connections to other terrorists."

Mitton-Wells steered his friend to one of two leather club chairs that sat either side of an antique mahogany table inlaid with a chessboard. Every Thursday Mitton-Wells and Simon played chess and reinforced their shared social, political and economic views.

Handing Simon a single malt scotch with one ice cube Mitton-Wells said.

"I expect the intelligence and security agencies are very busy, but Simon, how fortuitous these attacks are for us. My only regret is that there haven't been more casualties."

"I suppose your right Anthony, although as you know I don't condone mass killings and I am glad that you have agreed to limit the deaths from our plan to tens and perhaps a hundred rather than thousands."

The pang of pending betrayal struck Mitton-Wells hard and he turned away from Simon to hide his guilt. Simon drained his drink and swirled the ice cube around the glass.

"You are certain that the time is right Anthony?"

"My dear Simon, the timing could not be better. Remember those clashes between EDL protesters and counter-demonstrators in Walsall and the protest by hundreds of EDL members in Manchester city centre. All those marchers with flags of St George and anti-Islam banners, and the street battles against the left-wing group Unite Against Fascism?"

"Yes Anthony I remember. The protest gave me, well MI5, an excellent opportunity to gather intelligence on the UAF."

Mitton-Wells, his racist fervour increasing, continued as though he hadn't heard Simon.

"Then in April, Simon, six Muslim terrorists guilty of plotting an attack on an EDL demonstration with a home-made bomb, guns, knives and a machete and on top of that the bombing of the Boston Marathon."

Mitton-Wells paused, held Simon's eyes, and said.

"If these events were not enough Simon, the disgusting and savage slaughter of a British Army soldier in May in broad daylight by these bloody Islamic animals should be enough to drive every Englishman to action."

Pain and compassion fought with anger as Simon nodded acknowledgment of the murder of Fusilier Lee Rigby of the Royal Regiment of Fusiliers. Simon's father had served with the Fusiliers and the honour of the regiment had been a constant theme of Simon's childhood.

"As you know Simon there is much more. Mosques attacked with hand grenades in Essex and Kent; petrol bombs thrown into a mosque in Grimsby by two former soldiers; the Al-Rahma Islamic Centre destroyed by a fire; and another fire at an Islamic boarding school in southeast London. And most encouraging, a senior Metropolitan Police officer confirmed there had been an eight-fold increase in the number of Islamophobic incidents since Rigby's death. On yes Simon, I am very sure the time is right."

Simon, an excellent and committed chess player, rolled a white knight chess piece in his fingers and motioned Anthony to commence play.

Sitting down Mitton-Wells said.

"Before I thrash you with my variation on the Edward Lasker 1911 game Simon, we should attend to business."

"All right Anthony," said Simon smiling, "but I know this is just a tactic to try and put me off my game. What do you need to know?"

"The first two phone calls between Egypt, London and Berlin. Have you thought about the dates and have you found an appropriate person to make the calls?"

"Yes, the arrangements have been made. The calls will occur on August 29 and 31. As we discussed, the dialogue will be brief and only indicate to intelligence agencies that a date has been established."

"And you are sure these calls can and will be intercepted?"

"Yes. The calls will be made to phone numbers associated with known terrorists and I have ensured that those phones are in the hands of our operatives."

"Good, that's very good Simon. What about the second part of the plan, do you have a body?"

Simon placed the white knight on Ngf3 and chuckled at Anthony.

"I don't have a body yet Anthony. The body has to be fresh if people are going to believe the body belongs to the person who made the calls. Don't worry, life is cheap in Cairo. After our man has made the calls he will be dispatched and a good citizen will let our American friends know where to find him."

Succumbing to the challenge of the white knight, Mitton-Wells pushed a pawn to e4.

"One thing does worry me Simon. What will happen if a good citizen reports the activities of our little Muslim patsy to the authorities? We can't have the authorities arrest him before everything is in place."

"No need to worry Anthony, we have sympathisers in the Manchester Police and I have arranged that all intelligence and reports about Muslim extremist activities in Manchester will be routed to MI5 for analysis and action. I will simply stagger and delay the wider distribution of any public-spirited information that might surface until it's too late to stop anything."

"Excellent Simon, I'm glad everything is under control."

Simon, who had lifted his own pawn, paused mid-move and said.

"We do, or might have, one small wrinkle Anthony. Chris Thornton, a former MI5 analyst who now works in the Joint Terrorist Assessment Center is paying undue attention to one or two reports I authorized."

Mitton-Wells, snapped away from his concentration on the chessboard, by the comment, arched an eye at Simon.

"Don't worry Anthony; I will deal with him."

Unworried, Mitton-Wells played his variation on the Edward Lasker 1911 game, but failed to beat Simon.

~

When Simon left, Mitton-Wells reclined with a last scotch and reflected on his thirty-year dream to create a manipulated or contrived anti-immigrant uprising. Since 1979, when he had been twenty-one and easing his way through a four year Bachelor's degree in history and economics at the University of Oxford, he had, on account of his social status, become an associate 'member' of the Conservative Monday Club. The club was a British right-wing Tory pressure group, once renowned for advocating for a policy of voluntary, or assisted, repatriation for non-white immigrants.

At the same time, England's principle anti-immigrant and racist party the National Front won almost 200,000 votes in the May General Election.

Although the National Front declined and splintered during the 1980s, and reached relative insignificance in the late 1990's, Mitton-Wells had seen the possibilities of an anti-immigrant, or as he preferred to call it, pro-English, grass roots movement.

Since the decline of the National Front, Mitton-Wells maintained a keen but discreet tab on right wing, pro-English movements, providing anonymous financial contributions to keep the movements going. With the aim of ensuring an albeit shallow well of malcontents, Mitton-Wells provided quiet support to groups such as Stop Islamisation of Europe, the British National Party, the Christian Council of Britain.

'Yes', thought Anthony Mitton-Wells to himself as he savoured the last drop of the Jura Vintage 1973 Single Highland Malt Scotch Whisky, 'the time is definitely right'.

Fourteen

May 2013, Manchester, England

SOCIOPATH, PSYCHOPATH; MACKENNA had been called both. Laypeople use the terms interchangeably and psychiatrists often consider and treat sociopaths and psychopaths the same, but criminologists treat them as different because of their outward behaviors. A predisposition to violence and impulsive, erratic and excessive risk taking placed Mackenna firmly in the psychopath camp, however, his tendency to appear superficially normal in social relationships, placed one foot in the sociopath camp. Splitting hairs over Mackenna's psychiatric diagnosis meant nothing to his victims who, if they had the courage to remember, would simply call Mackenna an evil, sick bastard.

Like Darren, Mackenna heard from Marshall before he discovered a cell phone in his belongings and true to his impulsive nature, he answered it on the first ring and spoke first.

"This is Steve Mackenna. Who the fuck are you?"

Despite Simon's caution, Mackenna's aggressive tone caught Mitton-Wells off guard.

"I said who the fuck are you?" repeated Mackenna.

Regaining his composure, Mitton-Wells responded in his superior upper class Oxford educated voice.

"My name isn't important Mr. Mackenna. What is important is that we both share the same objectives and that I can..."

"Fuck you. You sound like Prince Phillip. You talk as if you have a cock in your mouth. You a shirt-lifter then?"

Shocked by Mackenna's profanity, Mitton-Wells hung up the phone. A few minutes and some deep breaths later Mitton-Wells recalled Mackenna. This time Mackenna said nothing and Mitton-Wells changed tactics and spoke to the silence.

"Would you like to hurt people Mr. Mackenna? Do you want to hurt the Pakistanis, the Muslims, the blacks and all the foreigners that poison and pollute England with their presence?"

"I already do that. What do you want?"

"I want, Mr. Mackenna, to help you do more of your good work. I want to help you to do whatever you want to them. I will give you money for your work. I will make people look up to you, make you a hero to all English men and ensure you never go to prison."

"You're full of shit. You think I'm dumb enough to fall for that. Are you the best that the police can do?"

"I assure you I'm not with the police or any other law enforcement authority Mr. Mackenna."

"And I'm supposed to believe you?"

"No Mr. Mackenna, a man of your intelligence and accomplishments would need some proof. I understand that."

"Go on then. What's you proof?"

"My proof will be waiting for you when you return to your home."

Back in control, Mitton-Wells terminated the call.

Mackenna, startled and unnerved by the certainty in the caller's voice, clenched the phone and placed it in a pocket.

~

Unsettled by the phone call, Mackenna hurried to his home. One door fronted 378 Lytham Road and from that one door led left into Barry's and one door led right to stairs and the flat above.

378A Lytham Road housed a barber shop owned and operated for 28 years by Barry, a chauvinistic, self-promoter who had been everywhere, done everything and could not keep a secret if his life depended on it. Gaudy gold chains hung from his neck and fake gold rings cut into fat fingers. Patrons, exclusively male, could browse through decade old editions of Playboy and fantasize over the topless females that occupied page three of The Sun newspaper. Jokes, sexist, homophobic, racist and juvenile, flowed effortlessly from his lips and tidbits of 'insider' information and local gossip entertained and shocked his loyal customers. Barry didn't hold with political correctness and equality and despite his antics, he prospered where many failed.

Besides cutting hair, Barry also provided another service to select customers: marijuana, ecstasy and various uppers and downers provided to him by the person who occupied 378B Lytham Road, a small two bedroom flat above his ground floor barbershop.

Mackenna entered the main front door, turned left into Barry's, and signaled Barry with a sharp tilt of his head. Barry, midway through a joke about a dwarf, a police officer and a politician, put his joke on hold and went to Mackenna.

"Barry, has anyone been around today? Has anyone asked for me or looked funny?"

Affable and light, Barry responded with "Just the usual. No one particularly funny except maybe old Mr…"

"I'm not fucking around Barry. Has anything or anyone out of the ordinary been asking about me?"

"No, nobody, it's just a regular day man. What's up?"

Mackenna peered past Barry into the shop and surveyed the waiting customers: Four bling-laden, over scented, teenage wanabe gangsters struggled to stifle erections as Playboy images fed unrealistic sexual expectations; two middle aged men lingering over topless models on page three, and two pensioners, in for Barry's 'over 75' special between 2 and 4pm: The usual crowd.

"Nothing Barry, get back and cut hair."

~

Placated, but still cautious, Mackenna turned from the barbershop and unlocked the door that led up to the flat. The quite chime and rhythmic pulse of the red light on the alarm key pad mounted on the wall to the left of the doorway reassured Mackenna that no one had entered his home. With an audible, 'fuck you' to the claim of the person on the phone Mackenna climbed the stairs to the second door and the second alarm system. This one too chimed and pulsed, as it should. Few people knew about the second alarm system. A necessity due to the drugs, cash and stolen goods Mackenna kept on hand. This one, wired through Barry's barbershop and independent of the other alarm included cameras focused on the stair well and the inside of the door to his flat. Confident in Barry's vigilance and the two-alarm system, Mackenna entered his domain.

A narrow hallway led to three doors. The first two doors, one left, one right, opened on to bedrooms. Left faced the street while right looked over a small unkempt yard into the alleyway that ran between the two rows of pre-WWII houses. Habit and paranoia sent Mackenna to check the rear-facing bedroom. Two padlocks, both intact and undamaged secured the door. Mackenna sighed. He actually wanted someone to break in and steal the white power, colorful pills and shaggy leaf neatly stacked on the table beside a scale, plastic bags and cigarette papers. Then he could check the cameras, identify the intruders and then hunt them down and make an example of them. Best of all, the drugs were 90% fake. His kept his real drug stash hidden under the floorboards in the kitchen.

Door number three, straight ahead and always open, led to the living room, kitchen and next to the kitchen the small bathroom. When he had first rented the flat from Barry he had asked a builder friend why the bathroom was through the living room and beside the kitchen instead of by the bedrooms. The builder, a terse non-nonsense man, responded that it was cheaper to keep all the plumbing in one place.

Mismatched IKEA furniture, most purchased from the 'as is' section of the IKEA warehouse, littered rather than decorated the living room. Black, beach and white bookcases covered the window wall and a dining room hutch filled the wall with the door to the kitchen. Floor to ceiling misaligned shelving, installed around a 50-inch flat screen plasma TV, filled the solid wall that separated the living room from the front bedroom.

Positioned to watch the TV a stained, creamy white, love seat fronted a scratched and cigarette burned black coffee table. To the left of the table, takeout food containers, beer cans and pornographic magazines littered the floor. Centered on the table, a folded 8 x 10 inch tent card with large printed black letters demanded attention. One word: 'PROOF' filled the card. In front of the sign, a tape player waited. Through the plastic cover, Mackenna could see a tape spooled and ready. Mackenna, impulsive, hit the play button:

Two frenzied male voices shouted expletives at one another as they discussed a third voiceless person.

"Fuck you. I'm first. I'm the one who put the roof-ie in her drink."

"Yeah well, who carried her out, eh? I'm first, so fuck you."

"No way. I'm not getting your sloppy seconds. It was my van."

"Your van, but who found us this place then eh?"

Sounds of a scuffle and panting then one of the voices began to laugh.

"What are you laughing at Steve?" said the other.

"Look, why are we fighting about this paki bitch. She has two holes right."

Snorted laughter followed by "O.K." ended the re-cording.

Mackenna knew there was more, much more. The girl, a teenager at a non-alcoholic dance party at a warehouse in Manchester, had regained consciousness as Mackenna and Bazzo callously switched orifices. The girl had gone crazy, scratching and punching and screaming she would tell the police. Mackenna, who was already on parole for assault, intended to hit the girl in the face, but she flinched and the blow struck her in the throat. Mackenna and Bazzo, both high on booze and drugs, simply watched the girl choke to death.

Mackenna swore. He knew Bazzo, who got his kicks by feeding his imagination with sound in a dark room, had made a tape of the rape, but when the girl died, Bazzo swore he would destroy it. Bazzo had died three years ago of a heroin overdose and Mackenna hadn't given Bazzo, the girl, or the tape much thought.

Sweat pushed from Mackenna's pours as he withdrew the phone from his pocket and placed it on the table beside the tape recorder. An hour later, as Mackenna twirled the tape cassette and downed a third can of Carling Larger, the phone rang. Less certain of his position Mackenna listened to the authoritative voice.

"Mr. Mackenna, I assume you have seen, or should I say heard, the proof. I am not with the police or any other official body. If I were, you would already be arrested and convicted of the crimes you committed on that tape."

Mackenna threw his empty can at the wall and shouted in to the phone.

"How the fuck did you get…?"

"You don't need to know Mr. Mackenna. However, don't worry, the original is in safe hands and will remain so. Now listen to me while I explain what you need to do and how you will become a part of an historic moment in the history of England and her people."

Fifteen

July 2013, Manchester, England

"FAT FUCK", YEAH he heard right.

Fat Fuck, or variations, had dogged Gary Boddie for as long as he could remember. Raised by overweight working class white trash parents on a diet of fish and chips, pie and chips, egg, sausage and chips and sometimes chips and chips, Gary Boddie hadn't a chance. By nine, Gary weighed the same as the average fifteen year old. By fifteen Gary was a two hundred pounds plus slab of lard. Now, at thirty-seven, Gary 'fat fuck' Boddie pushed the scale to three hundred and twenty-one pounds. He still ate chips, lots of them, with plenty of salt and vinegar, and since he was old enough, plenty of beer.

Gary's parents were dead. A heart attack killed his dad at forty-one and his mum drowned in the Manchester Ship Canal when she slipped into the water and was unable, because of her bulk, to pull herself out. Gary lived in his childhood home. The house, a rented 1920's era terrace on Railway Road within sight of the Manchester United stadium, was one of the few homes still owned by the local council. Under rent control regulations, the rent remained below inflation levels and Gary enjoyed a prime location for minimal cost.

Fatness burdened Gary with the all too common social, health, and physiological issues and problems.

Had it not been for his uncanny organizational ability and excellent memory, Gary Boddie would likely lead a solitary unemployed existence punctuated by meals and TV. Instead, Gary was a valued member of Manchester United's Facilities Management team. Fourteen years had passed since Gary joined United's work force as a cleaner. Now Gary co-managed a small army of full and part-time cleaners that worked 7 days a week to keep the stadium and immediate grounds dirt and garbage free.

"I might be fat, but I'm not the one cleaning the toilets. So get your skinny butt in the washroom and clean up the puke and shit now."

Gary didn't blame Brad for not wanting to clean anything. They both knew Gary could do little about Brad's indifferent and insolent attitude. The only card Gary could play was to suggest that Steve Lever, the other co-manager, might fire Brad. No matter what Gary might say; once Lever decided, Brad would be out. Gary did not know why anyone would go to such lengths to ensure a loser like Brad landed a job cleaning toilets at Manchester United. What Gary did know was that two months earlier a knock at his door had turned his life inside out.

~

Gary liked his chips hot. Reluctant to leave the half-eaten extra-large serving of chips he had picked up on his walk home from the stadium, ignored the knock on his front door. If he answered the door, they would go cold, so he ignored the knock a second time and continued eating. When the knock became rapid and loud Gary scooped a handful of greasy chips, dragged himself from the table and waddled to the front door.

"I'm coming; I'm coming, just a minute."

The banging stopped when Gary flicked on the narrow hallway light. He hesitated as he gripped the door latch with one grease-coated hand and leaned an ear against the dry wood of the dull brown door. Gary didn't expect anyone because no one ever visited.

"Who is it, what do you want?" said Gary into the wood.

"Never mind who I am. Open the door."

Apprehension contorted Gary's flushed face and sweat pooled on blotched skin.

"What. No. Go away. I'll call the police."

Squeak. Scrape. The sound drew Gary's attention to the mail slot in the door. A brown envelope emerged from the dark hole and hung half in half out. An odor of cigarette smoke crept in with the envelope.

"Open the envelope Gary. Then open the fucking door."

Gary pushed the envelope back out of the mail slot and shouted.

"No. I don't want anything. Go away."

The mail slot cover squeaked and snapped shut and Gary turned to retreat back to the kitchen and his cooling chips. A rough, mocking voice called out to Gary's back.

"Alright Gary, if that's how you want it. I will give the envelope to your boss at Manchester United and I'll send one to the Manchester Evening News. You won't have a job for long and you won't be able to stay in this house."

Unsure if he had heard correctly, Gary paused. Silence. Then one word punched Gary hard. "Veronica."

Flushed jowls quivered as Gary sucked air and braced himself against the hallway wall. Veronica was Gary's secret pleasure. No one could know about Veronica. She stayed upstairs out of site either in his bedroom or in the bathroom. He only took Veronica out twice a year and only far from Manchester. He told coworkers he went to Spain because he could not face the prospect of what his life would become if people found out about Veronica.

The mail slot squeaked again. This time the envelope flew from the opening and landed on the threadbare hallway mat. Gary's eyes tracked the envelopes flight and fixed on the thin rectangular object. A thump on the door and a shout refocused Gary's attention.

"Come on Gary, open the envelop and see what a fucked up boy you are."

Gary, afraid of what it might contain, didn't want to touch the envelope.

"Gary, you fat turd, I'm not going wait all night."

Breath caught in Gary's throat as he stumbled toward the mat. Unsteady hands grasped the envelope. Pudgy fingers tore the flap and reached in. Three 4 x 5 photographs slid out. An involuntary stir twitched in Gary's groin until the voice from the other side of the door spat.

"You're one sick, fat, bastard Gary. Now open the door."

A figure had crowded the doorway and a peaked hat cast shadow on the figure's face and obscured all but the bottom of a stubble-covered chin. An arm extended from the figure and a gloved hand extended from the arm.

Gary flinched and shook away the memory as Brad shuffled in to the washroom.

Brad Short had been the first person he had hired to keep the photographs from going public. The second was Aalim Hussein.

Sixteen

August 15 2013, London, England

ELEVEN THOUSAND TONS OF GREY steel, riveted together in 1938, punctured by a German mine in 1939, and exhausted by thirty years of service in Britain's Royal Naval, swayed on the cold murky waters of the Thames River. Chris Thornton, like hundreds of thousands of British schools boys, had stood on the deck of HMS Belfast and dreamed of battle and conquest. The cruiser, decommissioned in 1967 and turned into a floating museum in 1971, filled Thornton's vision as he looked up river from Potter Fields Park on the east side of the Thames River just below Tower Bridge. Lost in schoolboy memories Thornton did not notice the approach Simon Spencer, the Assistant Director of Domestic Terrorism for MI5, who touched Thornton on the shoulder before speaking.

"Hello Chris. It's been a long time since we last met. When was that?"

"Hello Sir; that would have been in November 2010. I prepared a report on threats to North Sea Oil rigs from Scottish Nationalists."

"Ah yes, that's right, a damn silly request from the Minister if I recall."

"Yes, although that's not what I wrote in the report!"

Both men smiled as they unknowingly shared an irreverent thought about ministerial requests.

Simon stepped to the cement wall that held people back from the water's edge and gazed out and upward at Tower Bridge. When Chris joined him, Simon said.

"Thank you for coming Chris. I expect you are wondering why I asked to meet you out of the office and unofficially."

Chris, wary of the man he used to work for, responded.

"Yes."

Spencer, still appreciating the view, spoke into the light breeze drifting in from the river.

"As you know from your time in MI5, and no doubt MI6, appearances can be deceptive."

"I know that, but what is MI5 doing and what has it got to do with me?"

"Nothing directly Chris, it's more to do with what might inadvertently occur if you keep asking questions about some JTAC reports I recently approved."

Chris, who had already guessed why he had been 'invited' to meet Spencer, took the initiative.

"You mean the reports about the EDL and Islamic extremism?"

"I always said you were a bright one Chris. Too bad we had to lose you to the JTAC. Yes, you are correct. I understand you have been asking why I, and not the JTAC Director, had final signing authority on the reports."

"Well yes and no. I mean, it is certainly unusual for someone else to sign off on the reports, but I am more interested in why the reports conclude that no follow up investigative or surveillance actions are required."

Spencer stiffened as he wondered if he had made a mistake meeting Thornton. Pushing a tight smile on to his face, Spencer explained MI5's involvement in JTAC reports.

"Two reasons Chris. The first is old fashioned bureaucratic cover your behind. The JTAC director didn't want her name on the reports and insisted, since I was the instigator of the final recommendations, that I should be the one accountable."

Chris thought about Heather Dewsbury, the JTAC Director, and accepting the likely truth of Spencer's statement asked.

"And the second reason, Sir?"

Spencer, displaying telltale signs of someone about to lie, shuffled his feet and blinked as he spoke.

"Ah well that's why we are meeting unofficially and why I hope I can count on your former MI5 status to understand and protect what I am about to tell you."

Thornton nodded and Spencer continued.

"MI5 is engaged in a massive and complex program to infiltrate both the English Defense League and several extreme Islamic groups. Naturally, we don't want investigative or surveillance operations to compromise our infiltration efforts. As you know Chris, lives are at stake."

"I understand," said Thornton "but don't you think we are walking a tightrope?"

"Of course Chris," said Simon, deliberately misunderstanding, "infiltration is always dangerous which is precisely why I need you to hold off your inquiries and questions."

"I don't mean the infiltrations Sir. I am concerned about what is happening with the EDL and how the public is reacting."

"What do you mean Chris?"

"The reports indicate EDL membership is increasing by thousands every week and anti-Muslim and anti-immigrant marches are occurring more frequently and with larger and larger numbers. In addition, the rhetoric of media and academia appears slanted against immigrants and is increasingly right wing. I worry that if the EDL is unchecked there will be serious conflict. How long will the infiltration program last?"

"That depends on its success. It's difficult to predict. You know that Chris. The important thing is that we get inside the organizations so we can be effective in thwarting whatever plans they may have."

"Yes, I understand that Sir, but aren't we running a terrible risk. If we allow the EDL and anti-immigrant sentiment more space we may reach a sort of social tipping point that would be impossible to stop."

Spencer, a little unnerved, but not surprised by Thornton's conclusions, waited to see how far Thornton's thinking had gotten him.

"What if we had our own Boston Marathon bombing here in London? What would happen if we had another bombing on the London Tube, or a 9/11, or an attack on a sports stadium? In the current anti-immigrant and anti-Muslim climate, anything could happen."

Fighting off an urge to stammer at Thornton's mention of the potential consequences of a terrorist attack on a sports stadium, Spencer attempted to assure Thornton.

"Of course we are aware of the risks, however, as you know current intelligence does not indicate any imminent threats. Besides, once we are inside the organizations we can stop any attempt to organize and cause problems. That's why we are doing this in the first place Chris. Now, can I be assured that you understand the situation and that MI5 can count on your discretion until we complete our infiltration program?"

Uncomfortable despite the logic, but certain now was neither the time nor place to push his concerns, Thornton said.

"Yes Sir. I understand and I will keep things close until the program is successful."

Seemingly satisfied, Spencer shook Thornton's hand and thanked him for his understanding and cooperation.

With Spencer gone, Chris surveyed HMS Belfast and thought of the loyalty and honour it represented. Across the river, high above the Tower of London, the fluttering Union Jack drew Thornton's gaze. Below the flag, sheltered by the top of the castle wall, Traitors Gate caught Thornton's eyes and shaped his thoughts.

Thornton was glad he had sent his friend Wilson an email and that Wilson's voice mail suggested he had understood the connection. When Wilson returned from his camping trip, they would talk.

Seventeen

August 27 2013, Manchester, England

DARREN'S INDEX FINGERS WERE BUSY. One spun a cell phone on the table and one pushed the 'channel up' button on a TV remote. Darren stared at the spinning phone with awe and willed it to ring. The cell phone had given Darren purpose and focus. The caller, whoever he was, had confidence and certainty, the instructions were clear and materials and money appeared as promised. Darren adrift and unfulfilled had become dependent on the phone and the tasks set by the caller.

Twirling and clicking, Darren reflected on his assignments so far. Manipulating Short to take the job at Manchester United and blackmailing Boddie had given Darren a taste of power and importance he had never before experienced. In fact, since meeting Boddie, Darren had decided the fight to make England a place for Englishmen did not include a home for men like Boddie. When Boddie outlived his usefulness, Darren would make sure Boddie did not contaminate the new world.

Internet research work followed the Short and Boddie assignments. Darren recalled the instructions that would reveal to him a world overrun with hate filled Muslim terrorists committed to cleansing the world of infidels.

"You will travel out of Manchester to different public Internet access providers such as cafes, shops and libraries. You will become familiar with websites related to Muslims, Jihads, Terrorists, and Radicalization. You will also seek bomb making sites and sites concerning large sporting or entertainment events in Manchester."

Exposure to extremist propaganda fed Darren's racism and hardened his resolve and conviction that he and England were at war: A justified war of self-defence against an onslaught of Muslim hatred.

"You must never return to the same public Internet access site, never take written or electronic notes and never log on to your own email account or any other personal service. You must also access web sites in Arabic and English."

Darren, as instructed, visited almost forty different Internet access points in towns and cities within a fifty-mile radius of Manchester. Darren couldn't understand the Arabic web sites and while he accessed them, he didn't spend much time on them. He knew what they were and he guessed that was the point. Darren soon developed and retained a solid knowledge of the sites as well as how to make different kinds of bombs from everyday materials.

~

Ring and vibration unbalanced the phone's spin and broke Darren's trance. Eager for action, Darren snatched the phone, pressed answer and smiled as the calm, posh voice spoke.

"Hello Darren. Are you alone?"

"Yes."

"Good. It is time for you to take the next step in our plan. You can stop your Internet research. You will need the knowledge later."

The Internet searches had stoked Darren with a desire to destroy, maim and kill. Anxious for knowledge Darren said.

"You want me to make a bomb then?"

"Shut up you fool! Do not use such words on the phone. The answer is no. Now listen carefully."

Slapped by the rebuke, Darren listened.

"You are to contact Steve Mackenna. He is an EDL member. You may already know him."

Darren did know Mackenna. He was also a member of the Wythenshaw Division, but never came to meetings. Instead, Darren had seen him at EDL marches. Mackenna was hard to miss, but not for the reasons one might expect of a right wing racist lunatic. Mackenna wore business suits, trendy overcoats and carried umbrellas no matter the weather. Except for the black Doc Martins boots, which he wore for comfort, speed and 'kicking abilities', he could pass for a bank clerk or government desk jockey. With short brown hair and soft features, Mackenna would be invisible in any city business crowd and that made him so noticeable in EDL marches because his bland conformity singled him out like a wolf among sheep. That is exactly what Mackenna was: a rabid wolf who hated non-whites. Hated and acted. What, thought Darren, did they want with that psycho?

"You and Mackenna will kidnap a Muslim man and his family."

Uncertain of what he had heard Darren spluttered

"What the fuck? How, I mean who is?"

"Don't interrupt Darren. You will receive detailed information and instructions. I will call you again in three days. If you have any questions, you may ask then. Do you understand?"

~

Darren had understood, but he had not really believed until he opened the bulky A4 sized envelope that appeared on floor behind his front door. As with the photographs of Gary Boddie Darren had not seen anyone deliver the envelope. No post marks, no delivery company logo. No identifying marks of any kind. Plain. Innocent.

The envelope contained an idiot's guide to kidnapping. Names, photographs, addresses, vehicles, keys, locations, routes, maps, identification, timing, dialog. The material had excited and frightened him. Excited by the prospect of action yet frightened at the prospect of kidnapping someone.

The instructions had not included what to do with the Muslim and his family except to take them to an address in the Lake District North West of Manchester and secure them in the basement. After that, he and Mackenna would leave the house and wait for further instructions.

Darren had studied until he could recite the material. Three days later, when the cell phone rang, Darren had only one question.

"When?"

"Transportation and accommodations will be in place by September 1. As long as the goods are secure by September 4 you can select your own day."

"How do I tell you we have them?"

"Don't worry Darren. I will know."

Darren was not worried. He had begun to believe. Really believe.

Eighteen

August 15 2013, Ottawa, Canada

WILSON'S FOLLOW UP ON THE Al Qaeda plot to attack the European high-speed rail network had not yielded any connections to the terrorists Raed Jaser and Chiheb Esseghaier, who had plotted to bomb a Canadian Via Rail train. With no connections to the Via Rail terrorists and with the recent Canada Day plot to bomb the B.C. Parliament neutralized, Wilson and ITAC's work had settled into routine intelligence analysis.

Draining his coffee, Wilson exhaled a satisfied sigh as he thought about the two week camping vacation he and his family would start tomorrow. Wilson and his long-time friend Joe and his family were going to Killbear Provincial Park on Georgian Bay, Lake Huron.

Relaxed, with half a mind checking equipment lists and meal menus, Wilson absently monitored his three computer screens and watched as emails arrived and automatically sorted into various inboxes.

Email arrived in ITAC in different ways via different communication systems. Unclassified email exchange between government departments and agencies occurred on a basic intranet service with standard firewalls and virus protection. Classified communication, up to Top Secret, traveled via a dedicated encrypted communications system called Mandrake, which connected key security related government departments. Canadian diplomats at Canadian overseas embassies and missions also used the Mandrake system. Classified email and documents transmit-transmitted between the Five Eyes intelligence sharing community use Stone Ghost.

Messages and information receive a level of classification, usually Secret or Top Secret. Addition of a caveat defining which of the Five Eyes may review the material control distribution. A Top Secret document intended only for Canadian officials has a "TOP SECRET - CANADIAN EYES ONLY stamp." Intelligence products shared with all Five Eyes intelligence allies were marked "SECRET - AUS/CAN/NZ/UK/US EYES ONLY."

Five Eyes members produced and shared hundreds of intelligence products and communications and analysts must be vigilant to grasp nuggets of intelligence. Wilson devoted several hours each day to scour shared intelligence documents linked to domestic terrorism and his counterparts in the Five Eyes were aware of Wilson's obsessive reviews and rarely sent Wilson personal messages to draw his attention to a specific report.

Which is why Wilson was surprised when an email from his friend Chris Thornton, who worked in the UK's Joint Terrorism Assessment Centre, dropped into his unclassified in-box. Intrigued, Wilson immediately opened and read the email:

Hi Craig, how are things? How was your flight back? It was good to see you and great to have the time to share a traditional English lunch with you. We should do it again, maybe in May like before. I hope you made the connection. Salam and bye for now.

Wilson, intrigue replaced by puzzlement, leaned in to the computer screen and re-read the message; it didn't make sense. Wilson pushed away pleasant thoughts of camping and reread the message a third time. Something was definitely wrong; their lunch in England at the Prospect of Whitby Pub had been in March, five months ago. In addition, there had been no 'connection to make' because he had taken a direct Air Canada Heathrow to Ottawa flight and May had come and gone.

Alerted by the two obvious, and Wilson was sure deliberate errors, Wilson assembled the cryptic clues. They weren't hard to find: 'traditional English,' because they had both chosen Indian curry for lunch instead of a traditional plowman's cheese, pickle and pork pie lunch; 'connection', because there hadn't been one; 'May', because May was out of sequence; and finally Salam, an Islamic equivalent to 'good day' was out of character for Chris.

Connection, May and Salam had made sense to Wilson right away. Something about traditional English and May connected to Islam. With the clues identified and arranged in black marker ink on a white board Wilson stood back and let his mind recall the lunch meeting with his friend Chris Thornton.

Wilson's mind wondered through the pub, the conversation about wives, children and the limited utility of a constantly raised terrorist threat level and onto speculation about European threats. Nothing in their conversation related to traditional English.

Wilson opened his mind to view the pub interior, the decor, the smells, the sounds. Nothing. Then, as Wilson subconsciously turned to leave the pub, a man flitted briefly in to sight. Behind Chris, a tattooed skinhead lingered and stared toward Chris. Chris had tensed and commented on how the man seemed familiar and quipped the man might be an 'EDL member keeping any eye' on him. That was it. Traditional English was a reference to the English Defense League. EDL and May connected Islam.

Two quick searches of ITAC's data system for EDL/May/UK and Islam/Muslim/May listed four reports from the UK's Joint Terrorism Analysis Centre. The first two were regular 'first week of the month' reports on EDL and Muslim extremism activities. The second two were supplemental reports.

The first supplementary report concerned the EDL and highlighted information indicating the EDL were engaged in a vigorous, well-funded and professional, recruitment drive. The second observed how domestic British media appeared to be devoting more coverage and more prominence to anti-English activities by radical and extreme Muslim organizations and individuals. Both supplemental reports noted no requirement for follow up investigative or analytical action.

Wilson consulted the reference code at bottom left hand corner of the two supplemental reports: UK/JTAC/CT/HD/BL/150513/ 1&2 - UK/Joint Terrorism Analysis Center / Chris Thornton / HD / SS / 15th May 2013. Wilson knew HD referred to Heather Dewsbury, the Director of JTAC. Her initials ended all JTAC report reference numbers. SS was new to Wilson.

Intended for Wilson's eyes only, Wilson transferred his notes from the white board to a flip chart. This way he could cover the notes and keep his thoughts and the information from inadvertent eyes. With more black ink, Wilson wrote key statements and questions:

EDL recruitment up with new financial resources - money from where? Media reports of Muslim extremism up, why? Why no follow up? Who is SS?

When he was done, Wilson covered the flip chart and asked himself why his friend Chris Thornton, a trusted former MI5 analyst, had covertly drawn Wilson's attention to these reports. In addition, Wilson wondered if Chris knew about the recent UK intelligence reports that British Muslims in Nigeria wanted explosives and chemical weapons and the apparent lack of UK emphasis what the weapons might be used for. Wilson checked the time: 4:15pm; 9:15pm in London. He called Chris at JTAC and left a voice mail.

"Hi Chris, I made the connection. Unfortunately, I am off for our annual two-week camping trip tomorrow. Let's connect when I get back."

Ending the call, Wilson wondered why Chris had not just called himself.

Nineteen

September 2 2013, Ottawa, Canada

THE DECISION TO GO ON vacation had been difficult, but his recent absence from several family events and concern for family cohesion had convinced him to go. In fact, Killbear Provincial Park, rugged, picturesque and peaceful had rejuvenated Wilson. Even the six and a half hour drive home on Sunday, the need to unpack, and his Monday morning task to drop his kids at 8am for the mountain bike day camp had not zapped the energy Wilson had gained on vacation.

During their camping trip, Wilson and his friend Joe had a rule to use no electronic media devices. Wilson, although he struggled with the rule, had not scanned media reports until they had stopped for gas about an hour outside of Ottawa. However, the closer Wilson got to Ottawa the more his brain began to work on the problems he had left behind. Thoughts of his friend Chris Thornton and his cryptic message about the EDL and Muslim extremist activities in the UK, the UK intelligence report about Nigeria and plots to blow up trains in Europe fought with domestic and family obligations and the post-vacation buzz.

With the kids off to mountain bike camp, Wilson steered his minivan into one of the hundreds of parking spaces that occupied a unprotected asphalted parking lot to the left of the pedestrian security entrance on the outside of ITAC's perimeter fence. Stifling in the summer and frigid in the winter, Wilson hated the parking lot.

~

ITAC, co-located with the Canadian Security Intelligence Service in Ottawa's east end, did not use flashing lights, sirens or bells to announce an intelligence crisis. Email, bland and pedantic, would request implicated analysts to convene, ASAP, in the boardroom for an analytical review.

At 8:48 am on September 2, 2013, Wilson's email summons to the boardroom vibrated his Blackberry. The review would take place in 12 minutes at 9 am. Wilson, stainless steel, double walled coffee cup in hand entered the boardroom at 8:55am. Director Priest stood at the head of the long conference table and nodded at Wilson to close the heavy, soundproof door. Wilson, it seemed, had arrived last. Steel shutters droned downward from recessed housings above the windows. Pot lights, synchronized with the shutters, blinked on and eyes squinted to adjust.

Seven bodies, all men, all-new to ITAC within the last 12 months, occupied seven of the twenty-two table seats. An eighth body, Director Priest, paced left to right behind his chair at the head of the wide rectangular table. Wilson, unused to arriving last, made for a ninth chair, arranged his note pad and sipped his coffee.

Priest nodded at Roger Cook and a white screen descended from the ceiling behind Priest. Lights automatically dimmed and a projector, secured to the ceiling above the table, hummed. Priest, in his element, stepped left of the screen, clicked a button on the remote in his left hand and spoke to the assembled.

"These transcripts," said Priest, pointing to the typed bold words on the screen, "were received from our US Five Eyes ally at 8 am this morning."

Eighteen eyes immediately focused on the screen.

> **One:** Cell phone intercept. August 29, 2013.
> From Cairo, Egypt to London, England
> Male voices, Arabic
> BEGIN:
> **Date?**
> **Almost. A question remains about the date.**
> **Why?**
> **To maximize casualties.**
> END:

> **Two**: Cell phone intercept. August 31, 2013.
> From Cairo, Egypt to Berlin, Germany
> Male voices, Arabic
> BEGIN:
> **Report.**
> **Date confirmed.**
> END:

Squeaks of leather creased and stretched by wriggled bottoms and redistributed torsos, cut the silence as the assembled drew hasty breaths. The potential consequences of the intercepted messages were clear: somewhere in Europe, a violent and painful death stalked people, probably innocent people.

Priest, after an inappropriate dramatic pause, continued.

"The cell phone calls were also intercepted by our own signals intelligence so we can be confident of their authenticity. I don't need to point out the seriousness of these messages and the need for you to coordinate immediately with other departments and agencies to review and analyze any intelligence that may have even the remotest connection to these intercepts."

Wilson, in unison with the other analysts, transcribed the cold indifferent words as Priest spoke. Unlike the others, Wilson counted the words while Priest continued.

"Roger will take the lead. Send everything you have to him. We need to provide a briefing note to the National Security Advisor by 5 pm today on what we know, what we are doing, and what our next steps will be: Any questions?"

Eager to begin, and in need of action, analysts squared note pads and pushed back from the table. Wilson, contemplative, raised a finger. He had questions.

"Yes Craig," prompted Priest, his face revealing irritation.

"Do we have an audio recording of the calls or results of the background noise analysis?"

Priest turned to Roger.

"Er, no, we only received the transcripts so far."

Wilson suppressed a groan to remain positive.

"I think we should have them as soon as possible. Background sound, voice timber, speech patterns, all can assist with analysis and cross reference."

Priest spoke for Cook and said.

"I'm sure that information is on its way. Roger, could you follow up and make the data available to everyone. Anything else Wilson?"

"Do we know what kind of phone was used? What time of day the calls occurred. What information do we have on the number called?"

This time Roger pre-empted Priest and said he would ensure they received the details Wilson wanted.

Wilson, thought processes already in motion and eager to get to his office and his white boards, made to exit the boardroom when Priest touched his arm to get his attention.

"Craig, you do realize this is Roger's file. I mean this is obviously an international and European file and there has been no mention of domestic or homegrown terrorist involvement. I asked you to the briefing so you would be 'in the loop', but as I said, Roger is the lead and he will provide the final analysis. I do not want you muddying the waters with any 'out of lane' information requests to your old contacts. This could be a big file. Do you understand?"

Wilson understood all right. The priority was to make sure a briefing note to the NSA was available by 5pm. There was no desire at this point to raise questions that could not be answered and thus delay the NSA's note. Wilson knew the drill. Without questions, a note to the NSA could provide only the concrete facts available: An intercept, the transcript, and next steps, which would probably be to 'engage our Five Eyes partners'. Priest wanted ITAC to be 'first' to provide the NSA with a written brief.

Experience assured Wilson that the head of CSE, Canada's own international listening and interception capabilities, had not only read and heard the terrorist calls, but had already informed the NSA directly via secure phone. ITAC should be analyzing the data, questioning what was missing, and formulating questions to guide the follow up investigation. Running to tell the NSA what she already knew would serve little purpose.

"Yes, I understand. If I think of anything I'll be sure to advise Roger."

~

Energized by apprehension that people would die, Wilson hurried to his office. Inside, he stood before his white boards, grasped a black marker, and transferred the words of the intercepted calls from note pad to white board. Then he added key words for the questions he had asked during the meeting. Background noise, type of phone, time of calls, and number called. To these he added dialect of speakers, word use, alternative interpretations of the original Arabic word, encrypted, and similarities with other intercepts.

Wilson knew he would add more to the board as he worked his way through these basic questions. Every answer always promoted more questions. Coffee was ready and Wilson perched on his desk edge and studied his initial thoughts as he dialed Chris Thornton's number in the UK. With no answer, Wilson left a message that he was back from holiday and was ready to talk.

~

Two days later, American CIA agents responding to an anonymous tip, discovered the mutilated body of a known Islamic terrorist in Cairo, Egypt. Written on the inside of his left bicep agents discovered the German cell phone number of the intercepted call from Cairo to Belin. The body and the phone number pushed the international intelligence community in to frenzied activity. In ITAC, Priest and his acolytes busied themselves with the preparation of another briefing note for the NSA.

Worried but less agitated, Wilson added the information on the dead terrorist discovered by CIA agents in Cairo, along with many more questions, to his white board. Cook, as requested, had supplied an audio recording of the calls as well as the background noise analysis. In addition, technicians at Canada's CSE, through analysis of the GMS/SIM card technology used to make the calls, determined the cell phone used was likely an iPhone or an Android based phone. The two last pieces of basic data Wilson had requested indicated the calls had been made at noon local time in Cairo and the numbers called, as expected, belonged to burner phones.

Wilson's white board had become a colored schematic. Dotted and bold orange lines connected black data, symbols and misplaced punctuation marks. Irregular shaped circles and ovals grouped the brown and orange lines, separating them into clouds of logic only Wilson understood. Squeezed between the clouds single uppercase red letters proclaimed Wilson initial single word conclusions: Open; Silent, Noon; Careless; Convenient; and Wrong. Wilson concentrated on the single words, and expanded, and contracted the reasons behind the words.

Open, unencrypted communications between terrorists was rare. Silent background noise was unusual. Noon hour wasn't the best time to call. It was careless to leave a body and convenient for the CIA to receive a tip off and for the cell phone number to be written on the arm. Use of high-end iPhone was wrong because why use a high-end phone if you do not intend to make use of its encryption capabilities.

A yellow marker, the color for revised conclusions, hovered in Wilson's hand, his eyes dilated and his heart rate increased. With purposeful motion, Wilson circled each of the red words in yellow and linked them all together under another single yellow word: Amateurish. Yes, thought Wilson with satisfaction, amateurish. The actions were those of an amateur.

However, Wilson was not satisfied. A niggle remained. Why? Why make the calls, murder one of their own, tip off the CIA and leave a body with a cell phone number written on it?

Immobile before his white boards Wilson waited. Not forced, not bludgeoned, not fitted. Gradually, Wilson's synaptic connections coalesced to corral the niggle. This was how it always worked. This was Wilson's way.

Wilson reached for a green marker and hurled his three word 'at a point in time' conclusion across the board: Disinformation or Fake.

Disinformation or Fake. That was Wilson's analytical conclusion and his recommendation to Cook and Priest would be that intelligence activities should focus on obtaining evidence to prove or refute one or both of Wilson's claims.

Priest and Cook would be resistant. They, and the majority of the intelligence and security community, were already committed to the conclusion a major terrorist event was imminent in Europe. Probably in the UK or Germany where security and intelligence agencies were on high alert as informants were pressured for information.

Wilson did not discount the possibility of a terrorist attack. He just wanted to understand the easy discovery of such obvious markers indicating a Muslim plot to conduct an act of terrorism. Forewarning Western intelligence and security entities reduced the chance of success and did not make sense.

Committed to his conclusion and duty bound to report Wilson headed upstairs to Priest's office. Better to explain his conclusion to Priest first before sharing with other ITAC analysts and partner agencies.

~

Priest didn't take Wilson's analysis and conclusions well.

"Facts Wilson is what we work with in ITAC. Facts drive intelligence, not your inductive magic show that creates something from nothing. Roger told me about your hocus pocus theory about the British Muslims in Africa. This is more of the same thing isn't it Wilson?"

"Yes and no. We have facts; the problem is we are only looking at them one way. I'm not suggesting that the threat isn't real, I just think we should be more open-minded about who the threat is coming from and what that might mean for possible targets."

Priest squared his shoulders and fixed Wilson with a hard stare.

"Listen Craig, you have a lot of experience and credibility in ITAC and the intelligence community, but you also have a reputation for doing things your own way. Well now is a good time for me to tell you what I've been thinking for a while. ITAC belongs to me and we will do things my way not Wilson's way. If you can't work with us then perhaps you should consider another assignment. Do I make myself clear?"

Staring right back, Wilson did not back down.

"I'm telling you Priest, it's too damn easy. The trail is a mile wide and foot deep. We are being led by the nose and we need to know who is doing it and why."

"You should leave now Wilson and think over what I said. And Wilson, I don't want morale and focus undermined by your theories. So keep them to yourself."

~

Back in his office, Wilson picked up the phone at one of those rare instances when an incoming call synchronizes with an intended outgoing call. Instead of a dial tone, the shrill voice of a distressed woman shouted Wilson's name in his ear.

"Craig. Craig is that you? Are you there?

Not recognizing the voice Wilson responded with caution.

"Yes. I'm here. This is Craig Wilson."

"Why? What did you do? Oh, god it's terrible."

"I'm sorry. Who are you? What's terrible?"

Huge sob and a guttural groan.

"He's dead. Chris is dead Craig."

Twenty

September 1 2013, Manchester, England

AALIM HUSSEIN BEGAN HIS DAY like millions of other Muslims: He woke and said.

"All praise is for Allah who gave us life after having taken it from us and unto Him is the Resurrection."

Between bed and bathroom, Aalim said the "Bismillah," followed by the supplication for entering the bathroom:

"I begin with the name of Allah. O Allah, I seek refuge in you from the evil and evil things."

Later, as Aalim sat bound and gagged in a damp widow-less room, he wondered if Allah had heard him that morning before he chastised himself for doubting Allah's will.

~

Aalim was a taxi driver. He drove one of those ubiquitous British Black Cabs with the odd rear-facing seats for Borough Taxis, a large taxi company based out of Oldham near Manchester. About seventy drivers were Muslim. The current chairperson, who had driven for the company since it opened in 1978, was also a Muslim. Aalim had obtained the job through a friend of a friend of a distant cousin for a small sum of money. For five years, he had driven without incident and without fear. White, black, Christian, Muslim, Oriental,

Indian, he never had any problems because Aalim was non-confrontational and polite.

He wasn't weak or a coward. Aalim gauged the odds or the moment and developed a tone and attitude that enabled him to retain his dignity and avoid conflict. Aalim was a good if not devout Muslim. He prayed when he could, which was quite often because Borough Taxis, with a large contingent of Muslim drivers, allowed its drivers time between fares to attend Mosque or to stop and pray where and when needed.

Aalim lived in Cheetam Hill, a working class suburb within Greater Manchester. He attended the Al-Falah Islamic Centre in Cheetam Hill because he liked the Egyptian Imam whose manner and speeches often used a strong dose of the sarcastic humour for which Egyptians were well known. Prayer times occurred six times a day. Aalim always attended the mosque for three of the six: Dhuhr at 1:10pm, Asr at 5:37pm, and Magrib at 9:41pm.

Aalim was predictable, which made it easy for his abductors. Nasreen and Masud, Aalim's wife and son, were also predictable. Every weekday Nasreen and Masud would walk the half mile to and from their two-bedroom terrace home on Wood Road and the Temple Primary School on Smedley Lane. School began at 8:30am and ended at 3:30pm.

~

Aalim had been relaxed when he arrived at the Al-Falah Islamic Centre. Three early morning trips to Manchester Airport, as well as decent tips from each, had assured him a good days earning. Content, Aalim prayed for almost twenty minutes. Invigorated by prayer Aalim sauntered from the Mosque to parking lot behind the Mosque, climbed into his black taxicab and backed out of the parking space.

Between reverse and first gear a man tapped on the passenger side window. People were always signaling for him to stop and while it was unusual to find a white man in the mosque parking lot a fare was a fare. Instinctively, without registering the man's bearing or appearance, Aalim signaled the man to get in.

Aalim realized something was wrong when the man flipped down the seat directly behind Aalim instead of the more comfortable and logical rear and front facing seat. Not wanting to promote conflict Aalim asked.

"Where to?"

"Piccadilly Station."

Relieved the passenger seemed normal Aalim exited the parking lot. The station was only a ten-minute drive.

Taxi drivers are cautious and curious. Most drivers installed additional rear view mirrors at different heights and angles to see what the passengers were doing behind them. Aalim, who shared the taxi with Samir, an older experienced driver, had installed three additional oblong mirrors. When Aalim had first started to drive the taxi, the extra mirrors had disorientated him. Now, after five years, Aalim could drive and observe with ease. Through oblong-bordered blocks, slightly shaken and blurred by the motion and vibration of the taxi, Aalim studied his passenger.

Black and shadow dominated Aalim's vision. A black baseball-like hat cast shadow across pasty off-white facial skin dotted with blond overnight stubble. Black rimmed, modern, glasses fronted blue eyes and a dark scarf, wedged between a black wool overcoat obscured the man's throat. Above the scarf, discolored and irregular teeth exposed themselves intermittently from behind cracked lips. The man turned to look right and Aalim noticed a fist sized blemish on the skin between the left eye and ear. Black leather gloved hands flexed and squeezed at the end of the coat's arms.

"What the fuck are you looking at? Keep your eyes on the road," spat the man.

Aalim had been wrong. This was no normal passenger.

Traffic was always dense in central Manchester. The traffic flow improvements along Deansgate, the main route into the city, were not working. Rumor said the road improvements relied on ten-year-old traffic flow data. Aalim believed the rumors. On the plus side, the meter ticked whether he moved or not. Eighteen traffic lights stood between the mosque and Piccadilly train station. Aalim had a habit of counting traffic lights. He and other drivers would compete to calculate the shortest route between two points with the fewest traffic lights. The flip side of course was that all the drivers knew how to take the longest route with the most lights. This came in handy when passengers deserved different levels of service depending on their attitude or manners. Aalim decided this passenger deserved the shortest route and the least lights. The sooner the passenger was gone the better Aalim would feel.

Traffic light 7 had the longest delay. Six roads intersected; four Roman era roads from all compass points and two more recent auxiliary bypass roads. Aalim's taxi reached the light as green changed to red. Two minutes fourteen seconds before red changed to green. That's how long it took the passenger to destroy Aalim's life.

The man turned sideways on the small jump seat behind Aalim. In the plastic barrier between Aalim and passenger, the 8 x 10 inch gap for passing money was open. A forearm rested in the space. The forearm withdrew and from the sleeve of the dark wool overcoat, the shape of tensed knuckles, outlined through taught black leather, jutted into the space. Thin fingers, attached to the knuckles, grasped a gun. The gun pointed at Aalim.

Alerted by the shift of the cabs suspension as the man angled his body to position the gun Aalim sought clarity from the three rear view mirrors fixed at different angles and heights in the front of the cab. All three mirrors reflected an image of a gun.

"What do you want? Take the money. I don't want any trouble."

"It's too late for that. You should have thought of that before you came here. If you want to see your wife and kid again do as I tell you."

"What, what do you mean? What do my wife and son have to do with this? What do you know about them?"

"Your wife is Nasreen and your brat is Masud right? We know all about them. Don't bother driving to Piccadilly station. Drive to the shops on the corner of Smedley Lane and Cheetam Hill Road. Stop in the parking lot near Dan's Cafe. We need to have a little talk."

Bile rushed up Aalim's throat and he coughed and swallowed. Aalim knew Dan's Cafe. He had been there before, many times. Dan's was a one-minute drive from Masud's school. When Aalim wanted to surprise Masud and collect him from school, he would take a coffee at Dan's while he waited for 3:30 pm.

"Why are you doing this? What have I done, what do you want? I'm not going anywhere."

The light changed to green and traffic began to move on either side of the taxi. A horn blared behind them.

"Listen to me you rag head. You either drive right now or I get out of this cab and by the time you get home to you hovel on Wood Street my associate will have put a bullet in your wife: Your choice Aalim."

Aalim calculated. He considered the odds. A man with a gun knew all about his family and his home address. The odds were against him. He let slip the clutch and pulled away through the light.

During the ride, the man consulted his watch several times, but did not speak. Aalim's digital dashboard clock read 1:50pm. Masud, thought Aalim, would be safe in school until 3:30pm.

~

Aalim pulled into the parking lot and parked by Dan's Cafe as instructed. The radio sounded a general call for a cab to pick up at Piccadilly Station. Then a voice spoke directly to Aalim.

"Aalim, are you at the station yet? We have a call from one of our regulars, Mr. Simms. He is waiting by the west door as usual. Can you pick him up after you drop your passenger?"

Aalim turned to seek guidance from his captor.

"Tell him you have a fare to the airport."

"That's four airport fares today Aalim," said the dispatcher, this is a lucky day for you."

Aalim, a gun pointed at his back, did not feel lucky.

Nervous, but needing to do something, Aalim tried to talk with the man.

"Sir, there must be a mistake. I don't..."

"Shut the fuck up."

Time passed. Aalim sweated. The man held a cell phone expectantly. The shrill of the phone jolted Aalim. The man listened, and then hung up.

"O.K. Aalim this is what you are going to do. First, you will call your wife at home. You will tell her a man will arrive shortly. You will explain the man is an insurance agent come to discuss life insurance. Tell her you are on your way home and she is to let him in and wait for you. Do you understand?"

"What are going to do with my wife? I won't..."

"Hey, like I said before, you can cooperate or I will get out of the cab and my associate will shoot your wife dead when she opens the door. You can either have her let the man in and give him tea or whatever you fucks give to guests or you can go home and arrange your wife's funeral."

The man consulted his watch. Aalim calculated the odds. They were still against him. He made the call.

Three minutes after Aalim called his wife the man answered his phone.

"Good boy Aalim. Your wife is making tea for my associate. Now you have another call to make."

The man instructed Aalim to call the school and say that he would collect Masud early today. At 2:30, the man told Aalim to get Masud.

"And remember, my associate is in your home with your wife. One call from me and she will suffer before she dies. Do you understand?"

Tears of impotency welled behind Aalim's eyes as he strode the asphalt path toward the school's main entrance. Through the glass door, he could see his son wave and hop up and down with excitement and expectation. Aalim calculated. If he remained inside the school with Masud and called the police, Nasreen would die. If he returned with Masud, Nasreen would remain alive. Because they hadn't killed him or Nasreen, he calculated they must need them alive: Nasreen was better alive now than dead now. Aalim held back his tears, collected his son, and returned to the taxi.

Masud, excited to see his father and pleased about riding home, climbed eagerly into the cab. Masud faltered when he saw the man and remained standing in the cab, his head grazing the top of the cab's interior. Large, brown eyes contracted as happiness at his father's unexpected arrival at school changed to apprehension as the man in the cab barked at him.

"Sit down now."

Masud turned to his father who nodded a slow agreement with the man. Assured by his father's presence, Masud sat in the rear sat, fastened his seat belt as he had be taught and squeezed tight up against the cab window as far away from the man as possible. Unbidden, a tear breeched Masud's eye and trickled down to quivering lips in response to an instinct that something was wrong.

"What now?" asked Aalim.

"We go home to pick up your wife. Call her now and tell her you have already gotten Masud and to be ready. Tell her the insurance man is coming with us and you have a surprise for her."

"My wife will be suspicious. This is not the kind of thing I would do."

"I don't give a damn what your wife thinks. You convince her or you will bury Masud as well as your wife."

Frightened by the man's words, tears and sobs spilled from Masud and he peered in the rear view mirror to seek comfort through eye contact with his father. Instead, moist frightened eyes stared back.

~

Neighbors were not surprised when Aalim's black cab stopped outside his house or that his wife joined him in the cab. Across the street, an old white widower, who had lived in the terrace for fifty-nine years, and who, as he approached his eighty-seventh year, conceded to his few remaining friends on the rightness of human equality, did muse aloud to his cat as to what Aalim and his family were doing in a cab with two white men.

~

Through the mirrors and torn between safe driving and concern for his family Aalim's face creased as he snatched quick glimpses of his wife and son. Nasreen, eyes hard with fear and questions, wriggled to create space between her and the men who flanked her on the cab's back seat. Masud, breath rapid and body twitching, clung to his mother's bosom. Aalim prayed.

Aalim drove to an abandoned warehouse near central Manchester on the west side of the Pomona Docks built in the late 1880s as part of the Manchester Ship Canal network designed to allow ocean-going ship to travel inland to Manchester. Only dock number three remained intact to provide a link for small pleasure craft to travel between the Manchester Ship Canal and the Bridgewater Canal. Inside the warehouse, at gunpoint, Darren forced Aalim, Nasreen and Masud into the back of a windowless white van. An hour or so later the van lurched to a stop. The passenger side door opened and Aalim heard footsteps crunch gravel. A screech sounded the opening of a door. The van reversed, the doors opened and three black hoods landed on the van's steel floor.

"Put these on."

Aalim had feared this moment all his life. As a child in Mubarak's Egypt, abduction and detention by the Egyptian State Security Investigations Service or the Central Security Forces was common. Aalim's father and three of his brothers, all detained and questioned as security forces sought to protect Mubarak from repeated assassination attempts by people opposed to his position against Islamic fundamentalism and his diplomacy towards Israel, suffered under the regime.

Aalim, a child, had not understood the beatings and detention his father underwent and wept with his mother as each detention and beating broke his father and crushed his spirit. Aalim's father died of undetermined causes in 1993. After his father's death, he and his mother endured an impoverished existence as the second wife of her brother in law. The arrangement provided food and shelter for Aalim and his mother in exchange for dispassionate sex and domestic slavery. His mother's pitiful existence ended in 2010 and Aalim made his one and only visit to Egypt to stand at the grave of the woman who gave him life and apologized for leaving her.

Aalim could not say when he decided he would leave Egypt and seek life elsewhere, but in 2004 he and his wife Nasreen had saved enough money to buy passage on a ship to Southern France on the pretext of visiting a relative of Nasreen. Once in France they made their way to Calais and boarded a ferry to Dover.

With wry reflection, Aalim struggled to comprehend how, in a land absent a dictator, and where the rule of law and respect for human rights held sway, he found himself hooded and detained like his father before him. Worse, how and why had they taken his wife Nasreen, and innocent son Masud? What, he begged, was Allah's plan?

Many times Aalim had stood by impotent in Egypt during the 1980's when the then President Mubarak's security forces had hooded friends, relatives and neighbors before forcing them into unmarked vehicles. Most returned, blooded, subdued and no longer trusted by their community. Many did not. Impotent again, Aalim soothed his wife and son as he placed the black hoods over their heads.

Mackenna led the captives from the van to a damp basement and separated Aalim from his wife and child. Aalim, bound to a chair, listened as Masud's whimpers battered Aalim's heart and he asked himself again what Allah wanted with him.

Aalim sensed his wife and child were close, perhaps separated by a wall or partition thought Aalim. He could hear Nasreen's voice as her calm words wrapped themselves gently around and between the fear-filled sobs of his six-year-old son Masud. Masud, meaning lucky, had come late to Aalim and Nasreen. Ten years they had waited for Allah to bless them with a child. Then, when Masud was born, the umbilical cord stuck around the neck and he and Nasreen waited several long minutes before the midwife slapped and massaged life into Masud's body. Aalim loved Nasreen and Masud. He would do anything to keep them safe.

"Aalim, Aalim are you here Aalim?" called Nasreen.

Aalim stretched open his jaws and pushed his tongue against the rough cloth blocking his mouth.

"Aalim. Please Aalim. If you are near…"

"I am here Nasreen, screamed Aalim, I am here." His voice, confined by the cloth, failed to carry from his lips.

Nasreen, despair weighing each stretched word, called softly.

"Aalim. Please Aalim. Help us."

Impeded by the gag, Aalim's voice bounced back in to his head. Mixed images of his father, Nasreen and Masud, their bodies beaten and broken, mingled with Nasreen's pleas and lacerated his mind.

Then the sounds began.

Twenty-One

September 6 2013, London, England

AIR CANADA FLIGHT 888, direct Ottawa - Heathrow touched down at 9:58 am on September 6, twenty-seven minutes early. The return flight left Heathrow Sept 11. Wilson had five days. Five days to discover the truth about Chris' death and how and if it was really linked to the terrorist calls. Wilson's announcement to Priest that he was going to the UK had not gone well.

"You can't just leave Wilson. Terrorists are planning an attack and we need everyone in ITAC."

"Like I told you before, something isn't right about these intercepts. It's too easy."

"For god's sake Wilson, you honestly believe the terrorist calls are fake? What about the body in Cairo, was that a fake too?"

"I agree that an attack is being planned but I think we are looking in the wrong direction. We are missing a connection and I think that connection is in the UK."

"Craig, I realise that the UK analyst…"

"His name is Chris Thornton."

"Yes, yes of course, I realise Chris was your friend but you can't just drop everything and run off to England to, to… Well to do what exactly?"

"I'm going to dig, to turn over rocks, to find out why Chris was murdered and to talk with Chris' wife.

Chris was murdered for something he knew and I think it's connected to these terrorist calls."

"Wilson, you don't have any vacation time left. If you walk out of here you will be absent without permission. Do you understand?"

"What I understand is that my friend is dead and the UK authorities don't seem to be doing very much about it. Chris worked for the UK JTAC on domestic terrorism and he was a former MI5 analyst. MI5 and the domestic authorities should be in frenzy about one of their own being murdered. Instead, the press are doing a character assassination of Chris and no one is defending him."

"If you go AWOL Wilson, I can't be responsible for what might happen. You're not a field agent Wilson!"

"Do what you need to; I'm going to London".

~

The murder of a current member of the U.K.'s Joint Terrorism Analysis Centre made good copy for both print and electronic media and Wilson downloaded the public reports. During the flight, Wilson analyzed the reports.

Reports said a street cleaner had found Chris' body in the emergency exit doorway behind the Admiral Duncan pub on Old Crompton Street, Soho in the heart of London's gay district. Tabloids had shown little restraint and had speculated wildly on the location of the body and the possibility Chris had perhaps been a client of the many male prostitutes who frequented the area.

Death, said the tabloids quoting official sources, was due to blunt trauma to the head. Wallet, jewellery, and cell phone were all missing. Only his government

ID card, which had been tucked into an inside zipped pocket of a shirt under a sweater, remained to provide an identity. No witnesses had come forward and no CCTV footage, which was very unusual for London, had been available. The proprietor of the Admiral Duncan pub later explained to investigators and media that CCTV surveillance at the back of the pub was usually turned off between 10pm and 2am to respect the privacy of patrons who might step out for a 'breath of fresh air'. Some of the more lurid tabloids had a field day with that claim.

A side story in the Daily Mail noted the Admiral Duncan pub had suffered a bomb attack, carried out by Neo-Nazi David Copeland on 30 April 1999. The bomb killed three and wounded seventy. The bomber wanted to stir up ethnic and homophobic tensions by carrying out a series of bombings. The end of the article included a throwaway line that despite regular police patrols and vigilant patrons occasional sightings of Neo-Nazi types still occurred near the pub.

Wilson, sticking with reality, suspended the gay angle due to lack of evidence, but remained open to its possibility. Chris was his friend and was married, but neither discounted discreet pursuits. Robbery seemed more plausible, but if true, the question remained. Why was Thornton in Soho in a well-known gay pub? Less probable and more disturbing, Wilson also considered a connection to Chris' email and the JTAC reports.

~

At 11am, Wilson's rental car sped along the M4 toward Soho in central London and his first stop the Admiral Duncan Pub. Before entering, Wilson walked the alleyway behind the pub. Left over crime scene tape, attached to the handle of a dumpster, marked the general location of Chris' death. A dark irregular stain, like a bruise on the concrete, pinpointed the exact place Chris had died. Wilson studied the area and noted the CCTV camera above the doorway. Angry and dismayed, Wilson left the alleyway and entered the Admiral Duncan through the front door.

Daylight and sobriety did not flatter the Admiral Duncan. Tired, seedy and gaudy sprang to Wilson's mind as he made straight for the copper-topped bar and asked the bar tender if he could have a word with Phillip York, the proprietor of the Admiral Duncan.

"Phillip," called the bar tender in the general direction of the pubs interior, "another one of those ghastly reporters is here to see you."

Wilson didn't correct the bar tender as a man, well over six feet, muscular and sweating stepped from the gloom and tore into Wilson.

"Look, I'm sick of you bastards coming in here, asking questions and twisting everything I say to sell your fucking newspapers. Now get the hell out."

Arms down Wilson held the man's stare and spoke soft words.

"The man who died, Chris Thornton was my friend. My name is Craig Wilson. I am not a reporter and I am not interested in twisting your words."

Wilson's demeanor halted the man's aggression and more kindly, the man said.

"You're not from London?"

"No. I'm from Canada."

"That may be, but I don't know what else I can tell you that I haven't already told the police."

Wilson had given this a lot of thought during the flight and had boiled his needs down to three questions.

"I only have three questions. Would that be alright?"

The man nodded.

"First, who knows the CCTV cameras are off between 10pm and 2 am? Second, do you or anyone else actually remember him being in the pub? Third, can I see the CCTV tapes?"

"OK, well, everyone knows the cameras are off. People use the alleyway for, well you know, and no one needs to be on camera for that. Now it's funny you should ask about anyone actually remembering the man in the pub."

"Why, what's funny?"

"Well, even though Friday night is busy your friend would have stood out."

"What do you mean?"

"The reports said he was wearing a sweater over a shirt."

"I don't get it, what do you mean?"

"Look, I don't want to endorse stereotypes but shirts and sweaters are not exactly de rigour in the Admiral. Anyone not showing biceps or chest would stand out like a sore thumb."

"So no one remembers him actually being in the pub."

"Yes, that's right. I told that to the police and reporters, but none seemed to take any notice."

"OK, now how about seeing the CCTV tapes?"

"Alright if you want to but there is nothing to see. I told you, CCTV is off from 10 till 2."

"I know, but I want to see if anyone was in the alleyway between 9 and 10. Just because the cameras are off at 10 doesn't mean people go away."

Phillip reviewed the tape with Wilson. One person, identified by Phillip as Billy, a local vagrant who frequented the alleyway in search of discarded drinks and cigarette ends. Billy had been on camera at 9:45.

After giving Phillip his cell phone number and eliciting a promise to call if Billy showed up, Wilson headed for St. James's Park. Before leaving Ottawa, Wilson had contacted several JTAC workers to talk about Chris. Only one of Chris' colleagues, Laura Paige, had agreed to meet him.

~

Laura, furtive glances left and right of the pathway that ran along the park's lake, responded to Wilson's greeting with bad news.

"JTAC circulated a bulletin about you today stating you are not on official business and we should not discuss any ongoing investigations or classified information with you."

"Then why are you here?"

"Chris was my friend and my mentor. He talked about you and your deductive reasoning methodology all the time. Besides, I am not going to tell you anything that is classified so please don't ask. I want to help, but I don't know if or how I can."

Wilson knew about Paige from Thornton and while he was certain she and Chris were close, he was not sure how much he could or should trust her. Not wanting to reveal that Chris had drawn his attention to the JTAC reports about the EDL, Wilson poked around with generalities.

"Laura, did Chris display any odd behaviour recently or appear particularly stressed?"

"No more than usual. No, I don't mean his behaviour, I mean stress. You know the job can be stressful, especially after that awful murder of the solider Rigby in London last May. I mean we were all under pressure at JTAC."

"Did Chris mention anything he was concerned about, reports or investigations?"

"I said I can't talk to you about investigations, I…"

"Sorry Laura, I don't want any specifics, I just meant did Chris have any major concerns about something, maybe about domestic UK terrorist or groups or anything?"

"What are you getting at? Do you know something I don't?"

"No, no not at all, I'm just desperate for some reason why Chris would be murdered."

Laura raised a tissue to her face and dabbed moisture from her cheeks. Swallowing a sob, she said.

"I have thought about it for days. There is no reason. Chris was good man. Everyone liked Chris. He never hurt anyone."

On the lake, a duck quacked and took flight as a rowboat oar slapped the water. Laura tucked the tissue in a pocket, got up to leave and said.

"I think I should go now. I'm sorry I couldn't be more help."

A step from the bench Laura turned.

"There might be one thing. Chris was hurrying to leave one day and I joked he had a hot date. He replied with something like 'hot and dangerous but definitely not a date'. Chris could be a bit dramatic sometimes, so I don't know if it meant anything or not."

"When was this?"

"I'm not sure, maybe early or mid-August."

After Paige left, Wilson checked his email. Chris had sent him the cryptic email about JTAC reports a few days before Wilson had gone camping. Chris had met someone 'hot and dangerous' shortly before he sent the email. The two had to be connected.

Wracked with guilt, Wilson stood wearily from the park bench. Across the small lake, sparsely populated by end of season boaters, a bright reflection flickered. Too far to be sure, Wilson thought a shadow dodged behind a tree. He had expected surveillance, but who was watching.

With Billy and Chris' mysterious meeting to follow up Wilson succumbed to fatigue and went to eat and rest at his hotel. He hadn't told Kathryn, Chris' wife, he was coming to London and he needed to gather his thoughts before meeting her.

~

Morning, noisy and frantic, arrived before Wilson met Kathryn. After hard tears, Kathryn apologized but she didn't want small talk and sympathy.

"I don't understand why Chris was in Soho. Every Friday we go out for dinner. We both have drinks after work with our colleagues then we meet at Caxton's at 7:30 pm. It doesn't make sense Craig."

Wilson asked Kathryn the same questions the police had with the same results. Nothing in Chris' behavior indicated any intention of visiting Soho and there was no evidence Chris had been there before.

Wilson told Kathryn what he had learned at the Admiral Duncan and what Laura Paige had told him.

"Something isn't right Craig. I can feel it."

"I can feel it too Kathryn, but I can't grasp it yet. Look, I'm going to follow up on this Billy character and try to find out who Chris met in August. Is there anything I can do for you or the kids?"

"Only one thing Craig: Find the bastards who did this."

~

For the remainder of the day and night Wilson beat the proverbial bushes without success. Priest had declared him persona non-grata, and no one in JTAC, MI5 or any of the other intelligence or law enforcement organizations would talk to him. Wilson contacted several reporters but all they wanted was an angle for another installment of their tabloid smut: Was Wilson a former lover? Did Chris have many male 'friends'?

~

Wilson's third day in London began well. A 9 am call from Phillip at the Admiral Duncan told him that Billy had been in the alleyway that morning and he should get over there if he wanted a chance to find him. By 9:45, Wilson stood in the alleyway with Phillip.

"What time was he seen?"

"The cook saw Billy about an hour ago when he chucked rubbish in the dumpster."

"Which way did he go?"

"Cook said he was probably headed for St. Anne's Church on Wardour Street. The church gives out free breakfast around ten each morning. It's only about half a mile. Go to the end of this street and turn left. You can't miss the church."

"How will I recognise Billy?"

"That's easy. He wears an old-fashioned Admiral's hat. He got out of the dumpster after our New Year's Eve party and I don't think he has taken it off since."

With thanks, Wilson set off and Phillip called after him.

"Oh, if you do find Billy, you might want to have some fags and a bottle of something with you. They will help Billy remember, if you know what I mean."

~

The hat and its owner were easy to find. Billy, already fed, lay sprawled on the church steps in a sliver of morning sun. Wilson sat beside Billy and offered him a cigarette from the package he had bought at the Booze and Fags shop on the way. Two more cigarettes disappeared before Billy spoke through a hacking cough, few teeth and swollen cheeks.

"Eh way and ja want what ya damd ya?"

Uncertain what Billy had said, Wilson offered another cigarette.

"No, ja want. You want ja what somfin I think ya."

Wilson's slow, steady and patient dialogue, coupled with a bottle of cider and more cigarettes, yielded Billy's story by noon. Billy remembered a car and three men. Three men came, two went away and one stayed on the ground by the door. Billy could not say what day it had been or what time, but he was certain about the place. Billy remembered two other things: Doc Martin boots laced up high over the ankles and a large umbrella one of the men had hung on the passenger door when the men got out of the car.

Billy would never make as a witness in a court of law but for Wilson it confirmed what he suspected. Chris had never been in the Admiral Duncan pub. He had been killed somewhere else and dumped behind the pub to muddy the trail. All he needed now was a man or men who wore Doc Martin boots and carried umbrellas.

~

The day got even better at 1pm when Laura Paige called and said she had checked Chris' desk and note pad again and found a reference to Potters Fields Park in August. Paige did not know if it meant anything but the reference seemed the only thing out of place.

By 2pm, Wilson stood in Potters Fields Park and gazed out at the River Thames, HMS Belfast and Traitors Gate. No evidence existed that Chris had been there or that he had met anyone, but it felt right to Wilson. The questions were who and why? Wilson felt sure that the why was related to the JTAC reports. Wilson was less certain about who. Could it have been someone mentioned in the reports? Maybe Chris had met an EDL member, a Muslim extremist, an undercover operative, or a colleague who shared similar concerns. Christ it could have been none of these. Perhaps Chris had really meant hot and dangerous in the sense of an affair.

Frustrated Wilson walked upriver under London Bridge, past Shakespeare's Globe Theatre, on past the National Theatre, Queen Elizabeth Hall until he stopped at the London Eye.

On impulse, Wilson brought a ticket and rode the 135 meters in to the air in search of inspiration. At the apex of the ride, Wilson stared east toward Westminster and Big Ben. Beyond Westminster and Big Ben Wilson recalled another venerable building that loomed over the river, Thames House; and within Thames House, MI5 headquarters. It wasn't science and Wilson had few solid facts but his deductive and intuitive reasoning methodology told him that Chris' meeting at Potters Fields Park had been with someone from MI5, but who?

~

Time was running out. More calls to intelligence colleagues he had met during the Five Eyes meetings and throughout his time in CSIS and with ITAC got him nothing. Priest had essentially blackballed him and while everyone was polite and sympathetic no one would meet, and no one had anything useful to add. The reflection from his watcher in Hyde Park had not led to any more sightings. They had stopped watching him or they were very good at what they did.

Wilson checked his watch. It was 1:30 pm on day four and his flight left at 10:30 the next day. Wilson sat in his rental car on a double yellow line outside MI5 HQ at Thames House for no other reason than he could think of nowhere else to go. He had less than 24 hours. Wilson wanted to stay longer, but he could only push Priest so far. If he was suspended or worse Wilson would have no access to information or intelligence and despite his need to find Chris' killer he needed to be on the inside looking in, not on the outside with the window blanked out.

Recalling the JTAC reports Wilson decided to play a long shot. Activating the GPS Wilson typed in 'Fern Street, Bedford'. Three options popped on screen: 1 hr 38 min via M1, 1 hr 49 min via A1 and 1 hr 54 via A40 and M1. Wilson pointed his car toward the M1. In less than two hours, Wilson would pay an unannounced visit to Morris Marshall, the leader of the English Defense League.

~

Marshall's pawnshop was open, but the layer of dust on the sparse array of goods indicated little business occurred. The pawnshop was a poor cover for other activities. Inside, at the rear, a long pub-like counter topped by a rigid mesh fence separated proprietor from customer. Behind the mesh, a door stood open and excited commentary on a horse race drifted from a TV or radio. Wilson tapped the bell on the counter. When the race ended, expletives filled the air and Marshall stepped through the door. During the drive to Bedford Wilson had made a plan about how he would engage Marshall. He began hard.

"You fucked up Marshall."

"What the hell are you talking about? Who the fuck are you?"

"There was a witness. He saw what happened."

"Saw what? I've been here all day."

"Not today. Friday night."

"I don't know what you are talking about; now fuck off before I call the police."

"The police? We don't want them involved. We need you to tidy up your mess."

Marshall waited.

"The witness, we have his name and location. We.."

"Look you fucking yank or whatever you are, I don't know what the hell you are talking about. Now get out."

Wilson, sensing his longshot had missed the mark, made one more attempt.

"Not many people wear Doc Martins and carry umbrellas."

A twitch or recognition, slight but definitely noticeable, ran across Marshall's face and his voice increased an octave.

"Who sent you?"

Out on limb, Wilson gambled.

"Who do you think?"

Marshall, a survivor, and a con man himself, visibly relaxed and said.

"You got nothing mate. Now fuck off before you get hurt."

As they faced each other, the shop door opened and a tough looking woman in a camouflage jacket entered. Wilson sensed a tension between the woman and Marshall as Marshall said.

"Sorry I couldn't help you mate."

Wilson, certain Marshall knew something about Chris' death, but unable to bluff more from the man, left quickly.

~

Wilson returned to his hotel and made a makeshift white board with A4 paper and pins.

> Chris sends me email
> Chris meets someone - MI5? EDL? JTAC? Affair?
> Chris murdered
> Chris dumped at gay bar
> Witness, Billy sees boots and umbrella
> Marshall flinched ref boots and umbrella
> Priest blackballs me in UK - ?

Unable to make headway, Wilson decided he needed air and space. The Cleveland hotel on Chilworth Street was a quarter mile from Hyde Park and Wilson entered the park from Lancaster Gate and made for the ornate and calming Italian Gardens. After a short walk, a park bench lured Wilson and he sat down and closed his eyes. The trickle of the nearby water gardens, rustle of trees and distant murmur of traffic lulled Wilson to sleep.

Twilight greeted Wilson's startled wakening and he peered in to the shadows. Unease heightened Wilson's senses and he strained his eyes and ears to see or hear the threat his sixth sense told him was nearby. Apprehensive, Wilson began a brisk walk back to Lancaster Gate. Three hundred meters from the gate, two hooded figures stepped from the trees on to the pathway. Wilson turned. Two more figures, shapeless and blurry blocked his retreat. To his right, a small squat building housed public toilets. With few options, Wilson ran for the toilets.

Wilson knew he had made a mistake. He had run himself into a dead end. Too late to exit, Wilson entered a stall and braced himself against the door. One thing in his favour was that the old style public washroom stalls had doors and walls that went from floor to ceiling. He might not be able to hold them off for long, but they would have to work hard to get the door open.

The pursuers were in no hurry. He could hear them enter the washroom area and kick open the other stall doors and an odour of alcohol, cigarettes and marijuana seeped in to his confined space. Whispered voices and the squeak of rubber-soled shoes on tile ended when a clear liquid trickled under the door. The whispers changed to uncontrolled giggling and laughter until two high-pitched voices alternated and sang while someone tapped on the stall door.

He knocked on the door of the house of straw
And he said "Pig let me in!"
The pig said, "No no no no no no way
Not by the hair on my chinny-chin-chin."
The wolf said he'd huff and he'd puff and he'd
Burn that house down.
The scared little pig didn't open the door
So he burned and burned and burned away.

Wilson dipped a finger in the liquid that had spread about ten inches under the door and into the stall. He lifted his finger to his nostril, lighter fluid. Not a lot, but the absorption stain on his leather shoe was a problem.

"Are you coming out little pig or are you gonna fry?"

Wilson took off his coat, undid his laces, eased his feet out of the shoes and braced himself with his feet between the toilet rim and the door. Hovering between toilet and door about two feet over the liquid, Wilson heard the scrape a match.

"Too late piggy, you should keep your snout out of things."

The initial whoosh was intense and scorched Wilson's pants before he smothered the flame with his coat. On the other side of the door, whooping and hollering signalled the depraved victory of the group.

Wilson jumped down and braced the door as vicious kicks pounded the door. Over the noise, a voice shouted.

"Fuck this man, the filth are coming. Get the fuck out. Come on. Leave him."

The crackle of radios and the beam of flashlights filled the air as Wilson grabbed his shoes and ran for the exit. He hesitated in the doorway long enough to see two horse mounted police officers chasing his assailants. With the police occupied, Wilson slipped away and ran to his hotel.

~

Wilson didn't drink much, but he made a dent in the hotel room minibar. By 11pm, he fell asleep with visions of booted, umbrella wielding men running amok in a burning MI5 headquarters while a drunken Billy, in full Admiral Regalia, cheered them on. The six am wakeup call brought Wilson back to an unsteady reality and he headed to the shower to wash away the booze and the fear.

Drying off, Wilson's cell phone rang.

"Craig, its Kathryn."

"Hi Kathryn, how are you holding up?"

"Shit Craig. I'm shit, what do you expect. Craig, I found a note in Chris' coat pocket."

"A note? Who to? What about? Not a...?"

"No, no, not a suicide note. Chris wouldn't have done that. No Craig, it's about you."

"Me?"

"Yes."

Afraid of what the note might say Wilson whispered.

"What does it say Kathryn?"

Kathryn, her voice cracking like dry timber, said. "The note says, 'Tell Craig to look again'."

The dry timber caught fire and Kathryn shouted at Wilson.

"What does it mean Craig? What are you to look at? Why is Chris' note to you and not me? I goddamn knew it had something to do with you?"

Wilson, felled by the weight of Kathryn's accusation mumbled.

"Chris sent me an email Kathryn. It was about some classified reports. The email came the day before I left for vacation and I..."

"What? Chris needed your help and you went on vacation. Damn it Craig, I think Chris died because of what he wanted you to look at. You had damn well better find out why my husband died and what was so important. I don't want Chris to have died for nothing and have people and newspapers telling horrible lies about Chris. You need to find out the truth. You owe it to Chris."

Kathryn hung up. Wilson needed to analyse those documents again. The problem was the documents were classified and only accessible at ITAC back in Ottawa.

Twenty-Two

September 12 2013, Ottawa, Canada

PREDICTABLY, PRIEST SUMMONED WILSON to his office moments after Wilson arrived at ITAC. Cook, probably on hand as a witness, flanked Priest.

"So Wilson," said Priest "what did you achieve in England aside from jeopardizing your career, irritating our UK allies and embarrassing yourself and ITAC?"

"Loose ends."

"What? Look Wilson, I don't have the time or patience for more of your cryptic inductive crap anymore. Did you discover anything related to these intercepted terrorist calls or not?"

Thirty thousand feet up at 1100 kilometer per hour, Wilson had asked himself the same question. His answer had been yes and no. The key was the JTAC reports but unless additional intelligence on the terrorist calls pointed more to the UK and the EDL in particular Wilson would not be able to make a case. He was certain that Chris had met someone from MI5, that the EDL were connected to his death and that in some way the entire terrorist plot was linked to the UK, MI5 and the EDL. His analysis and his intuition told him he was right but he could not provide the kind of facts Priest and his kind needed.

"No, I found no concrete connection between Chris' death and the terrorist calls."

Priest puffed up his chest and said.

"Effective immediately you are on a thirty-day probationary period during which time if you step out of your lane you will face dismissal. Do you understand?"

"Yes."

"Good god Wilson, what were you thinking? You run off like some kind of cowboy and come back with nothing. What a complete waste of time. You ought to…"

"Let's get one thing straight Priest. I said I didn't find any concrete connection to the terrorist calls. I did find things that don't fit into your myopic analytical processes that demand black and white images, symmetrical shapes and proven calculus. I did discover threats and loose ends connected to Chris' death that don't add up or fit in to a pattern; at least not yet. More importantly, I now know Chris wasn't the victim of a random robbery or some sordid liaison gone wrong. That wasn't a waste of time for me or for Chris' family. Chris was murdered for a reason connected to his work and I'm going to find out what that reason was."

Wilson didn't wait for Priest to respond and walked away before Priest pushed him too far.

In the sanctuary of his office, Wilson lifted the cover off the flip chart. The five statements and questions Wilson had written in relation to Chris' cryptic email almost a month ago glared at him accusingly:

EDL recruitment up with new financial resources - money from where? Media reports of Muslim extremism up, why? Why no follow up? Who is SS?

Heavy with grief Wilson chastised himself. "I'm sorry Chris. I should have done more."

Crisp knocks on the office door broke Wilson's grim reflection. Reluctant, Wilson acknowledged the second, more insistent knock.

"Yes, O.K. Come in."

Mitch Donaldson, one of the few surviving analysts from the pre-Priest era and attached to the European desk under Roger Cook, leapt through the door.

"Craig, have you heard? We have intercepted two more phone calls. The calls are similar to the phone calls from August 29 and 31. Priest and Cook are jumping like jack rabbits to get the info up the chain. They think it's a big one and…"

Wilson, thoughts still with his murdered friend Chris, shook his head and said.

"No Mitch. I hadn't heard. When did we get the intercepts?"

"Sometime last night, Priest has called a meeting in five minutes. I've come to get you."

Mitch, caught up in the excitement did not register Wilson's sombre mood and swept into the office and past Wilson. Mitch had joined ITAC a few months after Wilson and they had become close colleagues. Mitch, who respected Wilson's analytical abilities as well as his methods, nodded toward Wilson's white boards. After a few seconds, Mitch exclaimed.

"Disinformation or fake! That's your conclusion about the August 29 and 31 intercepts. Have you told Cook or Priest yet?"

"Yes. I told him before I went to England."

Mitch, concerned for his friend, said.

"How was England Craig?"

"I'll tell you later Mitch."

"Come on then, we had better get to the boardroom."

~

When Wilson and Mitch arrived, Priest and Cook had assumed their usual positions in the ITAC board-room. Priest nodded to Cook who activated the screen and projector. The projector light illuminated and eleven words chilled the room.

Cell phone intercept. September 10, 2013.
From Manchester, England to Egypt
Male voice, Arabic
BEGIN:
This is Musa. Target confirmed.
End:

Cell phone intercept. September 11, 2013.
From Manchester, England to Syria
Male voice, Arabic
BEGIN:
This is Ibrahim. We have access.
END:

Questions and comments remained unspoken as analysts listened as Priest provided additional information.

"The calls were made to two different phone numbers; one to Egypt and one to Syria. The numbers are on a known list of telephone numbers associated with Al Qaeda operatives or previous Al Qaeda activities. We believe these calls are a continuation of the two calls intercepted on August 29 from Cairo to London and August 31 from Cairo to Berlin."

Cook, prompted by a nod from Priest, projected the two previously intercepted calls on the screen.

One: Cell phone intercept. August 29, 2013.

From Cairo, Egypt to London, England
Male voices, Arabic
BEGIN:
Date?
Almost. A question remains about the date.
Why?
To maximize casualties.
END:

Two: Cell phone intercept. August 31, 2013.
From Cairo, Egypt to Berlin, Germany
Male voices, Arabic
BEGIN:
Report.
Date confirmed.
END:

Priest, not waiting for comments, established the ITAC position.

"Al Qaeda is plotting a major attack in Europe. These intercepts indicate the terrorists have established a date, a target and have gained access to the target. I cannot emphasis to you the seriousness of these intercepts and the lives at risk. The Americans intercepted the first two calls. We, or more accurately CSE, intercepted the second two messages."

Analysts, stimulated by the intercepts and challenged by Priest, fired questions at Priest and each other.

"Have we given the calls to the Five Eyes yet?"

"Yes."

"Did we get any data on the originating cell phone?"

"The originating cell phone numbers have been identified as part of a wholesale sequence of numbers assigned in the UK to disposable prepaid phones. Most of these phones are purchased for cash at anyone of thousands of kiosks in the UK."

"Are the cell phone purchases being followed up?"

"Tracing cell phone purchasing records has yielded little in the past and is a low priority for resource allocation."

"What about the destination of the calls, Egypt and Syria? What do we have?"

"As I said the numbers called are known Al Qaeda related numbers. The first call was made to the Khan el-Khalili souk market in the Islamic district of Cairo. The second call was picked up in the Muslim section of Damascus."

"What about targets?"

"The cities of Berlin, Manchester, and London are all directly implicated by being either the locations of either the origin or receipt of a call."

"Were the messages encrypted?"

"Apparently not, this is good news for us."

The questions continued as analysts zeroed in on their own areas of interest or focus. Answers and follow-up questions washed over Wilson as he fought to separate his guilt over Chris' death, the files Chris had wanted him to look at again and the messages, now four, that indicated a serious terrorist event was imminent somewhere in Europe. Wilson, distracted, did not hear Priest ask him directly what his thoughts were until Mitch, seated beside him, nudged Wilson on the arm. Priest, irritation clear, repeated his question.

"Craig, as one of our most experienced analysts, what did you conclude from the earlier phone calls and what are your thoughts on these latest intercepts?"

Wilson, reluctantly conforming to Priest's instruction to keep his conclusions to himself said.

"This morning I was uncertain about the seriousness of the threat but with these two new calls the threat appears real."

"Well Craig," said Priest with patronizing levity, "there's no harm in exercising that brain of yours. Let Roger know if you come up with anything."

Priest posed similar questions to the remaining analysts. Consensus, or group think, quickly cemented itself to confirm Priest's assertion Al Qaeda was well advanced in its intention to conduct a significant terrorist attack on a European city.

~

Dismissed, Wilson returned to his office subdued. He still believed something was amiss with the first two phone calls. As for the second two calls, he could not understand why the caller had not used an encrypted phone on a GSM network. In addition, the second two calls were one way. There was no second voice, no confirmation of an actual conversation. Yes, calls to voice mail were common enough, but leaving critical information to a voice mail seemed risky or amateurish or maybe something else. Wilson had a third reason within grasp, but it eluded him when he tried to force the thought from his head.

On autopilot, Wilson selected a strong espresso coffee capsule and slotted it into his Nespresso coffee machine. The hiss of steam and aroma of coffee broke Wilson's trance and brought him back to the present. Responding to a subconscious instruction Wilson grasped the flip chart with Chris' 'look again' information and placed it beside the white boards that contained his analysis of the first two terrorist phone calls. With a black marker, Wilson added the eleven words from the two new intercepts.

Halfway through his coffee Wilson stepped to the white board and scrawled the third possible reason why there had been no second voices or conversation on the second two intercepted calls: Maybe there were no second persons.

Twenty-Three

September 1 2013, Manchester, England

DARREN HAD BEEN ON EDGE for five hours since he and Mackenna had forced Aalim and his family into the white van and slipped out of Manchester to drive north to The Grange, a remote cottage in the heart of the Lake District. Adrenalin gushed, fingers shook and saliva dried until they had tied and gagged the man and locked the woman and kid in another room. Then, as instructed, he and Mackenna left The Grange.

Darren glanced at Mackenna as he maneuvered the white van through the narrow lanes of the Lake District. Excitement distorted Mackenna's blotched and puffy face as he boasted and over simplified the kidnap for the tenth time.

"I can't believe we did it man. Shit, it was so fucking easy. We should get more of them, kill them, and bury them in the forest. No one would know."

Mackenna's voice crawled across Darren's skin and he asked himself again why they need this whack head. Darren admitted Mackenna's business suit, trendy overcoat and umbrella made him a natural fit for the role of insurance man to call at Aalim's house, but Mackenna was crazy. And dangerous. With more sarcasm and disdain than intended given Darren's knowledge of Mackenna, he said.

"Yeah, well I think there is more to it than killing few families and burying them in the forest."

Cigarette smoke leaked upward from Mackenna's curled lips, past puffy cheeks, wrinkled eyes, and mixed and added to his sallow complexion and clung to his short, brown, greasy hair. The lips uncurled to form smoke and malice laden words.

"In my experience, it's dangerous to know too much."

Darren fixed on the white center-line of the road, thought about his companion. Although in his early thirties, most people pegged Mackenna as well north of forty. A pungent aroma of nicotine and alcohol, specifically unfiltered Woodbine cigarettes and Carling beer, a strong, low-priced ice beer with an alcohol content of 6.1%, preceded and lingered after Mackenna's presence.

Mackenna always disheveled and grubby, except when he donned his trademark business suit ensemble for a protest march, was a mini-Deity among EDL hardliners. Many members had readily shared stories and anecdotes, although every disclosure came with a caveat not to tell Mackenna they had talked about him. They were scared.

On the way back to warehouse in the Pomona Docks, Mackenna insisted they stop to buy cigarettes, beer and take-out fish and chips. Between the stop for supplies and the warehouse Mackenna, fortified with food and alcohol, belched, farted, and continued their previous conversation without any indication that an hour or more had passed.

"The thing is Darren, how do you know you know too much, and how do you know that someone else thinks you know too much. You see, the problem is not so much knowing too much, but not letting anyone think you know too much. Because it's not knowledge that's dangerous, it's the knowledge people think you have that is dangerous. Do you know what I mean?"

Unnerved by Mackenna's convoluted logic and unsure of the point Darren remained silent.

Mackenna had turned sideways to face Darren and the smoke no longer twisted upward, but drifted toward him as Mackenna spoke more riddled threats.

"I think you do. What's more, I think you know a lot more than you say you do, which is exactly what I mean. You are making me think you have a lot of knowledge about what we are doing. And that makes you dangerous, which is something I will have to think about."

Darren had no response and was relieved when Mackenna reclined his head on the seat and closed his eyes. Based on stories from other EDL members, Darren had reached some disturbing conclusions about his fellow kidnapper.

No one outright said Mackenna had actually killed anyone, but an undeniable theme of ferocious violence and detached cruelty against men, women, and according to some, children, permeated the achievements of Steve Mackenna. Victims were generally foreign. Most visible minorities, some white Eastern Europeans, some distinctly religious and a few just because they were in the wrong place the wrong time. Many were physically shorter and weaker, and Mackenna always attacked from behind. Brass knuckles, nightstick and feet were Mackenna's weapons. Brass delivered the sucker punch, the stick fractured skulls, broke arms, legs and hands and his feet, clad in Doc Martin boots, kicked and stomped vital organs.

Darren understood that Mackenna had not committed these assaults with impunity. He had a long criminal record and had spent seven of his thirty something years in government institutions. Many months of his non-incarcerated time also included wearing an electronic ankle bracelet. Darren was no psychologist but even he recognized that Mackenna's antisocial behavior, diminished capacity for remorse, and poor behavioral controls screamed psychopath.

Darren and Mackenna stayed in the warehouse for the night. Darren, organized and prepared, wrestled in and out of his sleeping bag on a bed of discarded cardboard boxes. Mackenna, after rummaging around the warehouse and cursing at his lack of preparation, slumped in the passenger seat of the white van. Both men dreamed:

Hollywood-like victim-filled explosions and white man Nuremberg-style mass rallies played across a canvas as Darren imagined himself humbled on a podium as thousands paid homage to his bravery and his role in ridding England of foreigners. Mackenna, restless and uncomfortable, dreamed in red and brown: blood and skin.

Twenty-Four

September 1 2013, London, England

HIGH DEFINITION CAMERAS, LINKED to an encrypted server, provided real time views of The Grange, a grand name for the modest cottage that hugged the south side of Beacon Hill in the North West region of England's Lake District.

Disguised on the centuries old oak trees that surrounded the cottage four cameras provided 360-degree coverage, ensuring no unseen entry or exit. Inside, additional cameras allowed viewers to witness every action of the cottages inhabitants. Microphones and speakers complemented the cameras and motion detectors, supported by external door and window sensors, announced visitors to the integrated surveillance system which communicated to a wireless transmitter that broadcast the sound and pictures.

MI5 had acquired The Grange during WWII. The cottage had belonged to William Charles Smithson, one of many well-to-do Englishmen who misguidedly sympathized with the German Nazi regime. Unfortunately, Smithson had done more than sympathize, and when authorities discovered the extent of his financial and intelligence support of the Nazis, he met an unexpected end and British intelligence seized his properties. In the post-war confusion, MI5 secured control of The Grange, and until 1999, official records indicated that the long deceased Smithson owned the land and property.

After 1999, ownership of The Grange changed to a holding company controlled ultimately by Mitton-Wells. Prior to the sale, Simon Spencer had ensured that the supposed 'decommissioning' of The Grange had been minimal and with little effort, Spencer had restored the facility to MI5 'safe house' standards and provided Mitton-Wells the keys, security codes, Internet server access protocols.

Mitton-Wells accessed the live audiovisual feed from The Grange moments after the front door sensor triggered an automated alert. Even in the twilight and the long shadows cast by the early setting sun of late summer the high-resolution cameras provided crisp images of a white van parked backward against the cottage front door. Mitton-Wells switched to the internal cameras.

Three hooded figures, led by Mackenna and followed by Blackley, stumbled through the narrow cottage hallways to the basement door. Another camera, angled up the basement stairs, watched the silent figures descend with timid steps. At the bottom, the three figures split: the two shorter figures forced left and the third, and taller forced right. Steered through a doorway, and pushed down onto a metal chair, plastic ties secured the lone figures ankles, legs, torso and hands to the chair. Over the hood, a thick cotton gag muted the mouth.

Mouth dry from concentration and anticipation, Mitton-Wells switched to camera right and watched as the figure, immobile and silent, slumped against his bonds. Satisfied, Mitton-Wells changed to the camera left of the basement steps and peered into another room.

A woman and child, the wife and son of the bound figure, huddled together on the floor in the far corner of the room. Increasing the volume Mitton-Wells listened dispassionately to the fearful sobbing of the boy and the reassuring murmurs of the mother.

~

Trembling with the power of dominance, Mitton-Wells recalled the advice and instructions from Simon.

"Control and authority Anthony, that's what you need to establish. When he is secure, take away his sight and manipulate what he can hear. I suggest you let him hear his wife and son. They will cry, whimper, and eventually call to him for help. The more they call for him, and the more he cannot answer, the greater the fear and uncertainty. After a few hours, you can introduce the other sounds through the speakers."

Simon had explained that the other sounds were part of the psychological torture techniques used by Israeli security forces to break suspected Arab terrorist before questioning. Content included the use of extreme stressors and situations such as mock executions, physical torture recordings, simulated violation of deep-seated social or sexual norms and repetitive noises such as human screams and pleading as well as denouncements of self, family and friends.

Mitton-Wells had listened to the sounds provided by Simon. Even safe and secure in his own home he had been frightened. After only fifteen minutes, with eyes and ears open and lights on, Mitton-Wells had sweat and crushed the supple leather of his armchair with clenched fingers.

"He's not a professional Anthony. He has no training so three hours should be enough to get his attention. When you do speak to him, the first thing to establish is control and response. Ask him simple yes and no questions, which he can answer with

a shake or nod of his head. If he hesitates, turn the sounds back on for five minutes. I doubt very much that you will have a problem though as he knows you have his wife and son."

Mitton-Wells had grimaced when Simon had said to give Hussein three hours of psychological torture. At first Mitton-Wells had observed the man's body arch and twist as the sound flooded unstoppable into his mind, straining against the plastic bindings that cut into the man's skin. Trickles of blood ran down brown skin, dropped, and pooled on the floor. Morbid fascination had trumped revulsion until a dark yellow stain spread across the captive's lap as urine leaked from an uncontrollable bladder. The prospect of more soiling repulsed Mitton-Wells and he had turned away from the screen and muted the sound.

Three hours to the minute, Mitton-Wells accessed the live feed from The Grange. The man, his body and clothes stained with blood, urine and excrement, hung limp and defeated on the chair. Mitton-Wells turned off the torture and listened to the room. Blood, evidence of bitten tongue and cheek, stained the white gag and incoherent murmurs trickled through the fabric and out of the speakers on Mitton-Wells' laptop. Mitton-Wells consulted the notes he and Simon had prepared and spoke to the man for the first time.

"Aalim Hussein. Is that your name?"

Lips stilled and the murmurs ceased, but no response came.

Mitton-Wells turned the sounds back on. The man convulsed. Despite Simon's instructions to wait five minutes, Mitton-Wells stopped the sound and repeated the question.

"Aalim Hussein. Is that your name?"

A nod, slight, but discernible.

"Good Aalim. Are you a Muslim?"

Another nod. This time a little more vigorous.

"Do you love your wife and son?"

Fast, repeated nods.

"Aalim, do you know where you are?"

Left, right head shake.

"Do you know why you have been taken Aalim?"

More left, right.

"Would you like to know Aalim?"

Yes, yes conveyed Aalim's bobbing head.

"Very well Aalim. Listen well."

Satisfied, Mitton-Wells explained to Aalim how the world should be, what Aalim's place in the world was, and most importantly, how he, Aalim Hussien, could save his wife and child. Done with dictating the new world order, Mitton-Wells asked his captive one last question.

"Are you ready to save your wife and son Aalim Hussein?"

Discolored and stained, the hood nodded agreement with two deliberate forward and backward movements.

Twenty-Five

September 3 2013, The Grange, Manchester, England

DARREN AND MACKENNA RETURNED TO The Grange twenty-four hours after they had left their captives. On the drive from Manchester to the Lake District Darren received a call with instructions to stop at the Motorway Services at Junction 32 near Lancaster, park the van with the keys in section D of the parking lot, and get a coffee.

When Darren and Mackenna returned, a blue Ford Escape had replaced the white van. Keys were inside and the gas tank was full. A sticky note on the dash read 'your shit is in the trunk'.

Mackenna, whose 'shit' comprised an assortment of porn magazines, a set of headphones for his Ipod and a bag of crumpled clothes said.

"They had better not taken my reading material or messed with my head phones."

Darren, irritated and annoyed by Mackenna's crass persona, ignored the comment and instead wondered at the ever-increasing level of organization and resources available to whomever was behind the operation.

"I guess were not taking the paki bastards back to Manchester then eh?" said Mackenna as he picked, licked and flicked the contents of his nose toward his feet.

"What," asked Darren, not following Mackenna's train of thought?

"The car you dip stick. Windows! We can't drive around with three people in the back with hoods over their heads can we? I guess we're gonna do them in? I never thought I would get the chance to kill some of them without any rush or interference."

Darren, caught off guard by Mackenna's conclusion, drummed his fingers on the steering wheel and tried to figure things through. He did not know the plan, but he doubted that they would just kill them in the middle of nowhere. Why bother with the elaborate kidnap just to kill them?

"What's the matter boy? You don't have the chops for it? Don't worry I'll do them."

Needing to assert control, Darren took a chance and said.

"You won't kill them. We have bigger plans than that."

A noncommittal grunt and narrowed eyes met Darren's assertion of 'bigger plans'. Unnerved by Mackenna's grunt and stare, and the substance of Mackenna's earlier comments about 'knowing too much,' Darren stayed silent for the remainder of the journey.

~

The moment Darren parked the car in front of The Grange and switched off the engine his phone rang. A familiar voice conveyed omnipotent awareness and direction.

"Ah, I see you have arrived. Inside, on the dining room table are two envelopes; one for you and one for Mr. Mackenna."

The line disconnected.

Startled by the call and knowledge of their arrival, Darren squinted at the Grange's walls and windows. Mackenna, who had scooped his 'shit' from the trunk of the car, said.

"Who was that and what are you looking for?"

"Nobody, nothing, let's get inside."

Darren led the way and strode to the dining room. Two brown envelopes, one thin and one fat, lay on the table. The fat one, its seal strained by the contents, had Darren's name on it. The thin one bore Mackenna's name.

Darren opened his envelop. A plain white paper, clipped to the front of a two-inch, three ring binder, held his first instruction. Darren read it and shuddered.

'Do not interfere with the activities of Mr. Mackenna'.

Darren turned to Mackenna who held the single sheet of paper he had withdrawn from his envelope. A vile smirk split his face as he read his instructions. He stared at Darren and hissed.

"That's more like it," said Mackenna as he turned to leave the dining room, "we will be having a little fun with the Pakis. Or at least I will."

Darren opened his binder. An index page, neat and alphabetized, in crisp bold print waited. Darren scanned the index: Daily routine; Electronic Equipment; Bomb Making Materials; Cover Story; Mosque; Mail; Travel; Control; Behavior; Money.

A slap of flesh on flesh, a roar, and a desperate, shrill scream, pierced the silence and broke Darren's concentration. Darren dropped his binder and ran to the basement door.

"Mackenna!" called Darren.

Sound, pain and fear-laden, filled the stairwell. Darren, caught between instinct and instruction, hesitated and shouted.

"Mackenna, Mackenna what the fuck are you doing? What's going on?"

Asthmatic like heaves and sobs replaced the screams as Mackenna appeared at the base of the steps and snarled at Darren.

"What do you want? Now fuck off while I get the job done. I'll come and get you when I'm finished."

Bile, thick and acrid, sloshed up Darren's throat. Mackenna was naked and erect. Perspiration beaded on his torso. A length of coarse rope hung around his neck and a thick short stick, a leather cord threaded through one end, hung on Mackenna's left wrist. Mackenna winked at Darren and turned to enter the room where Aalim sat bound and gagged. The screams chased Darren out of the house to stumble and vomit on the driveway.

Twenty-Six

September 3 2013, Manchester, England

MACKENNA HAD BEEN WRONG. Aalim and his family still lived. At least Darren thought Aalim's wife and child still lived. Mackenna had come to him about twenty minutes after Darren had fled in revulsion at what Mackenna was doing in the basement. Mackenna brought Aalim with him, pushing the bound but un-hooded man in the back with the end of a short stick. Aalim tripped and fell face first to the gavel driveway and Mackenna sprung onto Aalim's back and placed the stick under Aalim's chin up against his windpipe. Mackenna leaned in and spoke in Aalim's ear.

"You be a good boy for Darren now. If you don't your little wife and your sweet boy will get some of that special love and attention from their uncle Steve. You know what I mean."

Mackenna yanked the stick tight against Aalim's throat. Unable to breath, Aalim wriggled and spluttered as Mackenna braced a knee on Aalim's back for lever-age as he got off. Upright and glaring at the prostrate form, Mackenna hawked phlegm, spat on Aalim's back and said to Darren.

"He's all yours. I'm to stay here with the bitch and the brat."

~

Long evening shadows draped The Grange as Darren drove the blue Ford Escape away from the house toward the two stone pillars that marked the entrance to the 250-acre property. The first section of the binder 'immediate' instructed Darren to get Aalim cleaned and taken home to Manchester. Aalim, silent and submissive, slumped against the passenger door, head on chest and eyes fixed on his feet. Darren, cautious of the winding narrow road of the Lake District uplands, stole a glance at his victim. Disgusted, Darren threw cold words at Aalim.

"Listen you miserable shit. You have things to do tomorrow. First, you will contact Borough Taxis and tell them you have decided to quit taxi driving because of the long hours. Second, you will call your son's school and explain there has been a family emergency and he and his mother have gone to Egypt. You are not sure how long they will away, perhaps a month. You will contact them when your son returns. Third, you will tell the same story to anyone who asks about your wife and son. Do you understand?"

An almost imperceptible nod accompanied a shallow exhalation as Aalim acknowledged Darren's command.

"Good."

Faces and bodies twitched and contracted with unspoken thoughts and emotions as each man retreated into himself. Thick, angry, silence hung between them until Darren stopped the car on Lytham Street, two blocks from Aalim's home. Pressed against the passenger door Aalim did not acknowledge the car had stopped. Darren, tense and irritated, shouted at Aalim.

"Hey, shit head. This is where you get out. Here is a cell phone. I will call you. Keep the phone with you at all times. Now fuck off to your house, stay there, and contact no one except the school and the taxi company. I will call you tomorrow and you can start saving your wife and kid. Got it?"

Aalim squeezed his hands together between his legs and faced Darren. Nasal mucus, an involuntary by-product of emotional stress, streamed from Aalim's nose and mixed with tears that soaked Aalim's puffed cheeks. Pliant, yet strong, words seeped from Aalim.

"Why are you doing this? What have I done to you? Why do you take my wife and my son? Why?"

Anger and disgust suppressed pity and Darren barked at Aalim.

"Get out of the car".

~

Darren, exhausted and relieved to be away from Aalim, rushed to his newly rented two-bedroom apartment in the recently developed and burgeoning trendy area of the Salford Quays in central Manchester. Darren's previous one-room existence had ended soon after the first phone call in April. Money, plenty of it, had enabled Darren to rent the apartment and furnish it with modern, uncomfortable furniture and audio visual trappings that passed as indicators of success for people like Darren.

Before the largess of his mysterious benefactor, hapless foraging for morsels of something to give his life purpose and meaning had punctuated the day-to-day drudge of Darren's existence. Like many other unskilled men, Darren bumped from one black market 'job' to another, earning only enough to ensure shelter in one room houses in less desirable areas of Manchester. Occasional successes as a minor participant in petty crimes involving stolen goods, drugs, illegal gambling, or information exchange, provided rare highs and transient substances provided brief solace to stem the reality that Darren had no life, no purpose and no future.

Tired and stressed, Darren drank beer and rolled a joint. A second beer chased another joint and within an hour, Darren entered the 'sweet zone' of optimism and happiness that draws people to alcohol and drugs. Relaxed, Darren soared with recollections of his soccer zenith when, at sixteen years old, he had wowed and impressed the manager and owners of Oldham Athletic Soccer Club. Even more, how on one cold spring morning in 1996, the Oldham Athletic coach had whispered to Darren that a Manchester City scout had come to the training session to watch Darren.

Manchester City, long the 'second soccer club' in Manchester behind the dominant Manchester United, had filled Darren's dreams since his father had taken him to watch his first game in 1987. Mesmerized by the sky blue shirts of the Manchester City team players as they cruised to a 4-0 win over Crystal Palace, Darren had been a 'blue' ever since. Like many 'blues' Darren had dreamed of the day he would play for Manchester City. Unlike 99.9% of aspiring soccer players Darren actually had a chance.

Substance abusers, if they were able, would concede the greater intensity and longer duration of the low that follows the high. While better financial resources improved the quality and quantities of alcohol and marijuana, money did nothing to temper the inevitable post-binge memories.

When Darren's alcoholic and marijuana high began to subside, he no longer soared in a sky blue shirt of Manchester City but plunged into bitterness and resentment that centered on the instruments and symbol of his unfulfilled life: Manchester United, its supporters, and Sikhs.

~

Darren had been sixteen and a half in late 1996 when hooliganism, the disorderly, aggressive and often violent behavior perpetrated by spectators at sporting events, especially soccer, was, according to media and official reports, well in to a much-needed decline. Public hype, however well-intentioned and accurate, did nothing to prevent the indiscriminate and vicious beating meted by Manchester United fans to a small group of Manchester City fans who had become separated from the main body of their own supporters and found themselves isolated and vulnerable on a side street just 500 meters from Manchester United's stadium.

Darren, along with several friends from his high school soccer team, had gone to the game in the hope that Manchester City would beat Manchester United and knock United out of the highly prized FA Cup competition. Darren's hope was shattered when United beat Manchester City 2-1 and Darren and his fellow supports suffered the humiliating taunts of the United faithful as they slunk away from the stadium.

A left instead of right turn would have saved Darren. He and about twenty other Manchester City fans had exited the Manchester United stadium, and instead of making a hasty and direct line for the relative safety of the heavily policed main street, lingered and meandered through side streets until a boisterous crowd of about two hundred victorious Manchester United supporters blocked their way. As the twenty blues faced the two hundred reds both groups knew what would follow.

Young and fast, Darren would have escaped except for the Manchester City scarf that flapped three feet behind him and allowed a pursuing soccer fan to grasp it and haul Darren to the hard concrete of the sidewalk. Frightened and breathless, Darren tumbled and crashed to the ground at the base of a small unkempt hedge. Adrenalin gave Darren the strength to force his way head first through the hedge and up onto his knees to scramble to the faded front door of the shabby terrace house that hid behind the hedge.

Like hounds on the scent of a trapped fox, the Manchester United fans kicked in the locked wooden gate and paused to watch Darren pound and claw at the door for help. The door opened and a snarl of expletives polluted the air as five or six boys and men surged toward Darren. Chains, several of them, restricted the door to a six-inch opening. Darren, sensing escape, screamed through the narrow crack.

"Help. Help me for fuck's sake. Open the door. Open the door."

A frightened man, pupils wide and dark below thick black eyebrows, peered out.

Darren pushed his left arm in to the opening and tried to squeeze the rest of him through the unyielding gap. Darren's hand clawed for a hold until the impact of a blunt object splayed his finger. Pain shot up his arm. He jerked back and watched as a brown-skinned hand pushed his arm out of the opening.

"No, no, let me in, let me in. Please, help me."

Darren pressed his face to the closing door and croaked one last desperate plea as a turban-clad head shook with denial before the door banged shut. Trapped, Darren lunged out of the doorway and tried to jump the scrawny four-foot hedge that separated one miserable row house from the next. He didn't make it.

Instead, Darren jumped into the hedge and slid, with handfuls of ripped leaves and branches, to the ground. Without hesitation feet flew into Darren's torso and legs to inflict bruises that would takes weeks to heal and fade. Instinctive defense contorted Darren to the fetal position as stomps, the most indifferent and inhumane act of gang beatings, joined the kicks and punches.

The combined force of the blows and Darren's natural recoil pushed Darren into the base of the hedge and hindered the ability of his attackers to stomp. Bloodied and contorted Darren squirmed deeper under the hedge as sounds of whistles and sirens announced the arrival of police and emergency services. The attack paused and Darren, thinking himself safe, peered from the hedge. One beer gutted, tattooed Manchester United fan, unmoved by the prospect of law enforcement lingered long enough to inflict one last stomp on to Darren's left temple. With only concrete under his head the full force of the stomp pushed the orbital bone inward creating a permanent depression and a degradation of his vision that by his eighteenth birthday convinced professional soccer coaches Darren could never be a professional soccer player.

In forty-five seconds, the duration of the frenzied attack, two convictions cemented in Darren's psyche: hatred for Manchester United and hatred for brown-skinned people with rags for hats.

Through the fog of beer and marijuana, Darren spent the night studying the binder. The contents mirrored the kidnapping binder: Detailed instructions, maps, money, locations, and photographs. Separate sections for electronics, email, rental properties, cell phones and a vehicle. Everything he needed to manage and manipulate Aalim's Hussien for the next six weeks. Everything he needed to make Aalim a terrorist.

Twenty-Seven

September 21 2013, Ottawa, Canada

JANE WILSON UNDERSTOOD HER HUSBAND'S work. Nevertheless, she didn't always like what it did to him and their relationship. He was a bureaucrat. He did not spy on or arrest people or anything dramatic and hands on. He worked in an office and pushed paper. Jane was aware that her husband's office-bound paper analysis supported the people who actually did follow, spy and arrest bad people. The problem for Jane was Wilson's tendency to commit body and soul to an event to the exclusion of everything else, including his own physical and mental health. When Craig focussed on an event, he consumed nothing but coffee, didn't sleep and became distant and isolated. Worried for her husband, Jane worked hard to help Wilson to have some 9-5 Monday to Friday periods, which is why on Saturday September 21 Jane was frustrated with her husband.

"Why today Craig? We planned this dinner three months ago. You know how hard it is to get everyone together: New Year's Eve Craig! That was the last time we all got together."

Jane was right. For nine months the eight people, four couples, had tried to coordinate each other's personal and professional commitments to have a night out as they used to do pre-kids and everything else. Twice before, once in May and once in July, emergencies for one or other couple had led to a canceled or abbreviated night. Now, at 4pm on Saturday September 21, no one had called to cancel.

"Craig, I know you are worried about a terrorist attack and I understand you need to be involved. I worry about you and I just want us to have some time together with our friends."

"I want to go Jane. I really do."

Wilson did. Prompted by Jane, it had been his idea to indulge in an eight-course tasting menu complete with selected wine pairings. Le Baccara, an AAA, Five Diamond restaurant for 13 consecutive years, had needed to be reserved months in advance. Wilson wanted to go.

"Then tell Priest or whoever that you can't go in today. Surely whatever needs doing could be done by someone else."

Jane was partly right. The phone message intercepts about a plot to bomb a European city was not his file. He had been invited to the first two meetings because Roger Cook was new to the European files, there may have been a domestic terrorism component, and because Wilson was the longest serving ITAC analyst. Wilson, if he had been less modest, would also have mentioned he was one of ITAC's best analysts and despite his opinion of Director Priest's bureaucratic focus, Priest realized the value and legitimacy of Wilson's analytical contribution.

The email to attend an 'analytical review' at 5pm in the boardroom had come at 3:45 pm. While fending off Jane's understandable complaints Wilson had scoured the BBC and CNN websites for news of a terrorist attack in Europe. Relieved by the news coverage, Wilson assumed there had been an intelligence development.

"Jane, you're right. Someone else can always write the note, and the thing that is developing is not directly my file, but this is serious honey. I think this is real. More importantly, though, something about this isn't quite right. I don't know what yet. It's a feeling."

Jane sighed with sympathy. She knew how important his 'feeling' had been in the past. In 2008, Wilson had a feeling about a plot to hijack an oil tanker and blow it up in Rotterdam, Holland. His conclusions, contrary to those of the majority, had led investigators and police away from the hijack theory to focus on the use of harbour pilot boats as floating bombs. Wilson had been right. Two pilot ships, rigged with hundreds of pounds of C4, and the name and enlarged photograph of a US registered super tanker, had been discovered two days before the tanker's scheduled arrival.

In 2009, Wilson had spotted the link between credit card fraud and funding for international terrorist organizations. Criminal organizations, when they learned they were funding terrorism, had tacitly agreed with law enforcement agencies to end their relationship with these known terrorist organizations. The threat of prosecution for aiding terrorists, and the associated prison sentences if convicted, was more convincing than the prospect of a quick profit.

Concern and desire for her husband, Jane tried a different tactic.

"Craig, what about Chris. You need some distraction. You have hardly spoken about Chris' death. Getting out with friends, with good food and wine, might help. I'm worried about you Craig. Can't you tell Priest or Cook what your feeling is and let them deal with it?"

Wilson faced Jane and held her gaze.

"That's just it Jane. My feeling includes Chris. The more I think about it the more I am convinced there is a connection between Chris' death and these intercepted messages. Even if I did come tonight, I wouldn't be very good company."

"Alright Craig, I'll keep a seat for you. Text me if you can come. I love you."

~

Paper cups with plastic lids, sides printed with either Tim Horton's, Starbucks, or Second Cup logos, stood disorganized and haphazard on the boardroom table. Other cups nestled protected and obscured in the agitated hands of the ITAC analysts who sat or stood while they sipped. Wilson let the smell of coffee roll up through his nasal passages and regretted again his 'snobbery' of only drinking coffee of his own making. He had resisted the urge to slip into his office and brew a Longu coffee. While it had been the right decision, he still regretted it.

Wilson scanned the room. Priest, Cook, the European and Middle Eastern analysts and a new face occupied the space. Beside Priest, signaling the new persons importance, stood a man Wilson had known for several years, Bill Wycombe. Wilson groaned inwardly. Politics had entered the room.

"Right, let's get started shall we," said Priest. "First, for those of you who don't already know him, I would like to introduce Bill Wycombe. Bill is the Director General of the Security and Intelligence Secretariat at the Privy Council Office. Bill is here on behalf of the National Security Advisor to gain first-hand knowledge of events related to the recent phone intercepts indicating an imminent terrorist attack in Europe."

Priest nodded to Wycombe who smiled and said the complete opposite of why he was there:

"Don't mind me. I'm simply here to observe and keep updated on developments."

Peas in the proverbial pod thought Wilson to himself as he watched Priest and Wycombe exchange the knowing smiles of two cutthroat career bureaucrats who would tread, and had trodden, on many heads to reach their respective positions.

"Roger, if you please," said Priest.

Cook, pointing to the screen said, "We intercepted these messages on September 17 and 20."

Cell phone intercept. September 17, 2013.
From Manchester, England
Male voice, Arabic
BEGIN:
This is Nuh. Materials received.
End:

Cell phone intercept. September 20, 2013.
From Manchester, England
Male voice, Arabic
BEGIN:
This is Yusuf. Materials assembled.
END:

As you can see, the calls use the exact structure as the calls intercepted on September 10 and September 11. The calls also originated in Manchester England, and called cell phone numbers known to be associated with Al Qaeda.

Nervous excitement flooded the room as the implication of the words 'materials received and assembled' fed imaginations.

Priest stepped forward and took over from Cook.

"Based on these and the earlier messages I think we can be certain of several points. Al Qaeda has established a date, a target and a weapon. I believe we can be certain the date is imminent, the target is in England, probably Manchester, and the weapon is a bomb."

Priest paused as analysts' heads bobbed and nodded agreement. Mutual endorsement spurred Priest on.

"Our priority now is to focus on likely targets, dates and what kind of bomb Al Qaeda is most likely to deploy based on past experiences. Any questions?"

Andrew, an eager and immature analyst on assignment from CSE, interjected.

"Well, er, Sir, if the target is in England won't the British be working to establish targets and bombs types. What can we do that they can't? I mean, we're thousands of miles away and they know their country far better than we do."

Cook made to answer but Priest waved him silent and said.

"There are several reasons why we should and will devote all our resources to try and figure out what Al Qaeda's intentions are. First, and not least, we are allies. We have a duty to help. Second, the fact the Brits know their own country better than us can, and sometimes does, work against objective analysis and deduction; being too close to something can lead to missed conclusions. Third, there are tens of thousands of Canadians in the UK at any one time. We have a responsibility to protect Canadian citizens no matter where they are. Fourth, many Canadians have family in the UK. Fifth, Al Qaeda is a global organization with resources in many countries. The intercepts indicated that materials arrival and assembly. What if these materials arrived from Canada or if a radicalized Canadian citizen helped obtain the material? Be assured, no analytical effort, whether it produces or not, is wasted."

The rebuke of the newbie effectively scared everyone else off from asking any questions. Given direction from Director Priest, the assembled began to leave. Wilson, who agreed with everything Priest had said about why the Canadian ITAC should devote its resources to the threat, but disagreed with several of the Director's certainties, raised a hand to speak.

"Yes, Craig?" said Priest.

"Based on what we have so far I suggest that we don't limit our analytical focus to Al Qaeda and England."

"Why?"

"Our only evidence linking Al Qaeda is that the last four calls were made to phone numbers known to be or have been associated with Al Qaeda. None one answered any of the four calls. Just because a number is called and a message left doesn't guarantee the recipient of the call is a willing participant."

Cook, agitated and uncertain, challenged Wilson.

"What about the first two calls and the body found in Cairo with the German cell phone number written on his arm?"

"Yes, I agree the body suggests a Middle Eastern and Islamic connection. However, as of yesterday, unless notified otherwise, the CIA and the US have not confirmed the man, while he was a known radical Islamist, actually had ties with Al Qaeda. All we really have is the body of a man with radical Islamic views with an incriminating phone number written on his arm. I suggest that we don't limit our analytical focus to Al Qaeda."

Cook, bowing to Wilson's assessment, nodded agreement while Wycombe, contrary to his stated purpose, asked Wilson.

"You also mentioned something about England?"

"Yes. The last four calls originated in Manchester, England and if we take the caller's words literally, we could assume he was speaking about Manchester when he talks about receiving materials and establishing a target. However, we cannot be certain. The first calls, the ones from Cairo to London and Cairo to Berlin, might refer to one of those two cities being the target and the subsequent calls mean the same thing. It's also equally possible targets have been established in more than one city."

Cook perplexed and in danger of losing the thread, said.

"So you say not AQ, not England, well we don't have resources to analyze the world Wilson, were not omnipotent you know…"

Sensing his protégé might get the worst of the exchange, Priest interrupted to save Cook.

"You both make good points. I suggest Wilson maintains a wider lens on the outlying possibilities while we dedicate core resources to the more central possibilities."

Wilson suppressed mixed emotions and nodded to Priest his acceptance of the backhanded compliment and indirect dismissal. With access to the ongoing file and directed to look for the unexpected, which had been his intention anyway, Wilson harbored concerns about what he might discover. If, as he increasingly suspected, things were not as they seemed, he would have to challenge Priest and Cook and their myopic approach.

When Wilson rose to leave the boardroom, Wycombe, who had moved toward the door, intercepted Wilson and whispered discretely.

"I'm available if you need anything."

Without acknowledging Wycombe's offer Wilson strode from the room. Wycombe, as Director General of the Security and Intelligence Secretariat at the Privy Council Office, had connections and access. However, any assistance Wycombe might provide would come with a price: anyone could be sacrificed for the greater, or for Wycombe's, good.

Twenty-Eight

September 4 2013, Manchester, England

DARREN, HUNG OVER AND dehydrated, turned on to Lytham Street at 8.55 am and muttered to himself that Aalim had better be on time. Aalim was; he stood, eyes fixed on some distant point, inches from the worn curb with shoulders hunched against the drizzle of cold rain. Dirty water, splashed by Darren's car tire, speckled Aalim's light colored trousers that poked out from under the hem of his thobe. An impatient blast of the car horn jarred Aalim from his personal meditation and reluctant he climbed in to the car.

Unmoved by Aalim's defeated demeanor and sullen body language, Darren spoke harsh words at Aalim.

"We gotta lot to do today. I don't give a fuck about you. You are an instrument and you will do as I say. No tricks or signs, or any stupid attempts to fool me. Understand?

Aalim sat motionless and silent.

"I said do you understand? Look, you shit head, one call from me, one missed check in and your wife and kid will get some attention from that crazy bastard who is guarding them. I don't care how you do it, but if you want them to have any chance you need get on with things. The sooner we get done, the sooner they will be released."

Aalim perched forward to the edge of the car seat and began to rock back and forth. In rhythm with his movements soft words flowed as Aalim recited an Islamic Duas prayer for protection.

"O God, you are my Lord. There is none worthy of worship except You. I rely upon You, and You are the Great Lord of the Throne. Whatever God wills happens, and whatever He does not will does not happen. There is no power or strength except by God. I know that God is able to do anything, and that God knows all. O God I seek refuge in You from the evil in myself and every creature that You have given power over us. Verily my Lord is on the straight path."

Ignorant and uncaring, Darren blew cigarette smoke and mocked Aalim:

"Yes, very nice, very fucking nice. Now are you ready?"

Prayer had brought serenity to Aalim's face. "I am ready," said Aalim.

Darren drove from Aalim's home in Cheetam Hill to the Trafford Centre, a large indoor shopping Centre and leisure complex five miles west of Manchester city centre. The Centre is close to the Trafford Park industrial estate and less than two miles from the Pomona Docks where six days earlier Darren had forced Aalim and his wife from Aalim's taxi to the back of a white van. The Trafford Centre, the second largest shopping centre in the United Kingdom, with over ten thousand parking spaces, provided Darren perfect anonymity.

"What are we doing here?" asked Aalim as Darren slipped the car between a minivan and a sedan in the west parking lot.

"You have a phone call to make. Here is the number."

"Who am I calling? What do I say?"

"Your call is expected. Ask for Gary Boddie. When he answers, tell him your name and explain you want to apply for a janitors job. He will ask you to go for an interview. You will agree, thank him, and hang up. O.K?"

"Yes, but why?"

Skin, pale and red, tightened around Darren's eyes and jaw and his body arched toward Aalim who flinched and backed up against the car door.

"Let's get one thing straight right now. You do not ask me why about anything. You do, you do not ask. Got it? Do I need to call the house and have your wife punished?"

Forced to accept his fate, Aalim quietly answered.

"No, that will not be necessary, I understand."

Aalim made the call. When Aalim hung up a confused expression occupied his face.

"That was Manchester United I called. Why am I to work there?"

Darren snatched the phone from Aalim and pressed a pre-set speed dial button.

"You really are a dumb fuck aren't you? I told you no more whys."

Aalim, comprehending the purpose of the call, pleaded, apologized and promised he would ask no more.

Darren, ambivalent about the woman and kid, ended the call.

"Last chance Aalim, last fucking chance."

~

Obtaining a car, or more specifically a windowless van, was the next task for Aalim. Darren exited the Trafford Centre parking lot and drove less than a mile to Thrifty Car and Van Rental, on Twining Road.

Darren instructed Aalim to enter the rental agency slightly ahead of him. Darren would follow behind and watch while he waited his turn.

As Darren entered the glass fronted rental shop, a spotty faced twenty something sales clerk, introduced himself to Aalim with a level of enthusiasm and courtesy that would have impressed his corporate masters. Trevor, the sales clerk, with unexpected professionalism, acknowledged Darren, explained that he was alone now and would assist him as soon as he had finished with 'this gentleman' referring with a nod to Aalim.

Aalim, as coached by Darren explained he needed a small windowless van for a new delivery business he was starting in the Manchester area. Trevor recommend a new Ford Transit Connect five door compact van for a discounted price of 1,412 pounds for an extended two-month rental period. The sales clerk, keen to satisfy a new customer, included a free GPS system to help Aalim with his new delivery business.

When the paperwork was completed and Trevor conducted the walk around with Aalim to check for existing damage or scrapes, Darren left the shop and drove back to the Trafford Centre to await Aalim.

When Aalim arrived, Darren climbed into the Ford van.

"Good job. From now on, we will use this van and you will drive. Now drive to Elizabeth Street in Cheetam Hill. You know Curry's the electronics shop?"

Aalim nodded. The shop was close to his home.

~

Several factors made Curry's a good choice. The shop was small and employed only two sales clerks as opposed to the box shops with tens of clerks who interacted with countless people each day. Two clerks would talk about and remember customers. Second, when Darren visited the shop he pretended interest in security cameras for a lock-up garage and asked about systems with the longest back-up memory systems. The shop clerks had explained about a surveillance system that retained images and sound for six months. In fact, said the clerk, we use that system in our shop. Assured of lasting digital files, few sales clerks, and proximity to Aalim's home Darren had settled on Curry's.

During the drive, Darren explained what Aalim was to do and buy. Before entering the shop, Aalim wrote down a list of equipment dictated by Darren. Darren gave Aalim a wad of used twenty and fifty pound notes and sent Aalim to make the purchases.

Thirty minutes later, a smiling shop clerk held open the door as Aalim departed with a Sony Vaio Duo Touchscreen Convertible Ultrabook with IntelCore i5-4200U processor, Windows 8, and 4GB memory. A Printer, three wireless routers, headphones and an assortment of memory sticks.

Aalim reported the sales clerk had recommended something called PGP, or Pretty Good Privacy, to encrypt, and decrypt texts, and e-mails.

"The clerk said I could buy PGP online?"

"Don't worry, you won't need that."

~

Chaos, complained Darren to himself as he waited in Section D, row 8 of the Trafford Centre parking lot for Aalim to arrive. Five-thirty in the evening and everyone in Manchester had something to buy. For a moment, Darren regretted his choice of rendezvous location until he realized the chaos would mask his meetings with Aalim.

Darren had reversed into his parking spot to better observe other vehicles as they searched for a place to park. While he waited, Darren reviewed the section of the binder he had brought with him: 'cell phone communications'. The section contained two plastic wallets. A Sony IC voice recorder, about the size of two matchboxes, rested at the bottom of the first wallet. The second contained ten sheets of paper with typed sentences in English and Arabic. Each paper also included an international phone number, a date, a time and an Arabic name in the top right hand corner.

At five to six, ten minutes late, Aalim's white Ford van came into view as it crawled up row 8. Darren flashed his headlights and the van stopped.

"You're late," barked Darren to Aalim as he slide into the passenger seat.

"I'm sorry; the traffic is crazy, everyone heading home from work."

"I don't care. Do not be late again. Now drive to Starbucks on Oxford Road. When we get to Starbucks turn left on Charles Street and first left again into the alleyway then stop halfway down."

The alleyway, a cobbled dead end street, ran directly behind Starbucks and Aalim stopped as instructed.

"Wait here. I'll be back in a few minutes."

Impatient taps on the passenger window startled Aalim. Darren, a large Starbucks coffee cup in one hand, glared as he waited for the door to unlock.

"What the fuck? Scared someone might mug you?" said Darren as he maneuvered himself and his coffee into the van.

"Sorry, I must have pushed the lock button, I…"

"Never mind, now let's get to work. Open the lap top and let's see how good the Starbucks WIFI signal is."

Unfamiliar with electronic equipment and the Internet, Aalim struggled to follow Darren's instructions as he used Google to search for cell phones. After several searches, Darren directed Aalim to use his credit card to purchase ten disposable cell phones with pay as you go sim cards from TESCO's, one of the UK's largest retailers. Aalim paid extra for next day delivery to his home address; an easy trail to follow.

Raised eyebrows and angled head conveyed to Darren Aalim's unspoken question as to why he needed ten cell phones.

"I will give you a sheet of paper. You will dial the number on the paper, wait for the prompt, and leave the message written in Arabic. You will say the message once and hang up."

Aalim's face twitched.

"Don't even think about saying something different. I will hold a voice recorder as you speak. We will analyze each recording within an hour. If you have said anything different your wife will die and you will have her head to keep you company. If you do it again, you will live long enough to cradle your sons head before losing your own."

Fear replaced hopefulness on Aalim's face.

"Look you fucking rag head. We've thought of everything. Do as you told and things will be all right. Now give me the lap top."

Impatient with Aalim's poor computer skills Darren used the lap top to establish multiple email accounts with several leading UK email services including Outlook.com, Windows Hotmail, AIM Mail, Yahoo, and Zoho Mail.

When Darren completed the email account set-ups Aalim drove them back to the Trafford Centre and Darren's car.

"Tomorrow, after the cell phones arrive pick me up at the Trafford Centre at 7 p.m. section G, row 5. You have phone calls to make. And don't be late."

Soon, thought Darren as he eased his car out of the congested parking lot, Aalim would stimulate the world's intelligence agencies to action as they intercepted, translated and scrambled to understand cryptic communications from an unknown caller in Manchester, England to what Darren assumed would be other terrorists.

Twenty-Nine

September 9 2013, Manchester, England

GARY HAD TRIED TO KEEP the truth from Veronica but she caught him hiding the photographs and demanded to see them. They had cried together over the photographs and Veronica had wailed when Gary explained that because of the photographs, they would not be able to go to the Doll World Rendezvous this year. Veronica had tried to convince Gary that there was nothing wrong with their love and that they should not have to hide because people did not understand. Gary, his heart bursting with pride and love had agreed and once again promised that one day they would go public. After a while Veronica calmed and looked at him in her special way and they had made love. After he had washed, re-inflated, and tucked Veronica in bed, Gary had started to drink. Drunk, bloated and afraid, his blurred eyes searched past grease stained newspaper and crushed beer cans to consult the digital clock on the bottom of the cable box. 3:15 am. In four hours Boddie needed to be clean, sober, and in his office at Manchester United to manage the morning cleaning crew.

He had not intended to drink and eat himself in to such a state and the booze brought unwanted memories of the second envelope from his blackmailer. The second one contained a name, a photograph and a single typed page of terse instructions.

A Muslim. Not that Gary had anything against Muslims or any other darkies or foreigners for that matter. As long as they kept to themselves and didn't bother him, he didn't give a damn. Gary had tried to ignore the contents. Twice he held the photo and instructions over the gas stove to burn them. Each time he faltered, fear of exposure held him back. Hovering by the stove for a third time his cell phone rang. He knew who it was.

"Hello you dirty fat fuck. Have you opened the envelope?"

Gary held the phone at arm's length, as though distance might make the voice disappear.

"I asked if you had opened the envelope Gary."

Blubbering with self-pity Gary pushed out a weak response "Yes. Yes, I have. What do you want?"

"The rag head in the photo will call your office for a job appointment on Monday. Give him a janitor's job and make sure he works every shift with Brad Short. I want them to work together all the time. Do you understand fatty?"

"Yes. But why? What do you want?"

"What I want Gary is for you to shut the hell up and do as you're told. You are nobody Gary, just a fat sick bastard. If we make your little secret public Gary, I am sure some of those nice soccer fans will be happy to kick you to death one dark night as you stumble home with your chips and beer. Do you get it now Gary?"

"Yes, yes I do, but when will it stop."

The phone went dead. Gary understood. Gary did not really care. All he wanted was for it to be over.

The Muslim man had called on September 4, and on Sept 6, Aalim Hussein began to clean the floors, toilets and stands of Manchester United with his co-worker, Brad Short.

Thirty

September 10 2013, Manchester, England

SHOPPERS, LADEN WITH THE latest must haves, clogged the parking lot as Aalim edged the white van toward the main exit.

"Where to?" said Aalim.

"Altrincham," said Darren.

"Do you have the cell phones?"

"Yes."

Thirty minutes later Darren spoke again.

"Pull over and stop at the next layby."

Aalim stopped about six miles out of the Manchester City Centre just past Altrincham on the A56. Darren withdrew the voice recorder and a sheet of paper from his inside pocket and handed the paper to Aalim.

"Take one of the phones, I don't care which one, and dial the number. When the call goes to message, say the words on the sheet. And remember, I am recording what you say and if you mess up or say anything not on the paper, your wife and kid will suffer."

Darren leaned toward Aalim and read the English translation under what Darren assumed was the equivalent in Arabic.

<u>This is Musa. Target confirmed.</u>

Aalim pressed numbers and waited. No voice directed him to leave a message only the universal beep indicated Aalim should speak. Aalim spoke the typed words to the silence and ended the call.

"Good job," said Darren as he retrieved the paper and phone from Aalim and placed them both in plastic zip lock bags. With the first call made, Darren handed Aalim another sheet of paper and an electronic key fob and said.

"Drive to the address on the paper. When you get there, drive up to the steel roller door and press the key fob. The door will open. Drive in and close the door behind you. I'm going to get in the back of the van. Make sure you drive carefully. I don't want to be thrown all over the place."

"In the back?" said Aalim confused.

"Security cameras outside boy, I don't want to be seen with you. Now let's go."

Ten minutes later Darren emerged from the van and peered along with Aalim into the gloom of an industrial workshop. The space was narrow but long. Side by side and end to end, the space would hold about thirty cars. Darren stepped toward the closed steel roller door and located the light switch. His gloved hand flicked the switch and mesh covered lights buzzed and flooded the windowless room with industrial white light. A main power and fuse box hung beside the light switch. Darren opened the box and studied the panel layout. Fuses, indicating dedicated circuits, identified specific equipment. Darren called Aalim over, pointed to the light switch and fuse box and said.

"Turn the lights on and off and set all the fuses to on."

Darren led Aalim in to the workshop. Worn metal workbenches, many with discarded tools and automotive parts crowding the bench surfaces filled one entire wall. In the middle of the open space a caged area, about fifteen feet square, contained assorted portable equipment including acetylene tanks and welding equipment, air compressor, hydraulic metal cutters, and two portable tool boxes on large wheels. Behind the cage, a manual operated engine winch with thick chains and hooks stood surrounded by oil and lubricant drums. Past the drums and pressed up against the rear wall a single aluminum door to a paint spray boot hung open. Inside, suspended from wires, six bright red fire extinguishers gleamed in the overhead light.

Aalim, eyes searching left and right, his voice rasp with uncertainty, asked,

"What is this place?"

"It's your workshop."

"I've never been here before," said Aalim. "I don't know how to use this equipment. I drive a taxi."

Don't worry. You have a few weeks to learn. We will come here in the evenings and on the weekend. Each day, beginning in a couple of weeks, you will exchange two fire extinguishers at Manchester United for two I will give you. You will bring the two from Manchester United here. The ones in the paint booth you will use to practice your cutting, welding and painting."

"I don't understand. I don't want to."

"Shut the fuck up. I don't care about what you understand, or don't, or what you do or don't want to do. Like I told you before, you are an instrument. You're only purpose is to do as we tell you. You're only function is to serve our purposes. You're incentive and reward is the lives of your son and wife."

Indecision and uncertainty seeped from Aalim's taught body as shoulders hunched and teeth ground under the pressure of his clamped jaw. A hand drifted to a long handled steel wrench propped against a rust stained lubricant drum. Fingers wrapped the worn handle and tensed as the sinews sensed the weight. Darren, his pulse elevated and body tensed by Aalim's movement said.

"Go ahead. Hit me; kill me, if you want. There are thousands more like me. Thousands more rag head Muslims with wives and kids we could use. You only have one wife and one son. You can bet their deaths will be slow and painful. Your choice shit head."

Darren, poised on the balls of his feet, unclenched his fists as frustration and anger bled from Aalim and the wrench clanged to the cement floor.

"That's a smart choice. Now fuck off and start learning how to use the equipment. We have two hours to kill."

Tense from the exchange Darren retreated to the passenger seat of the van. Through the windshield, he followed Aalim's cautious progress as he picked, fumbled and studied the unfamiliar tools. A smile crossed Darren's face as he imagined the accumulation of Aalim's DNA and fingerprints on the equipment.

A plastic wallet from the binder slid from Darren's inside coat pocket. With a gloved hand, Darren withdrew a receipt for six months rental for the garage and placed it on the dashboard for Aalim to take home.

~

Darren did not know why he chose the Manchester Central Library. He had no connection with the library and could not recall the last time he had visited one. Darren had simply wanted a change of environment and a place where people sat for long periods without drawing attention.

Inside, Darren paused at the scale and grandeur of the 90-year-old building and the wall mounted plaques informing visitors that the library contents dated back to the mid-1800s. Through the grand entrance, Darren steered Aalim to one of the long wooden tables in the Wolfson Reading Room. Seated opposite each other, Aalim, silent, waited for instruction. Darren, overwhelmed by the large circular room and marble pillars, sucked breath and told Aalim what to do.

"Today you will use the Internet to obtain two books, conduct some research and buy three airline tickets. Now start your laptop and open your Yahoo email account. There will be one email. Open the email and copy the website link into Google. When the website opens, download these two pdf books."

Darren handed Aalim a slip of paper that contained two titles: The Mujahedeen Explosives Handbook and The Mujahedeen Poisons Handbook.

Aalim's hand vibrated as he read the words. He stared past Darren and said to the air.

"I won't kill anyone."

"Maybe, maybe not," said Darren, "but right now if you don't do as you're fucking told you will kill your wife. Now get the books."

Darren had not seen the books himself, but during his earlier research in to Islamic websites, he learned the Explosives Handbook was an 88-page bomb-making guide prepared and disseminated by global jihadists via the Internet. The book supplied details on how to prepare a bomb-making laboratory, purify bomb-making ingredients, mix the chemicals, and how to put them together.

Darren had also read how in 2002, Moinul Abedin, a 27-year-old native of Bangladesh, and a former waiter in Birmingham, England, had used the explosives handbook to gather large quantities of homemade explosives. Abedin got a twenty-year prison sentence for plotting a wave of terror attacks across Britain with homemade bombs.

Darren's research also revealed that the books used to be difficult to obtain via the Internet unless you already knew which website to access. Government anti-terrorist organizations and law enforcement agencies constantly blocked or disrupted these ever-changing websites because terrorist groups used the website for communication purposes. In 2013, the books had become easily available because intelligence organizations changed their tactics from prevention, which they could not achieve, to gathering intelligence on who was downloading the book. Aalim accessed a website monitored by intelligence agencies.

"OK, I've got the books," said Aalim.

"Good."

Darren withdrew another sheet of paper from his pocket and passed it to Aalim.

"What's this?" asked Aalim.

"Your next task; there are thirty words on the list. For the rest of the day you will conduct research on each of these words. For each word, you will download and save various documents to the hard drive. Don't leave. Don't talk. Just sit and learn. I'll be back in a few hours."

Most of the words on the list had made sense to Darren. Words like 'explosives', 'detonators', 'shrapnel', 'welding equipment', 'fire extinguishers', and 'storage facilities,' all fit with what he now assumed was a plan to place bombs at Manchester United's stadium. Two words were out of place though: 'Mustard Gas'.

Books, literature, and the arts had never held much interest for Darren and he could not understand why people stood, sat and leaned, in odd and uncomfortable positions, to peer into books and magazines. More used to the noise of soccer games, pubs and protest marches, the quietness of hundreds of people unnerved Darren.

Without purpose, other than a need to use up time, Darren meandered left, right, up, down until a display poster, placed in the middle of the corridor, smacked him back to reality.

The poster, glossy and professionally produced, proclaimed 'Islam & Christianity - Not So Different' transposed over pictures of happy, smiling brown and white skinned people. Beneath the headline, an invitation encouraged people to attend a free presentation by local Imams and Priests to discuss the shared messages and objectives of Islam and Christianity and show how coexistence among fellow believers was both possible and natural.

Enraged by the poster, Darren returned to Aalim and hissed into Aalim's ear.

"OK you bastard, that's enough for now. It is time for you to order some airline tickets."

Fifteen minutes later Aalim Hussein, his wife and son had reserved seats on a one-way flight on Egypt Air MS784 departing 18:30 Sunday October 6 from Manchester International Airport and arriving at Cairo International Airport at 23:45.

Skeptic disbelief unfolded across Aalim's face as he saved the pdf conformation to the lap top hard drive.

"Are you really sending us to Egypt?"

"Yes," said Darren with conviction, "you and every last one of you bastards will be put on planes, boats and trains and kicked the fuck out of England for ever. If you are a good boy, and if you are lucky, you just might get out first and alive."

Pressed lips and tight skin masked a cold, callous smirk as Darren watched hope flicker in Aalim's eyes.

Thirty-One

September 23/24 2013, Ottawa, Canada

THE ITAC MEETING ON SATURDAY had ended at
6:30pm. Wilson, given a backhanded mandate by Priest
to explore outlying data, had remained at the office
until past midnight and returned by 7am on Sunday
morning for another fifteen-hour session.

On Monday the 23, a summons to the boardroom
at lunchtime revealed details of a fifth cell phone
intercept snapped him out of it. Wilson, provided with
a photocopy of the fifth intercept returned to in his
office and with an expresso coffee to hand, studied the
intercept text.

> Cell phone intercept. September 22, 2013.
> From Manchester, England
> Male voice, Arabic
> BEGIN:
> **This is Lut. Packages sent.**
> End:

The message 'packages sent' put the ITAC team in
a frenzy of questions and speculation. Packages sent
had blown a massive hole of doubt in Priest and Cook's
certainties about the UK, probably Manchester, being
the target. The spectra of London or Berlin, the destination of the two first intercepted messages, loomed as

possible targets. Sent where, and why, they all asked. Why assemble them in England, possibly Manchester, and send them somewhere else? Why undertake additional risk to assemble in one place and transport to another. Unless, as Wilson pointed out, the initial assertion that the later calls had been about a Manchester target because the calls had originated in Manchester had been wrong and the calls had actually been about a target in Berlin or London, or even some unnamed city.

For the remainder of Monday and late in to Tuesday night Wilson did what he should have done on the weekend. He went back to the two reports Chris Thornton, via his wife, told him he should look again at.

With the two reports, UK/JTAC/CT/HD/BL/150513-1 & 2, in hand Wilson uncovered the flip chart and scanned the notes he had previously made. Five black coloured statements and questions stared back at him:

EDL recruitment up with new financial resources - money from where? Media reports of Muslim extremism up, why? Why no follow up? Who is SS?

Why had Chris Thornton drawn Wilson's attention to these reports? What had Chris wanted him to find?

Wilson began with the easy question first. Who was SS? The logical approach was to search for SS in the UK JTAC, the origin of the reports. All the Five Eyes JTAC's and ITAC's shared staff and contact lists for each other together with respective areas of responsibility or focus. The UK JTAC listed one SS. Sandra Sutton, Analyst, Pacific Region. The nomenclature of the report coding system dictated that the last person listed was the most senior. Wilson doubted the analyst for the Pacific Region was the SS he was searching for.

More logic suggested linking SS with Chris. Which was easier said than done. Chris was on assignment to the UK JTAC from MI5. MI5 did not provide staff lists to anyone without a very good reason and a very high level of authority. Wilson had neither. His few informal requests to contacts within the Five Eyes analytical community yielded little except raised eyebrows and Wilson expected some discreet calls to MI5 to report on the curiosity of a nosy Canadian. Wilson had of course been indirect in his requests and had not mentioned the initials SS, which, unbeknownst to Wilson, had been a very fortunate omission.

On the verge of relegating the need for SS's identity to a 'to do' basket, Wilson had gone to the public MI5 website. He got lucky. On a subsection of the 'About Us' page, an organizational chart listed the structure and titles of the principals who reported to Andrew Parker, the Director General of MI5. Without originality, a Deputy Director General, in turn supported by five Assistant Deputy Directors, supported the Director General. Each Assistant Director General was responsible for one of the five branches of MI5. The web page link provided no names, but gave Wilson an idea.

Twenty minutes and several Internet searches later the word search 'Andrew Parker-MI5-Domestic-Terrorism' yielded a London Times article from May 2013 reporting on MI5's Director General, Andrew Parker's speech at the Royal United Services Institute on the continuing threat of terrorism and how the Security Service are adapting to respond. The article included a photograph of Parker with another man identified as Simon Spencer, Assistant Director MI5 responsible for Domestic Terrorism.

SS must be Simon Spencer. Which did, and did not, make sense. Yes conceded Wilson the initial reports had both been about domestic terrorist entities. One about the EDL and one about radicalized Muslims. Why, asked Wilson to his white board would an Assistant Director of MI5 provide final authority on a report issued by the UK JTAC? That didn't make sense.

With SS identified, Wilson modified his notes: SS - Simon Spenser - AD MI5 - why approve JTAC report.

Questions about EDL financing and increased membership were next on Wilson's list. Business documents, tax receipts and financial statements were not available and even if they had, would not have been truthful. The money supply for the EDL, like many other socially despised extremist groups, came from a combination of anonymous donations, on street collections, and crime including drugs, theft and fraud. A consequence of these inconsistent funding mechanisms was in large part the reason many such organizations and groups remained small, marginalized and largely ineffective. They simply lacked the discipline and skills required to organize on a larger scale. Shared Five Eyes intelligence files suggested the EDL had links with the US Stop the Islamization of America campaign and that some funds from the US trickled to the EDL. Wilson noted that Pamela Geller and Robert Spencer, two high-profile bloggers who founded the 'Stop the Islamization of America' campaign, were invited to speak at the march to mark Armed Forces Day on June 29, arranged by the EDL. On June 26, 2013, the UK Home Office banned Geller and Spencer from entering the UK.

Other files speculated on the possibility that the EDL were puppets of Jewish Zionists who provided small amounts of money to the EDL to inflame anti-

Muslim sentiment in the UK. Whatever combination of funding the EDL traditionally received, it had never been enough to enable the EDL to engage in any kind of organized or professional recruitment drive. However, according to the UK JTAC report, the EDL had begun a national recruitment campaign in January 2013. The campaign incorporated modern media techniques, with advertisements and slick events with professional presentations, speakers and promotional materials.

The July report estimated the EDL campaign had cost in excess of half a million pounds, more than the EDL had officially raised in the previous three years. Moreover, the campaign showed no sign of slowing. Estimates of EDL campaign success indicated membership had ballooned from 10,000 to 120,000 in just six months, with thousands more joining each week.

Unsurprisingly, the report concluded the EDL either engaged in large-scale illegal activities, or had secured a source of private funding. A clear indication one of these situations existed was the EDL's habit of paying cash and responding to inquiries about money by asserting that anonymous donations provided EDL funding.

Investigations by police and security agencies, stated the report, found no evidence of significant illegal activities. Aside from a failure to identify the source of EDL funding, Wilson was aghast that the report stated no follow up investigation was required. How, thought Wilson, could the police and security services ignore a tenfold increase in the membership of an extreme far-right organization with a violent anti-immigrant agenda? Wilson devoted all of Tuesday to identify an individual or group to explain the massive increase EDL financial resources and activities. Wilson found nothing. Frustrated, Wilson slammed five thick black question marks next to a dollar sign beside the letters EDL. The question marks generated other questions. Why throw so much money into recruitment? Why now? What was the purpose, the objective? What would one do with hundreds of thousands of EDL members?

Unable to identify the source of EDL funding Wilson tackled media reports. Reason told him an increase in media reports about Muslim extremism would be due to an actual increase in such events. Wilson, a subconscious conclusion already forming, decided to coordinate his review of media reports on Muslim extremism with the increased EDL funding and recruitment activities, which began in January 2013. He would compare 2013 to 2012. Public Internet searches showed no noticeable increase in media reporting between Jan - March 2012 and Jan-March 2013.

Then, on April 11, 2013, MI5 published a report claiming there had been more than 2,000 Muslim terrorist arrests, plots, and attacks in the UK from 2001-2010. The statistics were not new. In fact, Wilson had seen the numbers and the details several times during 2011 and 2012 when he had attended various Five Eyes meetings.

However, MI5 had dedicated a specific report, an announcement and it seemed specific MI5 website space for people to view and digest the main points of the report. The report said that between 11 September 2001 and 31 March 2010, the UK had convicted 237 individuals of terrorism-related offenses, including murder, illegal possession of firearms and explosives offenses and the UK had invoked the Terrorism Act to arrest more than 2,000 foreigners.

Since the release of MI5 report in April, Wilson noted that numerous national media outlets reported or referenced the report on a weekly basis. Someone, or something, mussed Wilson, seemed to want a light shone on Muslim extremism activity in the UK.

Actual events throughout the spring and summer stimulated the profile of the MI5 report. On 22 May, two Muslim men with cleavers hacked a British soldier, Lee Rigby, to death on the streets of London. On June 17, a group of five Muslims attacked an American student with broken bottles in the Tower Hamlets area in London. In July, public actions and claims by a group called the Muslim Patrol, who cruised London streets to 'discourage' non-Islamic behavior, stoked claims of Muslim attacks on non-Muslims. In August, British media reported that the Muslim prison population in the UK was up by 200%; a rate eight times faster than that of the overall prison population. The media reports cautioned that Muslims, who make up roughly 5% of the British population as a whole, now made up 13% of the British prison population and that number of Muslim inmates created hotbeds of Islamic radicalization.

Black words, question marks and exclamation marks crowded Wilson's white board. To gain perspective, Wilson retreated away from the board and sipped at the coffee he did not remember making. Several sips and a burnt lip later orange and brown lines and circles competed with the black for space. Red followed brown and orange as Wilson jotted down some preliminary conclusions:

UK JTAC Reports - Muslim extremism up - EDL recruitment up - potential for conflict - no follow up - Simon Spencer - MI5

EDL money - source unknown - no follow up - MI5

Media reports - private and institutional - MI5

Wilson circled the three MI5 references. Then he swore. Of course, MI5 would be a common factor. MI5 involvement was natural and to be expected. Disappointed with the logic of the only commonality he could find Wilson rubbed out the three circles around MI5.

Wilson realized he was missing something. Something Chris had expected him to find, perhaps something Chris had died for.

~

The door to Wilson's office opened and Mitch entered unbidden and excited.

"Christ Craig. I've been knocking on your door for the past five minutes. Why didn't you answer? I thought something was wrong."

"Oh, sorry about that Mitch. What's up?"

"There has been another message Craig."

"Boardroom?"

"No. The message transcript is on our desktops via the intranet system. I came by to hear what you thought of it."

"I, urm…"

"You haven't even looked at the message yet have you? What have you been working on for the past two days?" said Mitch as he looked at the boards and flip charts.

"MI5? What are you up to Craig? What's this got to do with the bombing messages?"

Wilson shrugged and said.

"Nothing, maybe something, maybe nothing, I don't know yet."

Familiar with his friend's iydiosinracies, Mitch made to leave and said.

"Well anyway, when you do read the message, let's talk."

As Mitch passed out the door, he called over his shoulder.

"The name on your board, Simon Spencer, I had a beer with him and a bunch of guys once. Way back in 1990 something. He was an analyst then with the UK Foreign Office. He had some strong views about immigrants and foreigners. He is a damn good chess player too. I think he won some tournament. What's he up to now?"

Wilson, jolted by the news of another message intercept and just surfacing from his trance like analytical process, only registered Mitch's comments and question in the periphery of his awareness. However, the comment sowed a seed and a few days, and a few more clues later, the seed would sprout a fledgling root. While the seed sought nourishment, Wilson opened his intranet account and accessed the most recent message intercept.

> Cell phone intercept. September 24, 2013.
> From Manchester, England
> Male voice, Arabic
> BEGIN:
> **This is Isa. First five packages are in place.**
> END:

In addition to the obvious implication that destructive devices were in place Wilson discovered a clue about the identity of the callers in the last six intercepts. Musa, Ibrahim, Nuh, Yusuf, Lut, and Isa were all Islamic Prophets.

Thirty-Two

September 13 2013, Manchester, England

MANCHESTER UNITED'S STADIUM HAS TWO nicknames: Old Trafford, because the stadium is located in Old Trafford in Greater Manchester, and the Theater of Dreams, a name bestowed on the stadium by Manchester United legend Bobby Charlton. With a capacity of over 80,000, Old Trafford officially opened on February 19th, 1910 with Manchester United losing 3-4 to Liverpool.

Before 1910, and the building of the Old Trafford soccer stadium, the site was used for games of shinty, a cross between field hockey and lacrosse, and a traditional game of the Scottish Highlands. During the First World War, American soldiers used the stadium for baseball and in 1981, Old Trafford hosted cricket matches in the Lambert & Butler Cup.

During WWII, bombs fell on Old Trafford. First, on December 22, 1940, a German bombing raid on the nearby industrial complex damaged the stadium and the scheduled Christmas day game switched to Stockport's ground. Then, on 11 March 1941, bombs destroyed much of the stadium and forced the club to move a nearby facility. Eight years passed before Manchester United returned to play soccer in the rebuilt stadium. The stadium's highest attendance was in 1939, when 76,962 spectators watched the FA Cup semi-final between Wolverhampton Wanderers and Grimsby Town.

In 2012, the average attendance at Old Trafford for Premier regular league games was 75,387. During the 2008/9, soccer season almost 2.2 million supporters crammed into Old Trafford to witness Manchester United win the Premier League for the third year in a row, the League Cup, and reach the final of the UEFA Champions League and the semi-finals of the FA Cup. Old Trafford is the second-largest soccer stadium in the United Kingdom and the ninth largest in Europe.

Old Trafford, built, destroyed, rebuilt, and regularly improved for more than a hundred years has a rich and diverse history beyond the team players who come and go with the clubs highs and lows.

None of this history remotely registered with Brad Short as he shuffled, sullen and hung-over, through the double doors of the maintenance entrance on the south side of the Old Trafford stadium. Brad spat the mushy remains of a toothpick from his mouth toward a gleaming grey plastic trash can affixed to the brick wall beside the swipe card reader that registered his arrival and departure times. He missed. Brad did not care, but further into the entranceway someone else did.

"Pick that up."

Instinct and habit told Brad to respond with a venomous 'fuck you', but his instructions had been very clear: Cause no problems, be a model employee and no incidents, comments or confrontations with anyone about anything, especially racial stuff. For six months, Brad had been a model employee and the pressure was getting to him. Ahead of Brad, Steve Lever, the second facilities manager, who shared the role with Gary Boddie, Brad's immediate manager, repeated his terse order.

"Pick that up."

A few more weeks, thought Brad to himself as he stooped to retrieve the sodden sliver of wood from the cold cement floor, and his connection with Manchester United, Steve Lever, that fat fuck Boddie and the rag head Aalim would end. A few more weeks and he would give each of them a good kicking before he left.

"Sorry about that Mr. Lever," said Brad with fake meekness after he put the toothpick in the trashcan.

Steve Lever, disdain evident across his pinched face, turned and marched away toward the administrative offices, unaware of Brad's middle finger salute. When Lever was out of sight, Brad flicked another toothpick into his mouth. Some people chewed gum, some whistled and some sucked candy. Brad manipulated toothpicks. Mint flavored, with points at each end. Stung, as only small insecure and small-minded people can be by such a mild rebuke, Brad resolved to pass on the sting to the person he considered lower in the pecking order, Aalim Hussien.

Power over another was an addictive drug to someone like Brad Short. Self-righteous and unintelligent, Short was resentful, hateful, and envious. The prospect of 'working' with Aalim pushed thoughts of Lever away as he toyed with ways to insult and denigrate the Muslim under his care.

"Good morning my little camel jockey. What did you hitch your ride to this morning?"

Today was Aalim's fourth day at Old Trafford. Each day Short had greeted Aalim with a different derogatory salutation: Cairo Coon, Dune Coon and Fez had followed Short's 'good morning' greeting. Aalim, as on the first day, offered no verbal response, but physically Aalim's body quivered with restraint.

"Now, now, don't get shirty with me. It's not my fault you're stupid is it? Are you not speaking again then? Just as well, cause if you speak out of turn I'll put my foot through your fucking teeth. You understand you little rag head shit?"

Aalim remained silent and straightened the cleaning products, mops, brooms, bags and buckets on his four wheeled, two tiered utility cart. They had one each. Identical. For the next seven hours Short and Aalim would circumnavigate the stadium one level at a time to sweep, empty, wash, and restock each of the washrooms used by the 70,000 plus soccer fans who filled the stadium twice a week.

Loaded with supplies, Aalim pushed his cart out from the windowless storage / utility room where the carts remained when not in use. Already schooled in the order of things during the first three days, Aalim waited for Short to lead the way.

Five minutes later Short passed Aalim and said.

"A little variety today shit head. We have something different to break the routine."

Aalim made a noncommittal grunt and followed Short toward the washrooms in section A. While they walked and pushed their carts Short withdrew a sheet of crumpled paper from his trouser pocket and leaned on the cart to study the words on the paper. Darren Blackley gave Short the paper on Sunday when he had shown up unannounced at the Fox and Hounds, one of several pubs in the Moss Side area Brad frequented.

"What do you want?" had been Brad's terse welcome when Darren joined him at the rickety, copper-topped table in the pub's front lounge.

"It's time for you to earn your money Brad."

"What the fuck do you think I've been doing all summer? Cleaning toilets and mopping floors and…"

"Don't give me that shit Brad. Summer months at Old Trafford are easy. There are no games and only a handful of concerts. In fact, new turf was laid at the ground this summer so there was hardly anything going on."

"Yeah well, the games started in August and the place stinks after all those Man United shit head supporters piss and shit themselves silly all over the place. Anyhow, I got that fucking rag head to deal with now. He is such miserable shit. Never speaks."

"Why the fuck would he speak to you?"

"What are we doing there anyway? Why do we need him cleaning the place? How is his cleaning shit at Old Trafford going to get all those fuckers out of England eh? That is what I don't understand. I think you are just messing with me."

"Like I said before Brad, you don't need to know yet. I'll tell you soon. But now it's time for you to manage the rag head a little and make sure he does what we want."

"What do you mean? What do we want him to do?"

"I've made a list for you. It's not complicated, but you have to make sure everything is done properly."

"A list, what am I? Some kind of nigger who runs errands with lists? Just tell me what I need to do. I'm not stupid."

Brad had listened while Darren explained what he was to do. Afterward, Brad was relieved that Darren had given him a list.

Brad lifted his elbows from the cart and returned the crumpled paper to his pocket. He exhaled a huff at the idea of the first task on the list. It was plain weird.

"Hey, you're supposed to have a cell phone with you today. Do you have it?"

Aalim nodded.

"Right then you can start with the one over there."

Brad pointed to a bright red fire extinguisher attached to a bracket on the wall at the base of the steps that led from the common walkway up to the seating area in level four.

Aalim followed Brad's extended hand, but remained motionless, uncomprehending.

"Your phone you monkey. Take a photo of the fire extinguisher and the tag which notes its location and the next inspection date."

An unspoken why formed on Aalim's wide-eyed face as his head swiveled from fire extinguisher to Short.

Interpreting Aalim's expression Short snapped.

"You don't need to know why, just do it. Now. And when you've done that, you will take a picture of every fourth one on this level. After that, every fourth one on level five and six. After that hop up the steps and take a photo of the extinguishers at the top in the stands. Do you understand?"

Aalim nodded. He withdrew the cell phone Darren had insisted he keep with him at all times and took a close up photo of the extinguisher and the tag.

In addition to the covered common walkway and the open stands, Aalim took photos of fire extinguishers outside the Incident Control Room, used by the police to monitor the crowd and the Emergency Response Room that coordinated medical response. Finally, Aalim photographed two extinguishers that flanked the entrance to the 500 Club Executive Bar, on level five in the stadium's North East quadrant.

Two days later, Aalim had eighty-three photographs of bright red fire extinguishers all of which Darren down loaded from Aalim's phone to his laptop.

~

The next task on Brad's list was to instruct Aalim to purposefully enter and be seen in places he should, as a stadium bathroom and general area cleaner, not normally go including the players change room, the Manchester United Board Members room, the executive viewing lounges, the players tunnel and last of all the managers dug out beside the field. As intended, Aalim's travels drew the attention of other stadium staff who reported Aalim to Lever and Boddie. Lever, because Boddie had hired Aalim, and because Old Trafford awed most new employees, left Boddie to deal with Aalim and remind him to keep out of unauthorized areas.

In addition to loitering where he should not, Aalim had to ask questions about security and evacuation plans. The last instruction Brad had for Aalim was he should make false bottom in the large waste bin that hung on the front of his cart. The space, Short told Aalim, must hold two fire extinguishers.

Thirty-Three

September 13 2013, London, England

MITTON-WELLS RECLINED AND sipped chilled water as he watched the BBC evening news in his den. Reports of the Taliban attack on the US consulate in Herat, Afghanistan splashed across the screen and pushed other news items off the BBC's evening news agenda. The use of bombs and grenades by the Taliban pushed Mitton-Wells to thoughts of his own bombs and the efforts and compromises he had undertaken to obtain exactly what he wanted.

Initially, Mitton-Wells had been disgusted when Simon suggested using former IRA bomb makers to install the C4 explosives inside the fire extinguishers. Mitton-Wells considered the Irish Republican Army as much a blight on England and English people as Muslims, blacks and any other immigrants. With effort, Mitton-Wells could concede the IRA's desire for independence, but he drew the line at attacks on the English main land and the assassination in 1979 of Lord Mountbatten, a member of England's aristocracy and an example of everything 'English' Mitton-Wells held sacred.

"Simon, I cannot abide the thought of using IRA bomb makers. No Simon, there must be another way."

"There is always another way Anthony, but not a better way. The IRA is finished. The two or three men that can do the work languish in failure and are desperate for money."

"You can't trust them Simon."

"We don't need to. The scale of the bombing and the outrage that follows will keep them silent. Every law enforcement agency and military 'black ops' unit will hunt and destroy anyone connected to the bombing. These men are old and tired. They have no passion left. This would be a retirement fund job for them."

"I'm not sure Simon. These IRA animals have killed scores of English. The thought of providing retirement money to men who have killed Englishmen is obscene."

"My dear Anthony, I too loath these men and I have a great deal more knowledge of what they have done. Believe me I do not recommend them lightly. They are very good at what they do. We need their expertise. They are available and can do the work without difficulty."

Simon sensed Mitton-Wells' conflict and said.

"Anthony, I would recall to you the words of your own favorite philosopher: 'Whosoever desires constant success must change his conduct with the times.'"

Therefore, on the advice of a fourteenth century Florentine philosopher, Mitton-Wells accepted Simon's suggestion to contract former IRA bomb makers to turn fire extinguishers from instruments of safety and security into shrapnel laden bombs to kill and maim.

"One thing though Simon," said Mitton-Wells, "after the bomb makers have been contracted I want to have direct control of them. As you know, I will obtain the C4 explosives from my contacts in Iraq and I will provide the C4 directly to the Irish."

"Really," said Simon surprised his friend wanted to be 'hands on, "I would of thought the less you had to do with them the better?"

"Indeed Simon, but to borrow from Machiavelli as you just did, 'one change always leaves the way open for the establishment of others'. I think it would do me good to soil my hands with the Irish. Beside, we should minimize contact with you. You and your position are vital to our success and we must keep your involvement secret."

~

Mitton-Wells, more Machiavellian than Simon could imagine, had more to keep secret than Simon's position as the Assistant Director General of MI5's Domestic Terrorism. Charles Mitton, a second cousin on Anthony Mitton-Wells' mother's side, had been at Ypres, Belgium in 1917 when the German army used mustard gas against British and Canadian soldiers. Charles, a brash 23-year-old second lieutenant in the British 19th Division, was one of 160,000 British mustard gas casualties between July 1917 and November 1918.

Mitton-Wells had never met his cousin, but as a child, he heard family stories of the physical and psychological suffering and his ultimate suicide in 1922. Childish curiosity had prompted Mitton-Wells to discover the effects of mustard gas and he had been both fascinated and horrified by what he learned. Large blisters filled with yellow fluid, swollen eyelids and temporary blindness, bleeding and blistering respiratory systems, and severe and disfiguring burns had repulsed and frightened Mitton-Wells when he was young.

Now, Mitton-Wells had a righteous mission. The longer-term effects of mild or moderate exposure to mustard gas, which would require victims to undergo lengthy periods of medical treatment, as well as the mutagenic and carcinogenic potential for cancer in later life, were of more importance: The people of England would reap the hatred and bitterness toward Muslims sown by the mustard gas bombs for decades.

Mitton-Wells knew Simon would never have agreed to use mustard gas. In fact, Mitton-Wells had assured Simon that they need use only five bombs and casualties would likely be in the tens or perhaps a hundred. That Mitton-Wells planned to use twenty bombs packed with mustard gas with an expectation of thousands of victims could not be divulged to Simon. Keeping Simon away from the bomb makers had been one problem. The other was obtaining mustard gas from the only place Mitton-Wells knew the gas was available, Iraq.

~

The trick, or deception, needed the Muslim seller in Iraq to believe he had sold the C4 explosives and the mustard gas to fellow Muslims or at least to a terrorist organization who shared the radical Muslim hatred of the West. The deception required several intermediaries.

In early 2013, Mitton-Wells had begun his search for appropriate intermediaries in South and Southern Africa, home of apartheid, magnet for mercenaries, and a purchasing gateway for illegal armaments. His great grandfather, who had fought with distinction in the Second Boer War from 1899 to 1902, had established contacts with influential racist and pro-Christian/anti-Islamic landowners throughout the region. Many of those relationships had yielded armament and weapons deals for the past hundred years and initial enquiries for an intermediary had seemed promising.

However, in early June 2013, a statement issued by MEND, the Movement for the Emancipation of the Niger Delta, focused Mitton-Wells' attention on Nigeria. MEND, in response to violent acts by the Muslim terrorist group, Boko Haram, declared that "On behalf of the hapless Christian population in Nigeria, MEND will, from Friday, May 31, 2013, embark on a crusade to save Christianity in Nigeria from annihilation."

Mitton-Wells had no interest in MEND, although he did provide some financial and weapons support to ensure their anti-Islamic activities. Mitton-Wells was interested Boko Haram, the Congregation of the People of Tradition for Proselytism and Jihad. Mohammed Yusuf founded Boko Haram, an Islamic jihadist militant organisation based in the northeast of Nigeria, in 2001, to establish a "pure" Islamic state ruled by sharia law.

Boko Haram, according to media and information provided by Simon, attacked Christians and government targets, bombed churches, attacked schools and police stations, and even assassinated members of the Islamic establishment sympathetic to ideas of accommodation with non-Islamic peoples. Since 2001, the Boko Haram terrorist organization accounted for more than 10,000 deaths.

For Mitton-Wells, Boko Haram, a radical Islamic, anti-western terrorist organization, targeted by a direct uncompromising threat from MEND would be a natural candidate to seek explosives, weapons, and perhaps chemical agents, from their Islamic brothers in Iraq. Mitton-Wells had been right.

Utilizing shell companies, middlemen and personal contacts Mitton-Wells engineered the required deception between Boko Haram and the Iraqi terrorist organization AQI. AQI, Al-Qaeda in Iraq, also known as the Islamic State in Iraq and Greater Syria was a Sunni Muslim extremist group bent on creating civil unrest in Iraq and neighboring countries to establish a single, transnational Islamic state based on sharia law.

AQI was a perfect match for Boko Haram. After several months of negotiations, AQI, out of sympathy for its Boko Haram brothers, and for the sum of two million dollars, dispatched a weapons shipment to Nigeria. The shipment contained AK47s, RPG's, grenades, C4 explosives and 20 containers of mustard gas. The gas cylinders were similar to the ones by the Iraqi government against the Kurdish town of Halabja in 1988 that left 5,000 women, men, and children dead within days and more than 10,000 with long-term blindness, cancer, and birth defects. When the weapons arrived in Nigeria, money exchanged hands and the AK47s, RPG's, and grenades surprised a grateful MEND instead of Boko Haram. The C4 and mustard gas disappeared.

To bolster later intelligence connections to British Muslims, Spencer had arranged for several MI5 intelligence reports about British Muslims traveling to Nigeria to include a suggestion that the Muslims were trying to purchase explosives and chemical weapons.

A month later, in Liverpool, a port city on England's North West coast, two former IRA bomb makers puzzled over the twenty, fifteen by four inch steel containers nuzzled against the twenty bricks of C4 explosives. When Mitton-Wells contacted them on the cell phone provided by Simon to confirm the material had arrived, Patrick Oshea, the leader of the two bomb makers, wanted answers.

"What the fuck is in these containers?"

"Nothing for you to worry about Mr. Oshea, simply add the cylinder to the other ingredients."

"I don't like the look of them. What's inside them?"

"Let's say the contents will provide a little more long-term impact than the effects of the rest of the package."

"These things have Arabic writing on them. There not nuclear are they. I don't want to be working on any of that shit."

"No, no, not nuclear my dear man," assured Mitton-Wells casually. "Each container has pieces of shrapnel from American tanks that were used against Iraq in the Desert Storm war of 1991. Iraqi terrorist use the shrapnel in IEDs to send ironic messages to American's and the West."

"Why do we need them? We have plenty of materials and why the Arabic writing? What does it say?"

Mitton-Wells, feigned irritation and put the Irishman in his place.

"You don't need to know. You have a job to do. However, as you seem concerned, there is a need to have the blame for your creations laid at the feet of Muslims. The Arabic writing is some reference to Allah and death to all non-believers. Which I might add, would include you. Now do you think you could get on with the job?"

"Alright, yes," said Oshea. "The packages will be ready as scheduled. Just make sure the rest of our money is ready to."

Bloody Irish said Mitton-Wells to the static of the disconnected line. Then he chuckled and laughed at his own devious deceptions. First, the Irish would get their money, but because of handling the containers, trace amounts of mustard gas would leech onto their skin and into their bodies; no Irish killer of Englishmen would enjoy his retirement years with my money. Second, the irony of Muslim terrorist supplying an extreme anti-Muslim right wing organization with explosives and chemical weapons to frame the Muslims for what might become the most heinous crime in the 21st Century almost brought tears to his eyes.

Attributing the bombs and tracing the mustard gas to Iraqi Muslims, especially under the steerage of Simon, would be a simple and quick task. Oh how he wished he could see the faces of the AQI leadership, as through default they must take responsibility for the attack. After the euphoria of sticking it to the infidels, the Muslim world would realize that 'they' had gone too far. The backlash, according to Mitton-Wells, would be global, vicious and devastating.

While Mitton-Wells basked in his own devilry, an angry Boko Haram leader in Nigeria and a nervous AQI representative from Iraq argued and traded accusations about what had happened to the C4, mustard gas and guns destined for them. Despite their mutual mistrust, it didn't take them long to figure it out.

Thirty-Four

September 25 2013, Manchester, England

BOWELS, THROAT, AND lungs contracted with fear when the red metal cylinder fell to the concrete and rolled nosily across the floor to bump up against the base of the acetylene and oxygen tanks on the welding cart. Darren had been nervous and anxious from the moment he had opened the rear doors of the white van at the warehouse in the Pomona Docks. The early morning cell phone call had not told him what to expect.

"Good morning Darren. I hope you are well?"

"Er, yes thanks."

"Excellent. Today you will drive to the warehouse in the Pomona Docks. The one we used before. You do remember it Darren?"

"Yes why?"

"You will find a vehicle. You will take the vehicle to the workshop and unload the contents. Then you will return the vehicle to the warehouse. Tomorrow, our friend will begin the substitution process. He will exchange two items per day for the next ten days. Each item is clearly marked with the location of placement."

"What's in the van?"

"I am sure you will figure things out when you open the van. Do you understand?"

"Yes."

Inside the van, twenty red fire extinguishers had gleamed under the van's interior light. For several minutes, Darren stood and confirmed what he had already suspected. He now understood why Aalim needed to take photos of the fire extinguishers at Manchester United, why Aalim had cut up the extinguishers in the garage, why they needed welding equipment and spray paint facilities and why Aalim was made to touch and use all the tools and equipment. Like the cell phones, the calls, the computers, the rental car and the workshop, they all framed Aalim as a terrorist.

Darren froze when the extinguisher bomb hit the floor. He need not have worried though. The bombs were relatively harmless until detonated. Modern terrorist bombs used plastic explosives and electronic detonators. The Irish bomb makers had used instantaneous electrical detonators made from a copper tube closed at one end. The detonators, about 6mm diameter and 100mm in length, used an electric charge to set off small amounts of explosive material in the center and tip of the detonator. Two D sized batteries supplied electricity to the detonator and the remotely operated trigger. When the detonator explodes, the energy would ignite the main explosive.

C4, the main explosive, is often used because it is stable, insensitive to most physical shocks and requires the combination of extreme heat and a shock wave of a detonator to detonate. C4 is also malleable and can be molded into any desired shape and pressed into gaps, cracks, and holes. In this case, the bomb makers wrapped C4 around a small metal canister, the batteries, and an assortment of nails and ball bearings. The entire assembly was then sculptured to fit the inside dimensions of the extinguisher.

With the bottom of the extinguisher cut off, the molded C4 bomb had slid easily in before welding the base back in place and painting the extinguisher. To assure cell phone signal reception, the makers threaded an antenna from the detonator up through the extinguisher hose. In addition to being stable and malleable C4, when detonated, decomposes to release nitrogen and carbon oxides gasses, which expand at about 8,000 meters per second and create a devastating amount of force.

Chilled sweat cooled Darren's back as he righted the extinguisher bomb and added the last one to the neat cluster of nineteen that stood like bowling pins beside the paint booth. Curious, Darren stooped to read the extinguisher label.

10kg ABC Powder Fire Extinguisher. Quality kitemark certified to BS EN3. Suitable for A, B and C fires in offices, commercial premises and industrial premises. Capacity 6kg - Fire rating 27A 183B - Average discharge time 16.1secs - Height 51cm, (20 inches) Diameter 16 cm, (6 inches) Filled weight 9.5kg (20 pounds- Empty weight 3.5kg (7 pounds).

Darren lifted one up. It did not feel like twenty pounds, more like 15 pounds. Darren had been close. Each bomb weighed just 14 pounds: 7 pounds of extinguisher, 4 pounds of C4, 1.5 pounds for the small metal cylinder, and the remainder for batteries and detonator.

A crimped plastic tag, attached to the neck of each extinguisher, detailed the location and inspection history of the extinguisher. Darren realized each tag was an expert reproduction from the photographs Aalim had taken. When Aalim made the switch for the real extinguishers, no one would notice any difference. They were identical.

Done with the fire extinguishers, Darren pulled down his baseball cap and pushed up his Manchester City supporters scarf above his nose and below his eyes. Darren's instructions had included the need, because of the security cameras, to cover his face when he drove the van in to the garage. The van itself, assured the instructions, would be disposed of after he returned it to the Pomona Docks warehouse.

~

Darren dodged puddles as he hurried to his car. The line-ups at JD Sports in the Trafford Center had been long and slow. Darren, as instructed, purchased an official Manchester United Duffle Bag for Aalim to carry two extinguishers at a time into Manchester United's stadium. Five minutes later, Darren clutched the bag to his chest and he slid into the passenger seat of Aalim's van.

Withdrawn and sullen Aalim did not speak until he stopped the van for Darren to climb into the back before arriving at the lock up garage.

"I want to see my wife and son."

Darren, one hand on the door handle, paused and said.

"What?'

"I want to see my wife and son."

"Too bad. You do as you I tell you or you will see them all right. In pieces. Now stop fucking around."

"No."

"Are you stupid? Do you have any idea what the man at the house is capable of doing to you wife and kid?"

Aalim, agitation and stress evident in wide dilated eyes, shouted back at Darren.

"How do I know he hasn't already? How do I know they are alive? It has been almost two weeks since you took them. He, that monster at the house, might already have, have…"

Aalim, tears pooling in his eyes, blubbered.

"I don't care what you say. I must see them. I will not do another thing until I know they are alive."

Darren checked his anger as he realized more threats would not work.

"Alright, alright, I'll see what I can do. We can't sit here. While I am in the back, I will make a call. You drive to the garage. When we get inside I will tell you what has been decided."

Aalim's head began to shake in disagreement.

"Listen you fuck. Shake your head all you want. It's the best I can do."

Darren opened the door and stepped out. Before closing the door, Darren leaned in.

"You're taking a big risk. Now drive to the garage."

In the back of the van Darren held the cell phone and considered his options. Darren did not want to make the call. His instructions were clear. Only call in an absolute emergency. He could tell Aalim he had made the call and say his wife and kid were fine and if he pulled the same stunt again, Mackenna would deliver his wife's fingers in a matter of hours. What would he do if Aalim refused to move, or worse, tried to contact the police or something? What if Aalim attacked him and he killed him or something? The more Darren thought about it the more he decided it was an emergency. Desperate, Darren called Mitton-Wells. Unexpectedly, the call had gone well.

"I see," said the voice in response to Darren's explanation of Aalim's refusal to do anything else.

"Don't worry Darren. You did the right thing. Proof of life and a reminder of the consequences of disobedience may not be such a bad thing at this juncture."

"Tell our friend his family will call to your phone in one hour."

Aalim was combative when he opened van doors.

"Well? When will I see my family?"

Darren shuffled out and stood to face Aalim. Darren clenched his fists. During the ride, and after the phone call, Darren had seethed at the nerve of Aalim to make demands. Darren was in charge, not some stinking camel jockey who used his hand to wipe his arse.

Before Aalim could speak again, Darren craned his head back and delivered a vicious head but to Aalim's nose and jaw. Aalim staggered back as Darren punched and kicked Aalim until he fell to the floor.

"You ever speak to me again like that and I'll kill you. I don't give a fuck what we need you for."

Aalim pushed himself to his knees. Blood dripped from his nose and lips and cheeks had begun to swell.

"If my wife and son are dead I have nothing to live for. You may as well kill me now."

Violence had cooled Darren's heat and he smiled with malice.

"Oh, I'd like to kill you, you dirty fuck. Not now, not yet. Besides, I forgot to tell you. You wife will be calling in about half an hour. Now get the bag from the front seat and put two of those fire extinguishers in it."

Aalim made to speak, but Darren cut him off.

"Just shut up if you want to talk to your bitch."

Aalim collected the Manchester United duffel bag from the van and walked to the fire extinguishers. He opened the zip of the bag and thrust an extinguisher in to the bag. A second extinguisher followed and clanged against the first and the concrete floor.

"Hey, be careful with those for Christ sake. Do you want to kill us?"

Aalim stopped. He looked at the extinguishers. Darren could almost hear the wheels turning in Aalim's head as he made the same connections as Darren had earlier.

"These are bombs. You want me to plant bombs at Manchester United."

"Clever boy, yes they are bombs."

"Why?"

"That's not your concern."

"I won't do it. I don't want to kill anyone."

The 'bring' of Darren's phone stopped him midway toward Aalim and halted his intention to beat Aalim. Darren answered and Mackenna said he had Aalim's wife ready. Darren turned to Aalim and handing him the phone said.

"Hey, before you get yourself killed, why don't you talk to your wife?"

Darren listened to Aalim's side of the conversation.

"Nasreen, Nasreen, are you alright? How is Masud? Have they hurt you Nasreen?"

"Yes, yes I am alright. No they haven't hurt me."

"Just small jobs. I, I'm working for them cleaning and…"

A long silence accompanied the tension while Aalim listened.

"Yes Nasreen. No matter the price I will save Masud."

"Yes, yes I, I, promise, I promise Nasreen."

"Nasreen, Nasreen"?

Darren took the phone from Aalim's limp hand and said.

"Very touching. Now, if you want to save your boy, get the bag in the van. We are done here for the night. Tomorrow you will take the bag to work and exchange the extinguishers as indicated on the tags. Got it?"

Without response, Aalim placed the bag in the van and waited for Darren. As he climbed into the back of the van Darren chided Aalim.

"I don't know what you're so upset about. I thought you would be happy about bombing a whole shit load of non-believers."

Thirty-Five

September 27 2013, Manchester, England

GARY 'FAT FUCK' BODDIE was worried. More worried than usual and for very different reasons. Sexual perversions, secret trips, gluttony, work pressures, and social obscurity fed Boddie's natural inclination toward apprehension. This was different though. Since the blackmail to hire the nasty skinny white kid, Brad Short, and the not so bad Muslim, Boddie had worried about why the two men were at Manchester United.

Short arrived at Manchester United in May. Although surly and lazy, he had not caused trouble and his work had been good enough not to cause any problems with other workers or with Lever, the other manager. However, things had changed when the Muslim arrived. Short did less and worse work from the day Aalim started, often standing idle while Aalim did the work of two. Boddie liked Aalim a lot more than Short.

What bothered Boddie, aside from the blackmail, was why they forced him to hire two such different people. When time allowed, Boddie stole away from his managerial duties and huffed his way around the stadium to observe Short and Aalim at work. Aside from Short's vulgar and derisory treatment of Aalim in private, nothing seemed amiss until Aalim, at Short's insistence, used a cell phone to photograph fire extinguishers.

While Boddie was attempting to understand Aalim's photographic efforts, he heard from Lever about Aalim's unauthorized presence in the players change room, the Manchester United Board Members room, the executive viewing lounges, the players' tunnel and the managers dug out beside the field. Boddie, unable to make sense of the fire extinguisher and Aalim's unauthorised travels had begun to lose momentum and interest in discovering more about Short and Aalim until a chance conversation with the head of stadium safety.

"Your new boy, the Paki, he asks a lot of questions for a cleaner."

"What do you mean?"

"Oh, he was all over me to explain the evacuation plans for the stadium in case we had an emergency."

"What kind of emergency?"

"The usual kind, you know a fire or a stadium collapse or whatever. He even asked about earthquakes. Earthquakes for fuck sake! I told him we live in Manchester not up in the hills of Pakistan. Poor fellow, I told him we had excellent plans and not to worry. Still, he's a nosy bugger."

Taking photographs of fire extinguishers, asking for details of evacuation plans and entering restricted areas had made Boddie suspicious enough, but earlier Boddie thought he had glimpsed a bright red fire extinguisher in the garbage bin on Aalim's maintenance cart. Boddie had not been sure. He wanted to check, but was afraid to confront Aalim with Short present. Boddie also wondered about the link between Aalim and Short's activities and the person who had forced him to hire them. Torn between a desire to protect himself and Veronica and a growing certainty that Short was up to something very bad, Boddie decided he needed to learn more about Short and Aalim before talking with anyone else.

With access to personal files, Boddie noted the home address of Short and Aalim. Boddie, for no other reason than proximity to his own home, decided to visit Short's home on Wyford Street, in Moss Side. He had no plan beyond a desire to see where Short lived and a hope something might jump out to explain what was going on.

~

Home to Short was a run down five-story apartment building in Moss Side, a deprived inner city area two miles from Manchester's downtown business and entertainment center. Moss Side was not the kind of place Boddie would normally visit. Inhabited by violent gangs, drug dealers and prostitutes, Moss Side had a reputation as 'a great place to leave'. With a murder rate of 140 per 100,000 in the early 2000s, few people ventured into Moss Side unless they belonged or had business to undertake.

Graffiti, a mix of gang symbols, soccer club names, delinquent obscenity and an occasional misspelled literary quote pleading for help and understanding, covered the exterior walls of the building from ground level to about eight feet.

Opposite the apartment building, Boddie sat huddled on a cold concrete bench between two vandalized bus shelters. Eight buses came and went before Boddie, shivering from the damp and cold of a late September evening, and depressed by the parade of human misery entering and exiting the building, realized his impulsive quest to discover something about Short was futile and stupid. Worse, rain, hard driving rain, a staple of Manchester, had penetrated his outerwear. Miserable and despondent, Boddie sought refuge in a nearby pub to dry off before going home.

~

The Dirty Duck, a Moss Side landmark since 1899, sagged under grime that discolored its once white and cream stucco exterior. Steel bar covered windows and a heavy wood and steel door repelled rather than welcomed would be patrons. Boddie hesitated on the worn stone of the pub's threshold before weakness for beer and food sucked him in. He should have resisted.

Nicotine, heat and snarled, distorted vocals from ancient speakers smacked Boddie's jellied torso as he shook water and dankness from his coat. Leather and denim clad punks and beer bellied skinheads, tattoos proclaiming their belligerent and racist views, turned from the bar to evaluate the newcomer. Unconcerned and disinterested in a white male, the regulars returned to themselves. Boddie, nervous, but committed, scurried to the bar, obtained a pint and seated himself in an alcove out of direct sight from the bar and its occupants.

Just until the rain ends had been Boddie's intention, but the beer, McEwan's, was especially good and Boddie was weak. One beer led to two, and two to many. Fries and pie, and more beer followed until eleven pm when a drunken calculation concluded a taxi ride would get him to his favorite chip shop before it closed at 11:30pm.

Obscured sight lines work both ways. Nestled in his alcove, Boddie and the bar flies could not see each other. Although Boddie had ventured to the bar for numerous refills, he had drawn little attention. On his last refill run at 10:30 pm, dulled by drink, fatigue, warmth and food, Boddie failed to notice the man with spiked hair and chains who had arrived in the pub a few minutes earlier.

The man, seated at the far end of the bar, halted the left to right roll of the soggy toothpick that protruded from his cracked thin lips. Vindictive eyes followed Boddie's bulk as he shuffled away with his last pint. Short, tired of hiding his true self at Manchester United, repulsed by daily contact with a Muslim, and especially pissed because he perceived Boddie actually liked and respected the Muslim more than himself, smirked with malevolence.

Five minutes after eleven pm, when Boddie, buoyed with alcohol and eager to reach the chip shop, staggered from the Dirty Duck, Short slipped from his bar stool to follow.

The rain had slowed. Drizzle, light and constant, doubled the gloom of the poorly lit street. Disoriented, Boddie teetered kerbside and peered about for a taxi. Behind him, sound and light escaped the interior as the heavy door opened and closed. A sixth sense promoted Boddie to swivel his head. Indistinguishable in the shadow of the doorway, Short spoke and mocked.

"What the fuck are you doing here Mr. Boddie? This is little far for you to waddle isn't it?"

Boddie startled, blinked at the shadow and asked.

"What, er , who are you? How do you know my name?"

The shadow edged closer and spoke again.

"Gary, Gary, don't you recognize your number one worker?"

Breath, hot and moist, leaked from Boddie's open mouth as the shadow's words triggered recognition.

"Maybe you would recognize me if I had a little rag head Muslim by my side eh Gary?"

"I, I, Short is that you?"

"Fucking eh it's me you fat disgusting pig. You think that rag head Muslim fucker is better than I am don't you. You are a traitor to the white race. You're worse than them monkeys."

Boddie stepped backward off the curb and into the road.

"You, you can't talk to me like that. I'll have you fired on Monday. I, I…"

"Really, are you sure Gary? I don't think my friends will like that."

Boddie, eyes darting left and right in search of a taxi stepped back on to the sidewalk and walked away from Short.

Pensive, Short kept pace with Boddie and said.

"What are you doing in Moss Side anyway? This is not a place for you. What are you up to?"

"Nothing, nothing, I just wanted a change that's all."

"Gary, you know I live near here. Just over there in those apartments. You haven't been watching me have you?"

Too soon and too adamant, Boddie blurted.

"No, no nothing like that."

"You're a lying fat bastard Gary. I don't believe you. Let's get off the street and we can chat a little more."

Laughing, Short reached for Boddie's arm as Boddie began to run.

"Come here rolly. Where do you think you can run? This is my patch. Arrgh. I'm coming for you Gary. It's time you learned some manners."

Unfamiliar with the area, Boddie turned off the main street, onto a dim cobbled alleyway.

Short knew he had passed the point of no return when he followed Boddie out of the Dirty Duck. Short had blown his cover. Whoever he and Darren Blackley were working for would not tolerate him letting Boddie know who and what he really was. When Boddie sobered up and began to think about Short, an obvious rabid racist, making nice with a rag head Muslim, questions would begin.

Boddie, felled by the wet cobblestones, lay winded and whimpering among several blue City of Manchester Wheelie garbage bins. Indecisive, Short stood over Boddie.

"Get away from me. Get away. Help, somebody help. I know you and Aalim are up to something with those fire extinguishers and all those questions Aalim has been asking. I don't care about the photographs and I don't care what people say about Veronica and me. You are much worse than I am. I'll tell the police and everyone about you. You, you. I'll have your job, I'll, I'll…"

"That's the problem Gary. I can't have you telling anyone."

The steel toe protection of Short's work boot shattered Boddie's teeth and jarred the jawbone from its socket. When Boddie's hand reached instinctively to protect his face, a second steel-toed boot cracked and broke ribs. Forced through jagged teeth and ripped flesh, Gary uttered his last words.

"No, no. Please. Who will take care of Veronica?"

A third kick pushed the tip of a broken rib into a lung. Kicks four, five, and six obliterated facial feature. The seventh and final kick, unnecessary for death, and delivered with inhuman relish, caved the back of the head and careened vertebrae into the throat.

Short, satiated, gazed at the mangled mass at his feet. Liquid and matter, red, purple and grayish, distorted the shine of his black right boot. Annoyed Short wiped his boot on Boddie's coat.

"You should have stayed home you fat fuck."

Thirty-Six

September 27/8 2013, Ottawa, Canada

MUSLIMS IDENTIFY THE PROPHETS OF Islam as humans assigned a special mission by God to guide humanity. Wilson, hoping for guidance, stared up at the names of the six Islamic Prophets written across the top of his white board. None spoke to him. Wilson shuddered at the prospect of what message the Prophets would deliver to humanity.

After exhausting the messages for clues and leads, Wilson turned to instinct to guide his analysis. His gut said Chris' message and his death had links to the developing terrorist threat. Hours, caffeine and patience cemented one thread in Wilson's consciousness: The tattooed skinhead that lingered and stared at Chris in the Prospect of Whitby Pub back in March had indeed been an EDL member.

One of Wilson's primary tools to gain information on developing issues used automatic web searches for news items. At any one time, between eighteen and twenty-five searches scanned the internet to satisfy Wilson's need for information related to ongoing terrorism files or individuals.

The day after Chris' murder Wilson had added another automatic search the internet: 'violent assaults / murder / death / right wing / activists / skin heads /

punk / homophobia / religion or race / EDL / England'.

In the early hours of September 27, Wilson's desktop computer beeped with notice of a result for his most recent search. A headline in the Manchester Evening News, announced "Man Beaten to Death by Punk". Wilson read the article.

Greater Manchester Police have launched a murder inquiry after a man was found dead in Moss Side, Manchester in the early hours of September 27, 2013.

Gary Boddie, 43, was found beaten and bloody in a quiet alleyway, two blocks from the Dirty Duck pub.

Police say Mr. Boddie, of Railway Road, Old Trafford, suffered extensive facial wounds, a fractured skull, and multiple broken ribs and bruises.

Det Chief Insp Pete Jenkins, of GMP's Major Incident Team, said: "We believe Mr. Boddie died as a result of being assaulted by one or more persons."

"We have information he was drinking in the nearby Dirty Duck pub immediately prior to his death and that his assailant might have either followed him from the pub or chanced upon Mr. Boddie as he walked to a nearby taxi rank. We have already spoken with a number of people who have provided information to assist the investigation."

"It is vitally important that anyone who was in or around the Dirty Duck last night or who has knowledge of the incident come forward with any information about what happened."

"Mr. Boddie worked as a Facilities Manager at Manchester United's Old Trafford soccer stadium and was not known to frequent public houses in the Moss Side area."

The Dirty Duck, a Moss Side landmark for over a hundred years, is a known hangout for punks, skinheads and right-wing activists.

Det Chief Insp Pete Jenkins noted that the Dirty Duck was well known to police and that numerous violent, drug related incidents have been reported and investigated. "We cannot rule out the possibility that Mr. Boddie's death is somehow connected to the activities of the Dirty Duck and the type of patrons that frequent the pub."

Anyone with information is asked to contact the Incident Room on 0161 856 2027 call police on 101 or Crimestoppers on 0800 555 111.

Mindless beatings occurred across England in hundreds and thousands each year and while death was rare, nothing about Mr. Boddie's brutal and premature death fired any synaptic connections in Wilson's mind. Perversely, the only reason Boddie's death found a home in a far recess of Wilson's mind was the mention of Boddie's employment as a facilities manager at Manchester United.

Thirty-Seven

October 2 2013, Ottawa, Canada

FRUSTRATION GNAWED WILSON. HIS white board and flip charts, disorganized and jumbled, mocked and sneered as they silently challenged Wilson's self-belief in the power of reasoned analysis and deduction. Wilson, stalled by the shortage of analytical data, began to doubt his gut feeling that the murder of Chris and the imminent terrorist attack in Europe were connected. What evidence did he have anyway?

Two seemingly illogical reports related to UK domestic extremism authorized by the Assistant Director of MI5 for Domestic Extremism. What did Wilson know about the activities of MI5? For all he knew MI5 might be engaged in a major EDL or Muslim undercover or infiltration initiative and that was the reason MI5 had authorized reports that stipulated 'no follow up or further investigation'.

Yes, Chris had drawn his attention to the reports, but maybe that was just to let him know that the UK security services were seriously investigating the EDL and Muslims. He and Chris both advocated the art of deducting the meaning of something by what was missing. The reports and the message from Chris to 'look again' could mean exactly that: 'No follow up or further investigation' could mean the exact opposite and Chis simply wanted his friend to know that the UK intelligence services were hot on the tail two big domestic terror threats. And what about Chris' murder? What did Wilson really know? Was Billy really a reliable witness? The more Wilson thought the more he doubted.

Desperate, Wilson sought inspiration from his coffee machine and hovered over it expectantly as hundreds of dollars of chrome and steel gurgled and hissed. Wilson grasped his stainless steel double walled mug and lifted it to his flared nostrils. Sometimes, Wilson thought the aroma satisfied more than the taste. On the cusp of an almost erotic sensation, the door to Wilson's office flew open and Mitch, flustered and red faced, shouted at Wilson.

"Craig. More messages Craig. Oh god, it's getting close. Come on. The board room now."

Mitch, not waiting for Wilson, turned and headed toward the elevators.

Wilson's mug had no lid and loath to leave his coffee behind he followed Mitch as quick as he could to the boardroom.

People crowded the boardroom. Almost every ITAC analyst had squeezed in. Something, thought Wilson with apprehension, must have happened.

Director Priest wasted no time:

"The US intercepted and translated the following two messages." Cook clicked a remote. Words polluted the screen.

Cell phone intercept. September 28, 2013.
From Manchester, England
Male voice, Arabic
BEGIN:
This is Hud. All packages now in place.
End:

Cell phone intercept. October 1, 2013.
From Manchester, England
Male voice, Arabic
BEGIN:
**This is Adam. Activation codes established.
Glory, Glory, Our Men United Once More**
END:

Murmurs rumbled as close colleagues exchanged concerned opinions.

"Bastards," spat a young wide-eyed man from the back of the room.

"Oh my god, it's real. It's really going to happen," whispered, Gillian Stoker, a seasoned analyst on loan to ITAC from the Department of Foreign Affairs.

"All right everyone, alright. Let's stay focused," said Priest as he raised his hands to calm the apprehensive crowd.

"We know the threat is real and we have all worked hard to figure out what the target is and when the attack will happen. These intercepts are like the others. They use the same terse format. The callers are using names of Islamic Prophets and both messages are reports on the progression toward an event. However, this time we have something new."

Roger picked up from Priest.

"Two things stand out. First, the mention of activation codes which confirms our and the Five Eyes conclusion that we are dealing with an explosive device of some kind. Second, the use of the phrase 'Glory, Glory, Our Men United Once More' deviates from the previous seven messages and might provide a clue to the target and the timing."

"Thank you Roger," said Priest. "As Roger indicated it is the deviation from the established pattern and the inclusion of a phrase that obviously has meaning related to the attack that we want you all to focus on. Preliminary analysis by the US and UK have linked the words <u>Glory, Glory, Our Men United Once More</u> to Al Qaeda propaganda publications centered on how Jihadists can achieve the glory of Allah by destroying non-believers etc. Roger will provide you with details of the analysis in a few moments. However, I want you to dig deeper than propaganda slogans. I want you to find a specific reference in Islam or the Koran or speeches by the Bin Laden or other Al Qaeda leaders to link the words with a location. I am convinced the words point to a place, a target and if we can find that target we might save lives."

To Wilson it sounded like a slogan, a call to arms, and a chant before battle. Glory to this or that was replete in Islam and the Koran. Then again, Glory littered most religious texts, songs and prayer. Wilson asked.

"Do we have the original Arabic text?"

"No," said Roger, "it wasn't provided and I don't feel it is necessary. The US has the best translation capabilities of the Five Eyes."

True, thought Wilson, but experience cautioned about the limitations of single source intelligence - which is exactly what unchallenged translation was. Then the synaptic click happened: Glory, Glory Man United and the murder of Gary Boddie, a facilities manager at the Man United stadium.

"Wilson," asked Priest unexpectedly, "have your outlying ideas yielded any results or anything that should be shared with the group?"

Wilson, already out of favour with Priest for his ideas and on probation for his UK trip decided to gather more facts before telling Priest and risk being cut out of the loop.

"Nothing conclusive, I'm still analyzing information for connections."

"Have you found anything to suggest we are on the wrong track or that we should be looking elsewhere?"

"No, but I would like a copy of the original Arabic phone call and the translation."

"Roger?"

"Yes, alright, I will get that to you later."

Eager to analyse and research, no one responded to Priest's call for 'any other business or comments'.

Thirty-Eight

October 4 2013, London, England

Pulled back by the bulk of the backpack, Marshall's shoulders strained and stretched his coat. Four items filled the backpack. Two passports, a small toiletry bag and 250,000 pounds in used twenty and fifty pound notes. The money, skimmed from the anonymous donations from the man on the cell phone, weighed less than thirty pounds, but Marshall, who was wearing a thick wool coat, had not adjusted the straps and his shoulders scrunched. Marshall, conspicuous and guilty, paused at the door of his pawnshop to scan the street for plain-clothes police officers.

After many uneventful months, the police had withdrawn the 24x7-security detail, but Marshall did not trust them to leave him alone. Since the deluge of money from the unknown benefactor Marshall, as instructed, had undertaken a massive EDL recruitment drive. More than two hundred and fifty thousand people had officially registered and thrice those numbers were silent members. Yesterday, Marshall had received a call and a demand for an update.

"Mr. Marshall. What good news do you have for us today?"

"Things are going well. Our official membership is now around two hundred thousand."

"What about the unofficial membership?"

"About eight hundred thousand."

"So, Mr. Marshall we can count on approximately one million EDL members ready and willing to respond to a call to arms?"

"Yes. No problem."

"What about the plans for the rally on Saturday in Manchester?"

"Everything is set. It will be the biggest rally we have ever held."

"How many EDL members do you expect?"

"I'd say about a hundred thousand. The place will be crazy. I mean…"

"The route and timing of the march have been arranged as we discussed?"

"Yes, yes. They will be on the roads near Manchester United's stadium at exactly three o'clock on Saturday."

"Excellent Mr. Marshall, you have been most useful."

There had been finality to the last words from the voice on the phone: A finality that tweaked Marshall's paranoia and survival instinct and pushed Marshall to stuff a backpack with fake passports and a quarter million pounds.

Wary, but desperate to leave, Marshall stepped from his shop and turned left. Two blocks from his pawnshop, a taxi waited. The taxi had been arranged a day earlier from a pay phone in the rear of a seedy pub in Bedford's working class area. The taxi would take Marshall to the Bedfordshire School of Flying to meet up with Phil Williams.

Williams, a non-registered EDL member for two years and an ardent racist, owned and flew a four-seater Grumman Tiger plane. Williams had agreed to fly Marshall to Weymouth on the south coast of England.

From Weymouth, Marshall had arranged passage on a fishing boat to take him to the Guernsey, one of the two Channel Islands located off the south coast of England and just thirty miles from northern France.

Marshall's plans, made in haste, did not extend beyond Guernsey. He just wanted to be out and away from Manchester and whatever the lunatic, as he had begun to think of the man on the phone, had planned for Saturday October 6. Marshall had sensed he was a loose end to whatever was going to happen and experience had taught Marshall what happens to loose ends and he didn't plan on sticking around to find out how he would be 'tied off'.

Despite the damp cold October morning, the streets were busy. Pedestrians, trucks, buses, cars, bicycles and leashed dogs attached to human arms, jostled for primacy as each pursued their daily affairs. Marshall, his mind focused on taxi, plane and boat did not notice the serene expression on the brown-skinned face of the man who stood fixedly on the street a block from the waiting taxi.

Neither did he notice the serrated blade of the ten-inch knife clutched in the man's right hand. Only when the knife pierced his stomach, twisted, and rose up through his rib cage to cut into his sternum did Marshall's consciousness register the man and the knife. Only when the force of the attack raised Marshall to his tiptoes did he notice the *Taliyah* and *thobe* dress of a fundamentalist Muslim.

The man, calm and composed, withdrew the knife, stepped back and watched with Marshall as blood and intestine trailed the knife's exit to fall at their feet. Marshall fell to his knees as his hands flailed ineffectually to contain his guts as they slipped through his fingers. The man, dispassionate as though slaughtering a beast, grasped Marshall's hair and pulled his head taut to expose the neck. The point of the knife, red and sliver hovered between Adams apple and collarbone. The knuckles on the man's hand whitened as he tensed and pushed the knife through the windpipe and on into the nape of Marshall's neck.

Twenty feet away, a white man turned off the video camera on his disposable cell phone. Five minutes later the video clip of Marshall's brutal murder beeped or buzzed its way into the in boxes of every major news media service in England and Europe. Fifteen more minutes and the video appeared on multiple right-wing websites across the world.

An hour later, as Anthony-Mitton Wells joined millions of other viewers to watch an edited version of the gruesome video on the BBC, he silently complimented his friend Simon for having coordinated the same extremist British Muslims who had threatened to kill Marshall to carry out the attack. Contented, Mitton-Wells poured himself a small scotch and toasted Marshall's death with a short epitaph.

"Mr. Marshall, your death will galvanize your EDL faithful to a state of frenzy. You really have been most useful."

Thirty-Nine

October 4 2013, Ottawa, Canada

WILSON COULD NOT CONCENTRATE. Or rather, he could not concentrate on anything except his minds distortion of the latest terrorist message. For almost eighteen hours the same song, or chant, had looped endlessly inside his head. The message, 'This is Adam. Activation codes established. Glory, Glory, Our Men United Once More' had changed to become the opening lines of a Manchester United anthem song.

> Glory, glory, Man United,
> Glory, glory, Man United,
> Glory, glory, Man United,
> As the reds go marching on, on, on.

As a teenager, Wilson had chanted the song along with 70,000 other fans every Saturday from September to May. Each time Wilson attempted to conduct analysis on the message for meaningful links to Islam, the Koran, Jihad-ism, Al Qaeda or anything to do with terrorist propaganda, dogma or religion the song would butt in and distract him. Succumbing to the lure and nostalgia of the song Wilson found himself softly singing the second verse.

> Just like the Busby Babes in Days gone by

We'll keep the Red Flags flying high
You've got to see yourself from far and wide
You've got to hear the masses sing with pride.

A beep from his computer cut short a rendition of verse three as the automated search function found another news event. The event soon generated hundreds of thousands of hate-filled comments on websites around the world. A headline on the BBC World News website proclaimed 'English Defense League Leader Murdered in Street by Muslim'. A video, attributed to a passerby, showed with remarkable clarity the brutal stabbing death of Marshall by a brown-skinned man in traditional Islamic dress. The video allowed only one interpretation: a brown-skinned Muslim murdered a white-skinned Christian.

The implications of the murder finally broke Wilson free of the looped Manchester United song. As Wilson and millions of others clicked the BBC website for more information the automated search function began to spit out more news reports of violent incidents in England and around the world as extremists on all sides reacted with vicious deeds and bias words.

Every major national and international news agency carried the video of the EDL leader's murder. Spontaneous protests of outrage or support, along with counter protests and confrontations, followed as right, left and center competed with radicals and moderates for attention and recognition. Justification battled condemnation, celebration fought repulsion and as sides squared off, and positions entrenched, hate smothered compassion.

Wilson surfed through the avalanche of media reports as the speed and scope of global reaction threatened to choke media network capacity. From outside his office hurried footfalls and concerned voices joined the visual images on Wilson's screen as, thought Wilson, news of Marshall's murder spread through ITAC. Wilson's door opened as Mitch, propelled by the noise and activity behind him, called out.

"Craig, Craig, come quick there has…"

Wilson cut Mitch off.

"I know Mitch, I know. It is all over the news. I can't believe…"

"What do you mean? It can't be in the news. We only just found out."

"Well it's been on the BBC for the past half hour and it's all over the world now."

"What! It can't be. It's top secret."

"Marshall?"

"No, not Marshall: Munich!"

"Munich. What about Munich Mitch?"

"The terrorists Craig, they are going to bomb Munich."

~

Five minutes later, after sorting their crossed purposes, Wilson and Mitch sat beside each other as a grim faced Priest asked Cook to put the latest intercept message on the boardroom screen.

Cell phone intercept. October 4, 2013.
From Manchester, England
Male voice, Arabic
BEGIN:
This is Harun. Yellow. They will [never] forget Munich after this.
End:

A heartfelt cry from Werner, a second-generation immigrant of German heritage, broke the silence.

"Oh god, they must mean the 1972 Munich Massacre. What could they possibly do that will make people forget that."

Everyone in the room knew about the Munich Massacre when the Palestinian terrorist group Black September murdered eleven Israeli Olympic team members.

Wilson knew Munich too. Two years earlier, in October 2011, Wilson had attended a weeklong National Security and Intelligence / Military Interface course at the NATO training school in Oberammergau, a small town of 6,000 people in Bavaria. Before and after the Monday to Friday NATO course, Wilson had spent the weekends exploring Munich, including a hazy fifteen hours in an Oktoberfest beer hall.

Munich, reflected Wilson, the capital and largest city of the German state of Bavaria and the third largest city in Germany, straddled the River Isar just north of the Bavarian Alps. With more than one and a half million people within the city limits and endless sporting, education, cultural and seasonal events and structures, the potential for terror was immense.

People shuffled and squirmed in seats. No one would say it, but ITAC's analytical efforts over the past weeks and months had not discovered anything connected to Munich. All analysis had been driven by the first cell phone intercepts that had been made from Egypt to Berlin and London. Even then, with Berlin identified as a possibility, ITAC had produced nothing concrete to indicate a specific target. Priest, sensitive to the thirst for information and assurance that their efforts, no matter how unproductive, were not inferior to the rest of the Five Eyes intelligence community, relieved the tension.

"Munich is as big a surprise to our allies as it is to us. None of our allies, or at least based on the shared reports or communications, had identified Munich as the target. They, like us, were focused on Berlin and London."

"What do we do now?" asked a nervous analyst.

"With the target city identified, all European intelligence resources together with the UK and the US can be brought to bear," said Priest. "Given the scale of the intelligence resources available in Europe, we will stand down from proactive and predictive analysis to a watch and brief position. Roger, as Director of European activities, will maintain links with our Five Eyes allies and with other European intelligence agencies. We will produce daily updates for the NSA and appropriate bulletins for use by other government departments and agencies."

Body language conveyed group relief from responsibility and disappointment at their exclusion from the chase. Priest continued.

"I think we could all use a break from the strain of the last few weeks. I am sure we all wish we could do more to help prevent and catch the terrorists, but it is out of our hands. Thank you everyone for the long hours and commitment. Now, let's keep our fingers crossed and hope the Europeans can stop the terrorists before it's too late."

Wilson, deep in thought, raised his hand to get Priest's attention.

"Yes Craig?"

"The message, the word 'never' in brackets?"

"Yes, what about it?"

"Do we know why the word 'never' is in brackets?"

"Roger?"

"No not exactly. I assumed it is because there might be a question or ambiguity about the translation from Arabic. Why Craig?"

"It seems odd to me. Without the word 'never' the meaning would change to 'They will forget Munich after this' which doesn't sound right. If terrorists intend to do something more horrific than the Munich massacre then the word 'never' should not be there. No one will forget Munich after another attack."

"Well you've answered your own question Craig. The sentence doesn't make sense without the word 'never'."

"Then why is the word in brackets? I think we should establish if never was part of the actual text or not because if the word never is genuine and not an addition by translation its meaning could be something else. Would you mind if I follow this up?"

Roger looked to Priest who shrugged.

"Sure, but Roger will do it."

Wilson could not have explained why the word 'never' bothered him. He did not know. He wasn't even sure if it was the word or the phrase.

Forty

October 5 2013, Ottawa, Canada

WILSON WAS GOING MAD. His brain was stuck on the word never. He was still waiting for conformation from either CSE or Five Eyes on whether the word never was original text or an interpretation or translation addition. Fixation with the word never had brought an excerpt of Wilson's favorite Winston Churchill speech to mind:

"Never give in; never give in, never, never, never-in anything, great or small, large or petty - never give in except to convictions of honour and good sense. Never yield to force; never yield to the apparently overwhelming might of the enemy."

The excerpt rattled around his head taunting him to keep on trying while providing no assistance.

In an effort to ignore Churchill's call for unwavering resilience, Wilson grabbed a black marker and assaulted a blank flip chart with key facts and conclusions about the terrorist telephone calls.

> *Male voice. Arabic.*
> *Names of Prophets: Last nine messages.*
> *Dates and times: Random.*
> *Calls Made From:*
> *(1) Cairo to London / (1) Cairo to Berlin / (9) Manchester to a known terrorist number*
> *Terse Questions: 3, all one word questions.*

Terse Answers: 3 answers all no more than six words.
Terse statements: 7 all less than six words / 1 with
thirteen words and 1 with eleven words.
Dialog:
Date?
Almost. A question remains about the date.
Why?
To maximize casualties.
Report.
Date confirmed.
This is Musa. Target confirmed.
This is Ibrahim. We have access.
This is Nuh. Materials Received.
This is Yusuf. Materials assembled.
This is Lut. Packages sent.
This is Isa. First in place.
This is Hud. All in place.
This is Adam. Activation codes established. Glory,
Glory, Our Men United Once More
This is Harun. Yellow. They will [never] forget Munich
after this.

Wilson stood back from the flip chart and focused on the last two messages. He split each of the messages in to two parts by cutting out the first six words in one message and the first four words in the other message. Six words and four words were consistent with the previous seven messages. Wilson then isolated the extra words and placed them together:

Glory, Glory, Our Men United Once More / They will [never] forget Munich after this.

The more Wilson stared at the two phrases the more uneasy he became. They didn't belong. The words did not fit the pattern. The words were undisciplined, unprofessional, and almost personal. The earlier communications had been precise, cold and workmen like. They had no waste, no embellishment and no clues. Now the messages contained prose and a probable target city. Terrorists did not do prose and clues. Terrorist organizations used massive amounts of time and money to organize an attack and no terrorist would risk their investment by providing clues.

Almost, thought Wilson, almost as though there was a second hidden message, a message with a private or personal meaning or purpose. Wilson wrote the words <u>Glory, Glory, Our Men United Once More /</u> <u>They will [never] forget Munich after this</u> on an A4 pad and began to doodle around them. Doodles turned to drawings of a soccer ball and goal net and an airplane. Dislodging his thoughts a computer generated voice boomed down from the PA system speaker in the ceiling directly above Wilson's head.

"All analysts to the board room immediately. All analysts to the board room immediately."

Bemused and startled Wilson stared at the ceiling speaker and thought he was dreaming or nightmaring, if there was such a word. He had never before heard the PA system used, and certainly never to call a meeting. Fire drills used various speeds of a pulsating dong sound to communicate with employees. Half in denial at what he had just heard and half in an attempt to pick up ambient noise to either confirm or deny the overhead summons Wilson titled his head back and cocked an ear.

Raised voices, scurrying feet and banged doors convinced Wilson the voice and the call had been real. With A4, pad and pen in hand Wilson exited his office and joined the tail end of analysts heading to the boardroom. Worry and uncertainty clouded each face. Forty analysts and bosses worked at ITAC and the boardroom bulged with bodies. When the door closed, it did not take long for the air to stale as people used up vast amounts of air as they speculated and fretted about the reason for the assembly. Wilson, not last, stood elbow to elbow with two young men in flash suits and sparkling shoes. He didn't know who they were and he felt oddly out of place.

Director Priest, flanked by Roger Cook and three other regional Directors, stood stiff and tight lipped at the head of the table. Priest raised a hand and people quieted.

"During the last four weeks many of you here have worked on the intercepted terrorist cell phone calls that have made clear an intention and capability to commit a bombing attack somewhere in Europe. If you have not worked directly on the file then I am sure you are aware of the basic details. Two days ago, based on the latest intercept call that identified Munich as the target, I decided ITAC would stand down from proactive and predictive analysis to a watch and brief position. Our task would be to produce daily updates for the NSA and appropriate bulletins for use by other government departments and agencies."

Shuffled feet and paper crinkles filled the seconds taken by Priest to pause and swallow a breath before he delivered the bad news.

"However, this afternoon at one pm, we received a transcript of another terrorist cell phone communication. Accompanying the transcript was a request that we do everything we can to assist. Roger, would you please project the message."

Cell phone intercept. October 5, 2013.
From Manchester, England
Male voice, Arabic

BEGIN:
This is Ishaq. Green. On Sunday October 6, we shall celebrate as Allah's will is done.
End:

The meaning and the implications of the words, individually benign, collectively horrifying, sank in. Some gasped, some moaned, some uttered the universal OMG. Wilson counted words; sixteen. Questions blurted from fearful mouths and declarations of intent to 'find the bastards' or 'we must stop them' accompanied sombre shouts of 'what can/shall we do'?

Priest raised his hand again and spoke.

"Analysis from the UK, the US and other European agencies has concluded that they now know the exact target. As you know, an earlier terrorist message said 'they would never forget Munich after this'. This message, which indicates the attack will occur on Sunday October 6, just two days from now, coincides with the closing ceremonies of one of the biggest cultural and social events in Germany, Oktoberfest."

With a large European heritage and cultural base in Canada, everyone in the room knew about Oktoberfest. At least fifteen had attended themselves and most everyone else knew someone who had been.

"The Closing Ceremony signals the biggest celebration of the year as hundreds of thousands of Bavarians and visitors gather see out the summer."

Wilson knew all about Oktoberfest and the closing ceremonies. When he had extended his weeklong visit to the NATO school by two days so he could experience the end of Oktoberfest he had been overwhelmed by the scale of the celebration.

"Previous closing ceremonies," continued Priest, "have attracted more than 300,000 thousand people spread over several square miles in adjacent pavilions. In addition, numerous officials, celebrities and notables are expected. I don't need to tell you that the consequences of an attack would be absolutely devastating."

Analysts called for authorities to cancel or postpone the ceremony.

"Yes," said Priest, "all those options are being considered, but indications are that if authorities try to cancel the event then people will simply converge and parade on their own without all the emergency services support, police presence and coordination that would be vital if such an event was attacked. The ceremony is a key aspect of Oktoberfest and people will be on the streets no matter what. In addition, many of them will have had more than their share of German beer. The German authorities will make the decisions about the ceremony and any preventative actions. Our job, which is why I have brought all of you here, is to do everything we can to find some piece of information to help identify the person or persons behind this or a definite clue as to precisely where the attack will occur."

Priest, realizing his people needed to do something, became forceful and said.

"Effective immediately, every person in ITAC will drop whatever they are working on and analyze and dissect every piece of information we have and any others you may think relevant. Bring whatever you have to Roger."

Tight lips, sombre expressions and snapping folders and binders signalled the groups desire and intention to 'do something' and the boardroom emptied.

While others expressed shock, anger and determination, Wilson copied the latest intercepted message on to his A4 note pad. As with the last two messages, Wilson divided the sixteen words up at the sixth word.

This is Ishaq. Green. **On Sunday October 6, we shall celebrate as Allah's will is done.**

Excited, but not sure why, Wilson hurried away with the rest of the analysts. Back in his office, Wilson added what he now called the 'extra words' to his list on his note pad. Then he wrote the three sets of 'extra words' in black marker on a white board next to his multicolored analysis of the death of his friend Chris Thornton.

Glory, Glory, Our Men United Once More / They will [never] forget Munich after this / On Sunday October 6, we shall celebrate as Allah's will is done.

With growing certainty, Wilson feared the worst.

Forty-One

October 6 2013, Manchester United Stadium, Manchester, England

RAIN, FINE AND LIGHT, fell without prejudice or preference on the dense mass of soccer supporters as they walked briskly toward Manchester United's Old Trafford stadium. Anticipation crackled. Today's game was vital for both teams. A Manchester United win would maintain their contention for a record breaking 21st Premier League title. A loss would cast them twelve points adrift from their opponents Arsenal, the current league leaders. If Arsenal won today, they would open up a seven-point lead ahead of Chelsea, the second place team. Of equal relevance was the record of the clubs previous meetings: Manchester United had won 82, Arsenal 45 and 67 games ended in a draw. Regional differences, Arsenal from the South, was one of the big five London based clubs; Manchester United represented the pride of North Western England. History, status, location, honours, trophies, and many other measures and indicators of each teams 'pedigree' infused the expectant thirst and pride of the supporters as they marched toward the stadium.

Hawkers of scarves, hats, banners, pins, and match day programs plied their wares for cash and bulk discounts to fans to adorn and proclaim their allegiance. Pie, chip, burger and sandwich sellers tempted fans with fat, sugar and carbohydrates to fuel myopic loyalties and rabid devotion. Police, stewards and volunteers herded the human mass to narrow turnstiles embedded in brick walls.

Forty-Two

October 6 2013, Ottawa, Canada

DEFEATED PESSIMISM AND FRIGHTENED FOREBODING staved off the exhausted fatigue of the analysts crammed into the ITAC boardroom. Dust particles, infused with invisible molecules laden with the smell of discarded coffee cups, pizza boxes, and unwashed bodies swirled in the warm air created by the twenty or so computers hastily assembled to convert the board-room into a makeshift operations room.

No one worked. There was nothing they could do except wait, watch and pray. The 50-inch live TV coverage of the Oktoberfest closing Ceremony in Munich dominated and commanded the attention of everyone in the room. Within the coming hour, hand cannons and ancient rifles, an address by the lord mayor and costumed brass band pawnians would mark the last day of Oktoberfest with the Böllerschießen ceremony on steps of the Bavaria Statue.

Nearby, in the Thereisienwiese, a flat area of about 42 hectares in the Munich quarter of Ludwigsvorstadt-Isarvorstadt, thousands of revelers gathered in tents and gardens to drink the last of the estimated 6.7 million liters of beer consumed during the 16 day event.

With only hours of warning that Munich was the target, and without absolute confidence of the location or time, Germany authorities had reluctantly conceded it would have been impossible to cancel the closing ceremony and associated events.

Many experts had concluded that canceling the event would create more chaos and improvised and spontaneous celebrations would hamper security and consequence management should anything happen. Some analysts even suggested the possibility that the terrorists wanted the event canceled at the last moment to make it easier for them to plant bombs in the ensuing disorganization and confusion.

Priest stood at the rear of the boardroom to avoid the expectant eyes of the ITAC team who sought and needed an assurance he could not provide. Cook joined Priest as Priest answered a buzz on his Blackberry. Priest turned to Cook and answered his unspoken question.

"Wilson has asked me to his office. He has something to show me."

"What, now? He should come here. We can't be absent when something happens."

"Wilson says it urgent and confidential."

"Do you want me to come with you?"

"No thanks Roger, you stay here. I won't be long."

Forty-Three

October 5/6 2013, Manchester, England

MACKENNA CRADLED THE PHONE. The last call from the condescending prick who now controlled his life had been weeks ago to congratulate him for being so persuasive with the Muslim in the basement.

"An excellent job Mr. Mackenna, I don't expect we will have any trouble with the Muslim."

"Yeah, well, I know how to do my job. What do you want me to with the woman and kid now?"

"Keep them safe Mr. Mackenna. And Mr. Mackenna, no games. We will be watching. Understand?"

Mackenna had understood all right. Cameras and microphones monitored the entire place. He had been disappointed when instructed to only frighten the captives and not go all the way. Well, he had scared the shit out of them all right. Especially when he had dragged the sobbing boy in to the room and told the Muslim that when he was done with his wife, he would stretch the boy out with his stick."

Mackenna had no sexual interest in the boy. When it was time, he would just put it out of its misery with a tap to the head.

~

Mackenna had relived the mock rape scene repeatedly and the constant temptation of a captive and utterly helpless woman had become unbearable. Twenty-one days of sexual and violent frustration had eaten Mackenna's patience. He had lost count of the times, naked and erect, he had stood over Nasreen willing her to make a gesture to push him over the edge and justify a loss of control. However, Nasreen had done nothing save stare emotionless at some point Mackenna could not see.

The previous week, when the temptation to rape had become unbearable, Mackenna had decided to leave the house and seek a victim in the local area. Packing thin rope and rough builders tape, Mackenna had gotten less than fifty steps from the house when the cell phone vibrated in his chest pocket. Only one person could call him on the phone and Mackenna had expected the call.

"Mr. Mackenna, I see you leaving the house and the grounds. What are you doing?"

"I need some air and a chance of scenery. I've been cooped up with those fucking Pakis for three weeks. I can't stand the smell of them no more."

"Mr. Mackenna," said Mitton-Wells, "your instructions were very clear. You are not to leave the house until I tell you."

"Look, whoever you are. I need some space. I need to, to…"

"I know what you need Mr. Mackenna. The rope and tape you placed in your backpack last night make that very clear. However, let me make something clear to you. What I am doing is far more important than your disgusting and vile desires."

"You don't know what it's like with them. Stuck in…"

"Maybe not Mr. Mackenna, but there are two things I know for certain. If you do not fulfill your instructions to the letter, I will deliver the tape recording of your rape and murder of that young girl to the police within hours. More importantly Mr. Mackenna, I will ensure that every day of your fifteen years or so in prison you will suffer in the same way as your victims. Each day you will be violated and raped. Do I make myself clear?"

Mackenna, like many male rapists, feared his own rape more than anything and reluctantly returned to the house to seethe and plot to rape the woman and find and kill the man who belonged to the voice on the phone. His obsession with the woman, the unknown man, and the threats of abhorrent prison time, had bled into each other to produce tangled rape and murder fantasies in which Mackenna was both perpetrator and victim.

~

Sweating and aroused on the cot in his bedroom, Mackenna let the fantasy play over again in his head. The climax of the scene, a faceless man naked and prostrate over the woman pleading for mercy as Mackenna used the short stick to penetrate the man's anus as he thrust his own manhood into the woman, was broken by the incessant ring of the cell phone.

"Mr. Mackenna."

"Mr. Mackenna. It is time to allow you some satisfaction."

Disbelieving, Mackenna loosened his grip on his erection and his penis slipped from his hand.

"What? What do you mean?"

"You are to move the woman and the boy tomorrow. You will leave the house in the morning and take them to a lock up garage at the address that I will text you."

"What for, is it over...?"

"Don't interrupt Mr. Mackenna. No, it is not over its just begun. In the garage you will find a scarf."

Mackenna, anticipation and excitement resurging, said.

"What do you want me to do with the scarf?"

"That's up to you. I am sure you will think of something appropriate."

"You mean kill them? Strangle them"

"One very important thing, there must be no un-necessary marks on the bodies."

~

Mackenna squinted in the bright Sunday morning sun and angled the cell phone to place the screen in shadow so he could read the four-digit code for the key pad that would open the garage roller door. The code had accompanied the address, along with a warning about security cameras pointed at the door and the need to ensure his face remained covered. The car, a plain four-door sedan that had appeared with keys in it during the night at the house, was to be abandoned and set alight when he was done.

During the drive from the house in the Lake District to the garage in Manchester, Mackenna had gorged on the fear and helplessness of the woman and boy bound and gagged in the trunk of the car. Anticipation of what he would do to them had brought new heights of excitement and he had found it difficult to resist the desire to speed.

Inside the garage, with the door closed and lights on, Mackenna stood at the back of the car and listened as he snapped thin leather gloves onto his hands. Faint sobs mixed with soothing words in a language Mackenna did not understand seeped from the metal. A small smile broke Mackenna's face as he hammered his fist down on to the lid of the trunk. The sobs changed to screams and Mackenna's smile widened below eager eyes. Opening the trunk, Mackenna taunted his captives.

"What's the matter with you? Didn't you like the ride in the nice white man's car?"

Nasreen and Masud, entwined for mutual protection and comfort, had squeezed to the back of the trunk as though they might meld with the grey, black interior and remain undiscovered.

"Come here you fuckers," said Mackenna as he reached in and wrenched Masud from his mother's arms.

Masud screamed. His child hands, bound at the wrist, were no match for Mackenna's adrenalin-buoyed strength.

"Shut the fuck up you little brat!"

Mackenna shook Masud and slapped his face, but fear was in control and his screams continued. Mackenna held Masud at arm's length and regarded the boy with indifference. He hadn't found the scarf yet, and besides, he had his own little plan for the boy and his mother.

Thwack.

A short right hand jab to Masud's temple silenced the screams and Mackenna dropped the limp body to the floor.

Nasreen, penned in the trunk behind Masud's dangling legs as Mackenna shook him, wriggled to the edge of the trunk. Shocked at the sight of Masud's still body she fell to the ground and cradled the boys head.

"Now bitch. It's time to play," said Mackenna as he reached for Nasreen.

Pulled by her hair from her son Nasreen writhed and arched in futile attempts to strike Mackenna with her torso. Amused and excited by the woman's efforts, Mackenna kicked her feet from under her and dragged her deeper into the garage. Face down on the rough concrete Mackenna pushed his right knee between her shoulder blades and withdrew a length of thin nylon rope with a pre-made slipknot from a pocket.

The loop slid over Nasreen's left then right foot until snug on each ankle. Mackenna looped the middle of the rope over and around Nasreen's neck and pulled her up until she squatted on her knees with legs tucked under her at a brutal and painful angle. Mackenna adjusted the rope to allow a little slack. He didn't want her dead just yet. Sensing the slack, Nasreen moved to unfold her legs but the movement caused the rope to tighten on her neck.

"Nice eh, move your legs too much and you will choke yourself to death. I'll be back in minute and we can get started. You'll enjoy this. Well, I will."

The scarf lay folded on a workbench beside a spray paint booth. Beside the bench, on the floor, about twenty red fire extinguishers stood in a line like pins in a bowling alley. Mackenna ignored the fire extinguishers. He picked up the scarf with leather-gloved hands, wrapped it around his wrists, and clenched an end in each hand. A satisfying snap echoed off the cold walls and floor as Mackenna pulled the scarf taught between his outstretched arms.

Mackenna snapped the scarf as he sauntered back to the car. The boy, a red welt on the side of his face and temple, remained motionless on the floor. Mackenna's perverse plan, which he had concocted during the drive to Manchester, had included having the boy watch while he did his thing with mommy. Mackenna stared at the boy and debated the pros and cons of waking the boy or not or just strangling him there and then. A scuffling sound from the woman's direction distracted Mackenna from his indecision and he moved to see what was going on.

"Now where do you think you're going?"

Nasreen had crabbed her way toward the rear of the garage and lay sweating and panting as Mackenna mocked her efforts at escape.

"Now why would you want to run away from me eh? We are going to have a nice old time for an hour or so and then, well, we'll see."

Defiant strength projected from Nasreen's full brown eyes and tight dry lips as her head strained left and right looking for an escape.

"Let's put it this way you bitch. You do as I tell you or I'll bring that little runt of your over and you can watch while I squeeze the life out of him. Do you understand?"

Fear for Masud, the only thing that could force her compliance, broke her resilience and she sagged defeated. Glowing with callous control and inhuman indifference Mackenna began.

Lost in the ecstasy of his depravity Mackenna howled with lust and power as his brain prepared itself for the pleasure stimulus as he steeled himself violate the woman beneath him.

Pain instead of pleasure flooded Mackenna's brain as he slumped sideways and away from Nasreen. Blood, released from Mackenna's head by the blow of a claw hammer, gushed from McKenna's skull and sprayed over the trembling boy.

Masud, blood dotted on his face, dropped the hammer and rushed to his mother. Nasreen soothed her son until his sobs subsided and she was able to coax Masud to find a knife or saw to cut the nylon rope. Freed from her constraints, but sore and numb from confinement and abuse Nasreen stood over Mackenna's body.

Dark blood, like aged port, formed a place mat sized pool under Mackenna's head. A flap of skin, folded back over matted hair, revealed a piece of jagged bone scooped by the impact of the claw part of the steel hammer to protruded unnaturally from the skull's sphere. Nasreen knelt and sought signs of life. Faint breath exhaled from Mackenna's slack mouth.

Nasreen, swaying with exhaustion and fear, grasped the soiled hammer and weighed it in her hands.

"Masud, give me the scarf."

Masud's body heaved with stifled sobs as unsteady hands passed the scarf to his mother. Nasreen used the scarf to wipe Masud's prints from the hammer and tossed both to the floor beside Mackenna. Reaching into Mackenna back pocket she withdrew Mackenna's wallet and from his wallet a fold of bank notes.

Nasreen grasped her son's hand, pulled him to her, and whispered to his ear.

"Come Masud. We must go."

Forty-Four

October 6 2013, Ottawa, Canada

PRIEST, AGITATED AND DISMISSIVE, hardly listened as Wilson concluded his theory.

"The key is the word 'never'. Can't you see it? Look, if you remove the word never from last intercept you get 'they *will* forget Munich after this'. The statement is talking about a plane crash in Munich in 1958 that killed eight Manchester United players. The plane crash is sacrosanct to supporters and nothing could ever be worse than the Munich air disaster. That is what the statement means: the attack will be more devastating to Manchester United than the plane crash.

Look, Cook did not get me the clarification about whether translators added the word never to make the sentence more logical or if it was a mis-translation. Either way Priest, we can't ignore the possibility that this attack has nothing to do with Munich and everything to do with Manchester United."

Priest, tired, stressed and done with Wilson said.

"Why the hell would they tell us they plan to attack Manchester United Wilson?"

"I don't think they meant to tip us off."

"Oh, now it's a mistake is it? Jesus Wilson, you said yourself it's too easy. Now you say the tips off is a mistake."

"I'm not sure what's going on. The last three messages are different from the others. They change from using a terse minimalist tone to an almost taunting, personal tone."

"Of course its personal Wilson, these people hate us and everything we stand for."

"Just listen to me, the taunting statements, they…"

"No Wilson, you listen to me. Glory, Glory our men united is clearly about the terrorists working together and the statement about never forgetting Munich is a clear boast that they intend to do something more horrific than the 1972 Munich Massacre. The celebration on October 6 is a direct reference to Oktoberfest and is just the kind of…"

"Damn it Priest! October 6 is also the day Manchester United play Arsenal. I'm telling you that the additional statements are someone's personal message. Someone involved in the terrorist plot has a grudge against Manchester United and could not resist boasting about what is going to happen."

"Misdirection Wilson; the terrorists want us looking at the UK while they plant bombs in Munich. Two weeks ago, you came to me and said the messages were either disinformation or fake. Now that I agree with you, you say part of the messages are mistakes or a personal agenda item of one of the terrorists. I think you are getting confused by your own analysis Wilson."

Wilson squared himself to Priest.

"While I was in England, and despite your efforts to keep me from accessing people, I became certain that Chris was on to something, that he was murdered, and the EDL is involved."

"We have already discussed your cowboy act in England and in case you don't remember, you are still on probation."

"God dam it Priest. Someone tried to kill me in England."

"What. This is the first I've heard of it. Did you contact the authorities?"

"No."

"No. Why not?"

"I didn't have time or evidence and anyway the police chased them away. I didn't want to get involved and delayed. I had to get back here."

"That's the problem Wilson. You don't have evidence. This is more of your inductive reasoning isn't it Wilson. Well, I've told you before and I'll tell you one last time. We, I, deal in facts and so does the rest of the intelligence community. I am not going to run to the NSA to recommend she ask the UK to cancel a major sporting event because a Mr. Craig Wilson has a half-baked theory that terrorists are about to bomb a soccer game. We can't put our reputation on the line…"

"It's not about reputation Priest. It's about saving lives. Put my reputation, my job, my career whatever on the line. Make it Wilson said."

"Alright Wilson, if that's what you want. I will call the head of the UK JTAC and explain your theory. Then it's up to them whether they act or not."

"Good God Priest, Chris worked at JTAC and he was murdered because of this. Calling the UK JTAC is not enough. What if they are involved, what if…?"

"That's enough Wilson. You see conspiracy everywhere. I will call JTAC and that's it."

Priest, leaving, said.

"Wilson, this is on you. Do you understand?"

~

Wilson slammed his office door and stood before his boards and flip charts. It was more than just a theory. Analysis, facts, extrapolation, and 'intuitive analysis techniques' supported his theory. Weeks of intercepted terrorist communications had reported on progress toward bombing a Manchester United soccer game not an Oktoberfest parade in Munich!

Wilson had to act. Even if it was too late, even if he was wrong, he had to try. Wilson picked up the phone and dialed an unlisted Government of Canada ten-digit number provided to him in confidence a few weeks earlier in the ITAC Board room. Five miles away, on the third floor of an old heritage building on the corner of Sparks and Elgin Street above a Canada Post office, a phone softly tinkled. Bill Wycombe, the Director General the Security and Intelligence in the Privy Council Office and advisor to Canada's National Security Advisor, answered with polite efficiency.

Wycombe returned the receiver to its cradle. ITAC, under Priest had become a pandering bureaucracy. He had argued against Priest's appointment but Priest's years of service and multi-layered contacts had been enough to secure him the job. Wycombe and Wilson had history. Not all good, but not all bad either. Wilson went against the grain, but he had been right more times than wrong. However, this time Wilson, whose theory contradicted the entire Five Eyes intelligence effort and conclusions, had placed himself, and now him, on the extreme tip of a very long branch.

Wycombe considered his options. Ignore Wilson as Priest had done. This would be easy and defensible. Take Wilson's theory to the NSA and let the NSA decide. Without facts, a briefing note, concurrence of other intelligence community leaders like CSIS and CSEC, the NSA would not thank him for putting her in such a position. Besides, if Wilson was right, the bombing would occur while the NSA was rebuking Wycombe and telling him to get some facts.

Wycombe's third option was the informal route. He could call his long-time friend and counterpart in the British PCO, James Cox. If there was any hint of such a plot, Cox was certain to know. Wycombe checked his watch and did the time conversion: 9:15 am in Ottawa, Canada, 2:15 in London, England. Wilson said the soccer game started at 3pm. Forty-five minutes. Wycombe clicked his computer screen to Outlook, selected contacts, and dialed the fifteen-digit number that would connect him to the British PCO in London.

A crisp voice informed Wycombe that Mr. Cox was in a National Security Committee meeting at COBRA and contact by phone would not be possible, however, they could pass a note to him. Wycombe dictated a short note: *James, possibility target is Manchester United soccer stadium not Munich. Please contact me immediately.*

Forty-Five

October 6 2013, Manchester United Stadium, Manchester, England

DEATH HAD WAITED PATIENTLY FOR Aalim. From the moment the man entered his taxicab six weeks earlier, Aalim had known he would die. However, with faith in Allah, and desperate to save his wife and son, Aalim had complied and obeyed. Now, as he watched thousands of raucous soccer supporters pour thought Old Trafford's revered gates to witness the clash of a rising Arsenal team battle a declining Manchester United team Aalim's faith buckled.

For ten days, Aalim had loaded bright red fire extinguishers into a Manchester United backpack and brought them unchallenged in to the stadium. Then, hidden in a false bottom of his cart-mounted garbage can, he had wheeled the extinguishers around the stadium to exchange for the real extinguishers. Aalim had no engineering training or knowledge of explosion dispersal or impact effects yet he knew the placement of the extinguishers would cause massive destruction and thousands of deaths.

When Darren dropped him at Old Trafford, they had held each other's eyes and exchanged few words.

"Stay down in the basement area of the stadium in the storage room and you will be alright."

"What about my wife and son?"

"If you make it out of the stadium alive, they will be at your house."

"I don't believe you. How do I know they aren't already dead?"

"You don't. Perhaps you need more faith in your god. Don't all you fuckers believe everything is the will of God anyway? Well, whatever happens, blame your fucking God."

Darren's words had shaken Aalim's faith. Weeks of silent prayer and entreaties for guidance and help had gone unanswered. Alone in the storage room, and unwilling to concede Darren's words, Aalim kneeled and prayed. Mid-way through prayer the door the storage room door burst opened. Brad Short, Aalim's vile tormentor, entered flushed and agitated. Before the door closed, Brad aimed a kick at Aalim's vulnerable body. The kick, savage and dismissive, struck upper ribs and lifted Aalim sideways and onto his back. A second kick struck Aalim's pelvis and pushed him further into the room. More kicks and stomps, each punctuated with obscene denigrations of Aalim and his faith, careened in to Aalim's body.

"I've waited weeks for this you shit eating camel fucker."

A kick caught Aalim's jaw and blood spurted from burst lips.

"Every day I had to be near you made me sick"

Knuckles and fingers splayed under callous stomps.

"Now you gonna die."

Brad, ready for the kill stepped back to gain room for a short run up to deliver a fatal kick to Aalim's head.

Disoriented and in shock Aalim fumbled and grasped for a defence. Battered fingers and forearm reached above his head and curled around a ten-pound bag of mixed sand and grit used in the players' tunnel on winter evenings to prevent boot studs from slipping on icy concrete. Instinct and fear, and the sight of Brad's rapid approach, pulled the bag to Aalim. A combination of pulling the bag down and shuffling his torso up placed the bag between his head and his attackers boot.

Consumed by rage and hate Brad's consciousness did not register the bag and his fully extended and committed kick connected with the bag and brought his foot to a complete stop. The impact of boot on the dead weight of the sand and grit reversed the energy of Brad's murderous intent, snapping his ankle in two places and sheering his kneecap up and over his tibia. Brad, writhing in pain and screaming expletives and vengeance, fell to the ground. Aalim, his own rage and hate fuelling adrenalin to overcome pain, lifted the ten-pound bag and thrust it down on Brad's head. In the silence, bright thin blood flowed erratically around dirt and dust on the sloped floor, to trickle in to the drain.

Forty-Six

October 6 2013, London, England

LATE SUNDAY MORNINGS AND EARLY afternoons at White's hummed with the soft rustle and occasional snap of newspapers as club members worked their way through weekend editions of the Sunday Times. Some, seeking sensationalism, and occasional titillation, feigned disapproving tuts at the Sunday Express tabloid. Mitton-Wells, who arrived at one-thirty for a late lunch, sat at his favourite table by the window. A copy of the crass blue collar Sun newspaper lay folded open to the sports pages that, as always, shouted in overly large print and innuendo-laden headlines, the latest drama concerning England's Premier League soccer clubs and players.

Only one headline interested Mitton-Wells. *Man U v Arsenal Can Man U beat league leaders*. Mitton-Wells followed the article as it described Man United's poor start to the season under their new manager David Moyes and how fans and critics questioned his managerial abilities.

The press and pundits billed the game, which would kick off at three pm, as the 'game that would set the tone for the rest of the season'. Mitton-Wells chuckled inwardly and muttered how right the pundits would be, but for very different reasons. The article ended with assertions that the game a crowd or more than 76, 000 would pack Old Trafford to capacity and more than 100 million people in over eighty countries would watch the live television broadcast.

The magnitude on the impending event and the tension of years of dreaming and planning welled up in Mitton-Wells. Apprehensive, he thrust his hand into his inside jacket pocket and withdrew the instrument that held the power to kill, maim and generate deep and lasting hate. He cradled the nondescript cell phone in his hand and checked the battery level and signal strength. Reassured by full green signal bars he returned the phone to his pocket and glanced at his watch: Two-thirty. With only thirty minutes to go before the three pm kick off Mitton-Wells signalled the waiter. He ordered a bottle of champagne and told the waiter to take the champagne to the games room on the second floor where the clubs one and only television hung silently on a wall beyond two snooker tables. At two forty-five, with a chilled glass of bubbly by his side, Mitton-Wells arranged himself on an antique Wing Back chair facing the wall mounted TV and pushed the "on" button on the remote.

Vibrant images of a perfectly groomed soccer field filled the screen as the TV commentator used the minutes before kick-off to acknowledge the Manchester United's Old Trafford grounds staff for 'such a fantastic job of preparing the ground for this huge Premier League game'.

When the Manchester United and Arsenal players followed the yellow shirted match officials on the soccer field to line up for the obligatory hand shake and publicity opportunities Mitton-Wells pulled the cell phone from his pocket and held it with a clammy hand. On screen, Manchester United's two star players, Wayne Rooney and Robin Van Persie, hopped and bobbed on the centre spot with the ball between them as seventy-six thousand people in the stadium and millions worldwide held their breath in anticipation as the referee consulted his watch and prepared to blow the whistle to begin the game.

Synchronizing his actions with those of the referee, Mitton-Wells opened the contacts section of the cell phone and selected the only number entered. As the referee held his arm up to signal to the two goalkeepers the game would begin, Mitton-Wells pressed the send command on the cell phone and held his breath.

Forty-Seven

October 6 2013, Manchester, England

TWENTY ANTENNAS; EACH EXPERTLY hidden in the discharge spout of twenty-two bright red fire extinguishers, vibrated imperceptibly in response to the strong microwave signal emitted by the transmitter fixed atop the CIS Tower on Miller Street, Manchester. The signal triggered the detonator, the detonator provided the electrical charge to the small amount of explosives in the tip of the detonator, and the C4 plastic explosive changed from inert to active. Energy, released at 8000 meters per second, propelled fragments of red metal and assorted ball bearing, screws and nails in an indiscriminate 360-degree spread. Miniscule particles of mustard gas, blown, sucked, and then carried by the inward - outward dynamics of an explosion, mingled with the metal debris and spread outward in search of flesh.

The hot ragged metal shredded the first human flesh it contacted before mercilessly vaporizing the skin, tissue and bone. Less mercilessly, a group of humans twenty meters from the initial blast retained a short pain-filled consciousness as they watched and felt the laceration of their bodies. Still further, in small metal framed and walled buildings, eyes bulged in fearful disbelief as the walls buckled and imploded toward and around them to sever limbs and pierce organs. At the extremities of the blast, dodging falling debris, stunned workers and customers, stood rooted and sought understanding. Thankful for being spared dismemberment, burning and death, these bystanders would suffer the most and the longest as they inhaled and tasted the dust that rolled and swirled from the center of the blast.

Mitton-Wells, disbelief and panic pulling his face askew, repeatedly pressed redial on the cell phone as he searched for explosions, screams, obscenities broken concrete, twisted metal and mangled bodies. Instead, on screen, Manchester United's red shirted players raced forward to counter attack as Arsenal players back peddled to defend against the red surge. Arsenal's goalkeeper flailed in mid-air as a shot from Robin Van Persie, Manchester United's lead scorer and star forward, thudded off the cross bar. Mitton-Wells jumped and flung the cell phone across the room. Slumped in confused defeat, Mitton-Wells felt mocked by the roars and chants of the crowd that rose and fell with the ebb and flow of the game.

Unable to look away from the on screen reality of his failure Mitton-Wells registered an urgent ticker-tape news flash travel right to left across the bottom of the screen. Blinking away tears for an unfulfilled dream Mitton-Wells struggled to comprehend the news flash. "Reports of a massive explosion two miles south of Old Trafford in a small industrial estate are being investigated by emergency services."

Repeated vibrations in his breast pocket nudged Mitton-Wells from his trance. He withdrew his personal cell phone, stared at the call display and pressed answer. A terse six-second statement terrified Mitton Wells.

Forty-Eight

October 6 2013, Manchester, England

DARREN WAS TOO FAR AND at the wrong angle to see bodies and blood. He would settle for twisted metal, smoke and flying debris. He had wanted a tall building with access to a roof that overlooked Manchester United's Old Trafford stadium. He found several, but could not gain access to the roof. Desperate, Darren settled for a sixth floor room at the Holiday Inn Express on Waterfront Quay less than one kilometer South West of the stadium. The view of the stadium did not match the Hotel's promotional boast that Manchester United was a stone throw away.

The stadium, or more precisely, the upper steel support structures that held the roof over the home supporters 'Stretford End' were dimly visible but Darren needed to stand on a chair and employ 10x10 binoculars to see beyond the Stretford End across the space where the soccer field lay and onto the roof of the North Stand.

He hated Manchester United's success and assured smugness, but he hated the fans more. Many years had passed since a bloated, beer gutted Manchester United fan had stamped on his head and caused the irreparable damage to his vision that had ended Darren's soccer career. Darren smirked as he imagined the pain the words he had added to Aalim's last three cell phone calls would cause Manchester United fans. *Glory, Glory, Our Men United No More / They will forget Munich after this / On Sunday October 6, we shall celebrate as Allah's will is done.*

Darren's smirk widened to a full smile as he savoured his intention to post the words on a Facebook account he had established in Aalim's name.

Thoughts of Aalim and Manchester United recalled the Muslim who had closed his front door and left him to be beaten and stomped by the United's fans. Darren ground his teeth at the memory of the beating and the Muslim and chuckled as he recalled his last words to Aalim about staying in the basement of the stadium and that if he made it out alive his wife and kid would be waiting at his house.

Darren checked his watch. Two forty-five, fifteen minutes to kick off. The TV in the hotel room, tuned to Sky TV pay per view, provided live coverage of the stadium as red and yellow shirted players preened through their pre-match warm up routines. Darren had not been told when the bombs would be detonated but he figured the explosions would happen either at kick off or at the start of the second half.

~

The hotel window rattled from the explosion and Darren stared at TV confused. On screen, the play continued as Manchester United streamed forward to attack the Arsenal goal. Darren had heard and felt the explosion but nothing had happened at the stadium. Moments later, a 'breaking news' ticker tape ran right to left across the bottom of the screen announcing a massive explosion in an industrial estate near the Pomona Docks.

Enraged and in panic, Darren called Short. When he did not answer, he called Mackenna. With no answer from Short and Mackenna, Darren called the man who had controlled and directed his life for the past six months. He would know what had happened and what to do, but no one answered that call either.

Alone, angry and afraid, Darren weighed his options. If Short did not answer, then Aalim must have done something and gotten away. With mounting fear about what might happen to him if Aalim told the police Darren concluded he must find and kill Aalim. The last thing he told Aalim was that his wife and son would be at his home. As he ran from the hotel room, Darren called a taxi.

Forty-Nine

October 6 2013, The Grange, Manchester, England

WHEN THE BOMBS EXPLODED IN a small industrial estate, which Simon knew to be the location of Aalim's workshop, Simon repeatedly called Anthony. With no answer, Simon drove to White's but was told Anthony had left in a taxi shortly after 3pm. Unable to contact Anthony and certain the plot had failed, Simon pointed his car north and headed for The Grange. Endless calls and messages from his superiors and subordinates bombarded his cell phone, as he raced up the M1. Simon answered none. The only call he needed was Anthony's, but it never came.

Each call to Anthony had been reckless. Simon didn't care. The plot had failed. There had been no explosions at Manchester United. Instead, a massive explosion had flattened a half-mile square area of a sparsely used industrial estate in Manchester's dock lands. Initial reports indicated that perhaps fifty people who had been working, delivering, or cleaning some of the buildings had died in the blast. Secondary reports reported presence of a chemical agent thought to be mustard gas and more than a hundred people had presented at emergency departments for treatment. Evacuation and precautionary measures for people to remain inside predicted that final casualties would be minimal.

A failed plot with collateral damage was not what hurt Simon the most. Worse, much worse, was how Anthony had betrayed him. First, when Anthony had hatched the plot to conduct a significant terrorist event in the UK and frame the Muslim community for the atrocity, they had agreed casualties should be limited to tens and no more than a hundred if possible. All we need, Simon had argued, was a symbolic bombing. There was no need to kill many hundreds of innocents, especially the many women and children who would be at the game. Tens of deaths would be all the media, intelligence community and the EDL would need to galvanise public opinion.

Simon, having heard the scale of the devastation at the industrial estate realized that Anthony had planted enough explosive to kill tens of thousands! That was not what Simon had agreed to. Still worse was the reports of the chemical agent mustard gas. Simon had physically wretched at the thought of the horrific suffering that would have occurred had the bombs exploded in the stadium and the mustard gas dispersed in a contained area stuffed with over 75,000 people. Anthony was a monster. A monster that relied on their past relationship to manipulate and use him for a plot that Simon now realized had been madness from the first. Bitter tears welled as Simon thought of his friend's betrayal. He tried one more time to call Anthony but there was no answer and no voice mail. Anthony didn't want to speak to him. Simon's calls, which he had made on his MI5 government phone, had been to Anthony's home, office and disposable phone numbers. The call would later be traced, connections made and conclusions reached. It was all over. Simon didn't care.

~

Remnants of fear-laced sweat caught in Simon's nostrils. Pain had been the room's purpose. Pain designed to weaken physical strength, subdue spirit and erase resolve. Simon had been a part of that pain. He provided Anthony with access to the Grange, the Israeli Mossad sound recordings, and he supplied the psychopath Mackenna to supplement Aalim's torture with threats and actions against his wife and son.

A chair, soiled with human excrement and urine stood pretending innocence in the centre of the stark basement room. Black plastic bindings, cut and discarded, lay on the floor beside each leg. Simon picked up the chair and positioned it under a beam that ran the length of the basement ceiling. Coarse rope thread snagged on Simon's Oxford University alumni ring as he played a section out to match his estimate of the length needed to ensure his feet did not reach the ground.

Fifty

October 6 2013, Manchester, England

MACKENNA, VULNERABLE WITH PANTS and underwear by his ankles, blinked away warm blood from his eyes and felt the cold hard cement floor of the garage press against his thighs and knees. Pain pushed vulnerability aside as he raised himself up on an elbow and reached backward and down to tug at his jeans. Mackenna switched elbows and hitched some more. Light headed, he pushed himself to sit and wiped more blood from his eyes. Instinctively, he reached to touch the source of the numbness at the back of his head. Clumsy fingers entered the fracture and Mackenna screamed, gagged and passed out.

Moments later, face down in his blood, Mackenna woke. Tightness and pressure, combined with needle pricks, had replaced the numbness. Motor control of legs and arms stalled as blood hemorrhaged and cranial swelling increased. Prostrate, sticky fingers fumbled his cell phone from a front jean pocket and scrolled for calls received. Blue digital lights illuminated the only telephone number ever received. The number of the man who had called all the shots, the man who had promised him glory and the gratitude of the people of England, the man who had gotten him almost killed by some rag head. Well, he was gonna tell that man what he, Steve Mackenna, thought of the man's plan now.

Rage accompanied bile and blood in Mackenna's throat as he stabbed the button to initiate the 'recall' function. He watched the spiral of the icon turn as electrical signals and information bytes obeyed Mackenna's thumb and traveled through time and space to seek a connection with another phone. Mackenna's vision drifted above the cell phone and locked on the triangle of red fire extinguishers in front of the paint booth. Distorted by fading consciousness, Mackenna imagined the red cylinders shimmer, expand and hurl toward him as the final beep of a busy signal terminated the call and his life.

Fifty-One

October 6 2013, Manchester, England

NASREEN HAD BEEN LUCKY. The cab driver had been white and asked no questions. A fellow Muslim, picking up a woman and child, with torn cloths and obvious signs of distress, would have been suspicious and asked many questions. The white driver, overweight, smelling of tobacco and stale sweat, hardly acknowledged Nasreen and Masud's existence. The money she had taken from Mackenna pocket had been enough to cover the twenty min cab ride from the garage in the industrial estate to their home. As the taxi pulled away, Nasreen noticed the rustle of curtains from the window of the old man who lived across the street. Not caring what the old man might see, Nasreen clutched Masud to her as she lifted up the third of four plant pots that lined the short pathway from the street to the front door of her house. Underneath, wet and a little dirty, a spare key to the front door waited for Nasreen's eager grasp. Relieved, and still holding Masud, Nasreen wiggled the key in to the door lock and hurried inside.

Ignoring the disarray, the unfamiliar computer, books and empty cell phone packages, Nasreen stumbled to the kitchen and poured water for herself and Masud. Fighting her own fatigue and pain, Nasreen soothed Masud. He had not spoken since hitting the man with the hammer and he shook and sweated as

Nasreen held water to his mouth and calmed him with loving words.

A rustle and scrape from the outside the front door cut short Nasreen's efforts to calm and love her son. The sound of a plant pot scraping concrete, then a second, seeped under the door. Silence. Masud whimpered then jolted upright and tense as a knuckle or a palm tapped the glass of the front door. Rigid with fear, mother and son gripped each other. A squeak, short and tight, echoed down the hallway at the letterbox cover lifted. A voice, weak and unsure, followed the squeak.

"Nasreen, Nasreen, are you there Nasreen?"

Masud stirred. His tear filled eyes widened with hope.

"Papa, Papa."

"Nasreen, Masud, Nasreen it's me Aalim."

Masud broke from his mother's arms and stumbled to unlock the door.

Entwined, they huddled and sagged to the floor in the hallway. Love flowed from one to another giving strength and relief. Hurried words and disjointed sentences conveyed each persons' edited story until Nasreen, wiped tears from her cheeks, held Aalim and whispered,

"What are we going to do Aalim?"

Struggling to stand, Aalim lumbered to the small living room that fronted the house. A brown desk, worn and scuffed, stood wedged between sofa and wall. Aalim pulled open the only drawer and withdrew three sheets of printed-paper. He turned to Nasreen and held the paper to her eyes.

"We will use these Nasreen. They forced me to buy these tickets for a flight to Egypt tonight at 6pm. I think the authorities were supposed to find them as part of the evidence against me. Now we can use them to get away. We do not have much time Nasreen. You must pack a bag for each of us. Only enough to show we are going for a short visit. I will get our passports and call for a taxi to take us to the airport."

Bags in hand, washed and with fresh clothes, Aalim led his wife and child along the hallway to the front door. Aalim stopped abruptly. Nasreen and Masud bumped in to his back. A shadow silhouetted on the glass of the front door. The shadow pressed against the glass. Distorted human facial features squished. The shadow withdrew then lunged forward. The door broke open, wood splintered, and Darren Blackley, rage and triumph on his face, entered the hallway behind the gun held in his hand.

"Where the fuck do you think you're going?"

Darren, secure in his dominance, motioned with the gun for Aalim to retreat in to the kitchen. Nasreen, Masud clutched to her bosom, squeezed up against the sink. Aalim moved behind the small table to put distance between himself and Darren and place Nasreen and Masud out of Darren's direct line of fire.

Hate and loathing leapt from Darren as he spat words at Aalim.

"Where is Short?"

Aalim, relieved the blood from Short's crushed head no longer stained his changed shoes or fresh clothes, strained to hold his voice steady.

"I don't know. Last time I saw him he said he was going to get a drink at the stadium."

"What time did you see him?"

Aalim's eyes drifted downward and he faltered as an image of Short's lifeless body emerged from the kitchen floor.

"About 2:30. He, he said he had something to celebrate and said he was going for a beer and told me to stay in the storage room."

Darren recalled that he had told Short to leave Aalim in the basement and 2:30 would have been about the right time for Short to get out of the stadium. Forsaking Short, Darren pointed the gun at Masud and demanded.

"What about fire extinguishers?"

Afraid for his son Aalim moved into the table and shouted at Darren.

"You don't need to harm my son. Leave him…"

Darren stepped closer to Masud and placed the gun against the boys head.

"Get back. Come any closer and one bullet will do both of them. Now what happened to the fire extinguishers?"

Needing time, Aalim stalled.

"I don't know what you mean. I did everything you asked. Short was there, he can tell you."

"You're a fucking liar Aalim. A very bad liar and now your lies will cost you the life of your son."

Aalim had calculated the odds many times during the last month and they were still against him.

"Wait, wait, alright. I didn't plant them at the stadium. The fire extinguishers were identical. The first day I switched them Short watched me, but the second day I suggested he act as a look out and I pretended to switch them. I switched back the first two a few days later when Short was sleeping in the storage room. Short never checked. He was lazy."

Realization swamped Darren at the likely truth of Aalim's claim. Short was a lazy bastard.

"You mean you put the fire extinguishers in the lock up garage?"

"Yes. I stacked them by the paint booth."

Darren, unsure where or how to focus his anger lifted the gun to Nasreen's head.

"And you, you bitch, how did you get here? Where is Mackenna?"

"Mackenna took them to garage. He left them tied up, but they got away. We don't know where he is." said Aalim trying to draw Darren's attention away from Nasreen.

"I didn't ask you."

The gun wavered and moved back to Masud who had turned away from his mother to find his father's eyes. Masud shook and sweated.

Darren, his gun covering Aalim, reached for a towel hanging on the back of a chair.

"You think you're so fucking smart eh Aalim? You may have switched the bombs and somehow gotten away from Short and Mackenna but you won't get away from me."

The towel, dirty and damp, hung from Darren's hand as he draped it over the gun and wrapped it twice around.

As the gun leveled at Aalim's middle Masud vomited so hard it splattered on Darren's hand and the gun. Aalim lunged and Darren fired.

Vomit, and the table pushed by Aalim's lunge, forced the gunshot wide. As Darren recovered and pulled the gun back in line Nasreen pushed off the counter and plunged a short bladed peeling knife into Darren's neck. Darren's gun arm jerked upward and the second gunshot hit the ceiling. Aalim shoved the table into Darren and pinned him against the wall as Nasreen and Masud squeezed by and out into the corridor. Aalim followed and turned to watch as Darren, desperate to stop the pain, dropped the gun and reached for the knife in his neck.

Beneath the knife's blade, a large dark circle of pooled blood stretched and pulled the skin of Darren's neck as his heart pumped ever faster to circulate blood around a broken circuit. The knife slipped easily from the neck and pressurized blood spewed through the air onto the wall and bounced back on to Darren's face. In the illusionary moment of relief, Darren smiled at Aalim and bent down to retrieve his gun. His brain, already deprived of oxygen, failed under the sudden movement and Darren swayed forward, fell to the floor, and rolled on to his back.

Darren's consciousness remained long enough to watch Aalim and his family collect their bags and quietly close the front door behind them.

Fifty-Two

October 6 2013, Ottawa, Canada

WILSON HAD BEEN WRONG AND right. Wilson, like millions of others, watched the frantic media reports about explosions in Manchester and thanked God the bombs had detonated in the center of a lightly used industrial estate and not in Manchester United's soccer stadium. The media reports speculated that a gas leak or chemicals had caused the explosions and gave little thought to the possibility that terrorists would have targeted a small industrial estate. Wilson knew better. He was sure terrorist bombs made the explosions and that the bombs had been destined for Manchester United.

By three thirty Manchester time, news channels were looping initial footage of the area as reporters sought new information and images.

A quiet knock pulled Wilson from the media coverage and he turned to face the door as Priest entered and came straight to the point.

"Craig, I know, I know. You were right. Well, at least more right than the rest of us, but you must understand that there was no time to do anything. I called the UK JTAC and told them everything. Even if we had notified the NSA nothing would have happened for hours and the bombs would have gone off anyway."

Wilson swallowed a rebuke and remained silent.

"Look, there is nothing to gain by sharing your conclusions after the fact. We need to maintain the integrity of ITAC and ensure we do not compromise the confidence that the NSA and the government have in ITAC."

Wilson, contempt building, still did not speak.

"Christ Craig, what do you want from me? I'm sorry. Yes, all right, maybe I should have taken your theory more seriously, but that's all it was, a theory. We gain nothing by telling people about it now. What do you say Craig?"

No pleasure or malice infused Wilson's words as he told Priest what he had to say.

"It's too late. I called Wycombe at PCO an hour ago. The point is never about protecting integrity or maintaining confidence, it's about saving the lives of innocent men, women and children. How can you be certain our warning would have been too late? What if the bombs were timed to explode at half time instead of kick off? What if there had been a problem with the bombs and there had been time to evacuate the stadium? What if our early warning had mobilized emergency services to help the injured? I don't know what Wycombe did with the information, but I won't remain silent to protect your or ITAC's reputation."

Priest, his body arched forward made to argue or plead, but Wilson turned his back on Priest and continued to watch the media reports. The reports said that casualties were low and Wilson sighed with relief at the thought of what the casualties might have been had the bombs exploded at Manchester United's stadium.

Coordinated with Wilson's thought a BBC news reporter, filling space between images, said 'Thank god it wasn't at Man United's ground. Thousands would have been killed.' The news report widened their story on the bombing and showed coverage of a massive EDL rally underway near the Manchester United stadium and noted that marchers were inexplicably carrying banners blaming Muslims and all foreigners for the explosions.

Multi-sized and shaped placards bounced across the screen as thousands of protesters carried their hate-filled messages through the suburban streets adjacent to Manchester United's soccer stadium. Wilson read and made note of the vile messages: 'All Foreigners Out,' 'England for the English,' "Immigrant = Ignorant,' 'Bomb the bastards like they just bombed us!,' 'Act Now - Muslims Out,' 'Muslim Terrorists Will Bomb You Next!,' '

EDL's anti-immigrant and pro-English slogans were standard fare for Britain's right-wing thugs, but direct attribution for a bombing that happened less than thirty minutes ago was incredible. Wilson's mind raced with questions and answers to validate what he already knew and what Priest would not accept: Conspiracy.

How and why were the EDL present near Manchester United's stadium on a match day? How did they know, or why did they believe, the explosions three miles away were terrorist-related? How did they prepare banners and placards so quickly to blame Muslims for the explosion/bombing? Almost, thought Wilson, as though they knew beforehand what was going to happen? Almost, thought Wilson, as though the explosions, the EDL march and the placards were choreographed.

Synaptic connections ignited in Wilson's brain as disparate events and information began to align and create order.

Ten intercepted cell phone calls originating in Manchester, each using a name of an Islamic prophet, and the last three messages clearly, according to Wilson's analysis, pointing to United's stadium as the target.

Chris Thornton's suspicion about an EDL supporter watching him at the Prospect of Whitby pub in London and Chris' email pointing Wilson to UK JTAC reports on the massive expansion of the EDL and the increase in anti-Muslim and foreigner media coverage in the UK.

The direction in those reports for 'no follow up action' and that S.S. - Simon Spencer - the Assistant Director General of MI5's Domestic Intelligence - had, contrary to established protocols, signed off the JTAC reports.

How Chris' murder occurred at the Lord Duncan pub; a pub bombed by a right wing lunatic and one still associated with Neo Nazi thugs.

How, just days before the bombing, the EDL leader, Marshall, was stabbed in the street by a Muslim and conveniently recorded and published to world media sites within minutes.

How the brutal murder of Gary Boddie, a facilities manager at United's stadium, occurred just steps away from the Dirty Duck, a pub known as a hangout for right wing, anti-immigrant racists.

Now, on his computer screen, how tens of thousands of extreme right wing EDL members marched with pre-made placards that directly related to and sought to exploit an explosive incident that had happened only moments before.

Reconsidering his earlier 'point in time' analysis and the observation he had made and dismissed about MI5 being the common denominator in Chris' death, the EDL, and the JTAC reports suddenly made sense: A different kind of sense. Could MI5 really be engaged in fostering anti-Muslim and anti-foreign actions and sentiments? Wilson, excited and apprehensive, reconsidered his earlier conclusions. If not MI5, which was beyond even Wilson's ability to consider, then perhaps a faction or an individual within MI5 were involved.

No great intuitive leap induced Wilson to write Simon Spencer's name in large capital letters on the white board. Even less intuition led to add the words knowledge, intelligence, resources, contacts, and access. Together these words equaled the first fundamental component of a terrorist activity: capability. The second, intent, would be harder to establish.

Wilson added dotted orange lines to connect the indicators of capability to Spencer then extended a brown line away from Spencer to a blank area on the board where he used black to write 'accomplice' or 'leader'. Between Spencer and 'accomplice' or 'leader', Wilson wrote 'money'.

"Money, money money," said Wilson aloud to the white board. Money for the massive EDL media campaign and recruitment drive: money for bombs, money for logistics, money, thought Wilson to arrange for the murder of a man in Egypt with a phone number on his arm. Money thought Wilson for the EDL leader Marshall, who had almost a quarter million pounds in his backpack when he was murdered.

Wilson doubted Spencer had that kind of money and he doubted that Spencer could have used MI5 'operational dark money' without exposure; the amount was too large. With the need for money to finance the operation, Wilson circled 'accomplice' in red and linked the circle to Spencer with a dotted orange line.

'Leader'. A leader with money. To find the leader Wilson needed to know more about Spencer. Thoughts and snippets of information tumbled through Wilson's mind like a water through fingers. An eddy, created by the swirling information as its flow met an obstacle, appeared in Wilson's mind and the voice of his friend and colleague Mitch shouted words to Wilson above the noise of the rushing information.

"The name on your board, Simon Spencer, I had a beer with him and a bunch of guys once. Way back in 1990 something. He was an analyst then with the UK Foreign Office. He had some strong views about immigrants and foreigners. He is a damn good chess player too. I think he won some tournament. What's he up to now?"

A black marker scrawled Foreign Office and Chess on the board. Wilson pondered the three words for a way into Spencer's life. Accessing information about Spencer from his Foreign Office service would take time and draw attention, which at this point Wilson wanted to avoid. Chess on the other hand was a long shot.

Skeptical, Wilson entered a basic search in to Google. Chess/Oxford/Simon/Spencer/UK. The third Google result was a Wikipedia entry about the Oxford University Chess Club. Mid-way through the Wikipedia document, under other events, an entry noted that the Oxford University Chess Club won the1980-81 Oxfordshire Chess League and that Simon Spencer won the prize for best player with a remarkable 9/10.

Wilson cut and pasted 1980-81 Oxfordshire Chess League and that Simon Spencer in to the search engine. Of the five hits, the fourth provided a link to Cherwell an independent newspaper published since 1920 for students of Oxford University. Several layers down within the Cherwell, on-line since 1996 and with access to archived editions, Wilson found what he wanted. A mid-sized article reported on Spencer's 1980 Oxfordshire Chess League win and noted that his friend and fellow player Anthony Mitton-Wells, son of the Duke of Exeter, accompanied Spencer.

Wilson did not know Anthony Mitton-Wells, but the 'feeling' came on strong. Twenty minutes later, the Internet had changed Wilson's feeling into an intuitive certainty. Through the right lens, Mitton-Wells fit the role of 'leader'. Heritage, education, title, wealth, connections, club memberships, all portrayed a man with almost blue blood Englishness. Additional research yielded more connections with Simon Spencer as well as an article in one of the UK's notorious tabloid papers from the late 1990's that suggested a financial connection between Mitton-Wells and the then declining far right-wing National Front Party political party.

Convinced, Wilson added Mitton-Wells to his white board in the role of leader. Then, with reservations, but without any real option considering Priest's integrity, he called Bill Wycombe at the PCO to share his conspiracy theory.

At least to share the part about Spencer, the Mitton-Wells connection Wilson decided to hold back; it never paid to show all one's cards.

Fifty-Three

October 6 2013, London, England

STAGGERING IN DEFEAT AND DESPAIR, Mitton-Wells fled White's and the inquisitives stares of the doorman and club members who offered assistance. Through heavy wood doors, down worn concrete steps, Mitton-Wells flailed as though drunk. Curbside, engine running, a black cab waited for a fare. Habit-driven, Mitton-Wells stepped in to the cab and slumped dejected on the rear seat. His cell phone vibrated again. Simon, his co-conspirator, and life-long, had failed him and the cause. Gathering a dismissive disdain consistent with the narcissistic sociopath he was Mitton-Wells turned off the phone.

The cab door clicked to lock as Mitton-Wells commanded the driver to a destination. Without responding, the driver pulled into traffic and Mitton-Wells leaned forward to speak through the money hole in the hard clear plastic that separated driver from customer.

Instead of a 10 by 8 rectangle, a small one-inch hole, drilled through a piece of plywood positioned to cover the rectangle, filled the gap. A green garden hose, attached to the driver's side of the hole, led to a small metal cylinder attached to the passenger seat back by a wire. The cylinder, thought Mitton-Wells, looked familiar.

Confused and apprehensive, Mitton-Wells rapped on plastic divide. The cab, stopped at a traffic light, idled and a dark skinned face turned in response to the knock. A warm smile formed wrinkles in the cheeks of the driver's brown skin, contradicting purposeful eyes. The man reached in a pocket and withdrew a small cloth version of the Black Standard of ISIL: Boko Haram's flag.

Unnerved and afraid Mitton-Wells grasped handle of cab but could not open the locked door. The traffic light switched to green and the cab accelerated smoothly as Mitton-Wells slid across the seat to tug and pull at the other door. Through the side windows, Mitton-Wells watched as concrete walls rose to swallow the cab as it approached the entrance to the Blackwall Tunnel that ran east to west under London's famous Thames River.

Pressed up against the plastic Mitton-Wells shouted and pounded for the driver to stop and let him out. A hundred and fifty meters from the tunnel's entrance the driver reached back with his left hand. Mitton-Wells followed the hand and watched as fingers touched the hose and felt their way along the hose to the head of the cylinder. Transfixed and immobile, Mitton-Wells saw the hand locate a valve. The fingers turned the valve and Mitton-Wells followed the hose length back to the hole in the plastic.

Yellow-brown air, with a faint smell of mustard and garlic, leaked with a soft hiss from the passenger side of the hose and recognition exploded in Mitton-Wells' consciousness. Driven by fear, Mitton-Wells covered his mouth and nose with one hand and punched, and kicked at the plastic and the side windows with his other. Quickly exhausted and forced to breathe, Mitton-Wells inhaled. Light, dull and grey, bled in to the cab as it exited the tunnel and turned off the main road onto a side street. Mitton-Wells, aware of his fate, huddled against the back of the cab and sipped the air. Afraid of what was to come; Mitton-Wells pinched up the sleeve of his right arm and read the hands on his watch. 4:15 pm. He knew the mustard gas had begun to attack his skin and eyes, and that severe external and internal blisters would soon cover his skin, lungs and other organs. As he had planned for those who survived the bombs at Manchester United, Mitton-Wells knew the gas would not necessarily kill him but weave its insidious damage on his DNA for months and years to come.

Mitton-Wells slid from his seat to the floor and watched blurred images of London until the glow of a golden dome filled the cab's rear window. Up on one elbow Mitton-Wells peered at the huge dome as the driver's door opened, closed and locked. To the right of the dome a tall Minaret signalled Mitton-Wells' had reached his destination: The London Central Mosque, one of the largest in Europe, loomed over Mitton-Wells as his eyes watered and his skin itched.

Fifty-Four

October 6 2013, Ottawa, Canada

Smoldering images of wrecked buildings, vehicles and infrastructure choked news media outlets. Early images included deformed and charred bodies, isolated limbs and ragged pieces of clothing until black bags deprived the media of the gore factor.

Theories of an industrial accident, compounded by the possible storage of illegal chemicals, added to the refuted reports of a terrorist attack, which authorities and experts dismissed due to absurdity of the location being a credible target. Unknown sources had added speculation of the possible presence of buried WWI or WWII munitions, perhaps even mustard gas.

Wilson, fixed to the media coverage, vibrated between relief and frustration. Relived the explosions had not occurred at Manchester United's stadium, yet frustrated by the developing cover up. Wilson did not know why the explosions had occurred at the industrial park, but he suspected something had gone wrong with the terrorist plans. Official speculation about WWI or II munitions and illegal chemical storage made sense, but Wilson could not understand the addition of a throwaway line about mustard gas.

Motivated by professional curiosity and morbid interest, Wilson, like the majority of ITAC staff, had remained at ITAC to follow the event. Mitch had stopped by to report that PCO had summoned Director Priest to a meeting at the office of the NSA.

Wilson knew his call to Wycombe at PCO to explain his theory about the real terrorist target had shaken Priest. Wilson wondered what Priest would say if asked about ITAC knowledge of a possible attack on the UK instead of Germany.

Wilson did not care about Priest, Priest's career, or his own for that matter. Wilson also realized his conclusions about Manchester United being the target were likely too late to have saved anyone, even if the bombs had gone off at the stadium. That was history now. That was his bad analysis.

Wilson was concerned about the links he had uncovered about MI5, Simon Spencer, the EDL and Mitton-Wells. There had been a conspiracy to frame Muslims for the attack and Wilson was certain the conspiracy included members of the UK MI5. More personal, Wilson was convinced of a link between the bombing conspiracy and the murder of his friend Chris Thornton. Wilson decided to wait for Priest, hear him out, and then decide what he would do. Either way, Wilson was not going to let the 'spin-doctors' bury MI5's involvement and Chris' murder.

~

Contrary to his plan, Wilson left ITAC before Priest returned. A phone call had invited Wilson for coffee. The call and the caller had not surprised Wilson. Only two people in the Canadian Government knew about Wilson's Manchester United theory and only one of them knew about the MI5 connection. Priest knew about Manchester United and Wycombe from PCO knew about both. Wycombe had called him and 'suggested' coffee. Entering the Second Cup, Wilson wondered what Wycombe had to say.

Wycombe sat on a stool facing the window and a coffee sat on ledge indicating where Wilson should sit. Wilson sat and curled a hand around the paper cup.

"It's a latte with full milk, no sugar," said Wycombe "not your fancy machine coffee I grant you, but the best I could do."

A second hand circled the cup. Wilson lifted the cup and sipped foam from the small plastic opening. Through the window, under bruised clouds, humanity scurried on the darkened street in contrast to the blurry reflective image of the shop interior.

"What do you want Wycombe?"

"I've always respected your directness Craig. What I want is what's best for Canada."

Wycombe ignored Wilson's grunt.

"Silence Craig. That is what is wanted and required."

Wilson slurped coffee through the foam and said.

"If I'm right, and I know I am, MI5, the UK's own domestic intelligence and security agency, conspired to bomb their own citizens and frame Muslims. For all we know MI5 might have arranged the whole thing. For Christ's sake Wycombe, people died, someone has to pay!"

"Someone has paid Craig."

"What do you mean, who?"

"Simon Spencer is dead. Officially, his death will be an accident. Unofficially, Spencer hung himself at a former MI5 safe house North of Manchester not long after the explosions in Manchester."

Wilson processed the information and prodded Wycombe for more.

"That's convenient. Spencer was the only link to MI5. At least the only one I had discovered so far. There must be more. One cowardly exit is not enough. MI5 must have been involved. The scope and scale of the events is too large for one person."

"Yes, Craig you're right. But not in the way you imagine."

Wilson, his voice rising, faced Wycombe.

"Don't try to bullshit me. There must have been many people involved. There must be accountability. They can't be allowed to get away with it."

Unruffled by Wilson's agitation, Wycombe remained calm and explained the situation.

"More people were involved and many of them were MI5 operatives and agents. However, they did not know what they were doing. Spencer, as Assistant Deputy Director of MI5 for Domestic Extremism, had a great deal of access, autonomy and knowledge. Spencer used MI5 assets to conduct numerous activities related to blackmail, coercion, manipulation and all the other tradecraft skills that such agencies have at their disposal. The key point Craig is that the operatives and agents did not know the overall plan. Preliminary conclusions suggest Spencer expertly compartmentalized everything. Agents operated in isolation. They did not question anything. That's SOP."

Wilson thought about Mitton-Wells and his feeling that he was the moneyman behind the plot.

"Maybe Wycombe, maybe, but there has to be others. The EDL received hundreds of thousands of dollars, maybe millions. Where did that come from? What about the bombs? Who made them and paid for them? What about the reports of mustard gas? Who the hell was behind all this? I just don't believe Spencer operated alone."

Wycombe sipped coffee, pursed his lips and said.

"You are correct again. In fact UK authorities, using Spencer's phone, have already identified Spencer's accomplice."

Who?

Hesitant, Wycombe said.

"You don't need to know Craig."

Slamming his coffee on the ledge Wilson stood.

"Fine, you don't want to tell me. It will be all over the news anyway."

"Actually Craig it won't."

Wilson, not wanting to show his hand said.

"I doubt whomever it is will keep his or her mouth shut when they get to court."

"There won't be a court appearance Craig. None of this conspiracy theory or MI5 connections will make BBC news headlines. That's why I am here to request your cooperation in remaining silent and keeping your knowledge and theories secret."

"What do you mean?"

"The individual in question has already been dealt with."

"Dealt with, how?"

"The man met with a very tragic accident in the back of a London taxi less than an hour after the Manchester bombs."

"They killed him. You mean the UK authorities murdered someone?"

"No, no of course not, I mean someone has seriously injured him, but it wasn't the UK authorities. He will live for a while, in terrible pain, but he will die."

"So you're telling me that because Spencer and this other person are dead or about to die it's all over and no one needs to know what happened. That's bullshit. There must have been more people involved. Who made the bombs, who supplied the mustard gas, how did they expect to blame Muslims? How did they plan to get the bombs into Man U? Who helped them? No. I can't let this go because two people, who you or someone in the UK says were the main players, are dead."

"I have no doubt you are right Craig. In fact, the UK authorities agree with you and will conduct a thorough investigation to determine who else was involved and ensure they receive appropriate justice."

"You mean MI5 will investigate itself. What good that does? MI5 will just make certain the cover up is done properly and the truth never gets out. It's not right Wycombe."

"That may well be Craig, but you fail to grasp the bigger picture."

Wycombe placed his coffee on the ledge, spread his arms wide, and delivered what Wilson thought was a prepared speech.

"Exposing a terrorist conspiracy aimed at killing thousands of UK nationals involving a senior member of MI5 would seriously undermine public confidence in the UK security service and compromise their ability to perform. Handing real terrorist organizations information about such a plot would give them propaganda material they could exploit twist and manipulate for years. Acknowledging such a weakness in MI5s internal screening and security systems would erode the confidence of our international allies and damage intelligence and information sharing agreements that have taken decades to establish.

The big picture is what counts Craig and it is because of the big picture you can be certain any other people involved will be hunted down and dealt with. No one wants information about MI5 involvement or details of the plot to frame Muslims exposed. Do you hear what I am saying Craig. No one."

"Are you threatening me Wycombe?"

"No Craig, I'm not threatening you."

While Wilson thought, Wycombe spoke softly.

"There is one other matter Craig. Something that might compensate you for the need for secrecy."

"Don't offer me money Wycombe."

"Nothing so crass Craig. There is one loose end to this entire event that you may be interested in."

Wilson, expectant and puzzled waited.

"Chris Thornton," said Wycombe.

"You want to pay for my silence by offering me an opportunity to help catch Chris' killer. What if I say no? What if I go to the press with what I know and tell everyone about Chris and that maybe MI5 murdered one of their own to keep it all secret?"

"What would you tell the press Craig? You had a theory that turned out to be wrong. There were no explosions at Manchester United. Spencer from MI5 will have died in a tragic accident before the explosions in Manchester. There will no evidence linking him to anyone else. What can you prove about the man in the taxi in London?

Your friend Chris Thornton died a month before the explosions and I am sure that should you go to the press 'new evidence' about Thornton's 'life style' would suddenly surface. Do you really want to put his wife and family through that? All you have is speculation and you will face charges if you use classified material. Then of course, reporters would find 'evidence' of your own questionable conduct. You know how it would work Craig."

Wilson reflected on the truth of Wycombe's statements and concluding he could gain nothing by arguing asked.

"How?"

"How what?"

"How will I help catch Chris' killer?"

"I didn't say you were to catch Chris' killer, you have already done that."

Coffee slipped from Wilson's mouth as he spluttered an incredulous "What?"

"In Bedford, at Marshall's shop; Marshall was under police protection for weeks and of course that included observation. In Marshall's case that also included listening devices in his shop front."

"I don't understand, Marshall didn't tell me anything."

"You're right; Marshall didn't tell you who murdered Chris. You told yourself."

"What the hell are you talking about Wycombe?"

"Do you remember asking Marshall about anyone who wears Doc Martin boots and carries an umbrella? The description your witness Billy gave you."

"Yes, I remember, but Marshall said nothing."

"He didn't need to; only one candidate fits that description. Steve Mackenna."

"Who?"

"Mackenna was an EDL member with a long history of extreme violence and his trade mark is Doc Martin boots and an umbrella."

"Where is he? Do you have him? I don't care what you do; I want to talk to him. I want to find out who is behind Chris' death and why?"

"Mackenna is dead."

"Fuck you Wycombe. Do you expect me to believe that?"

"No. But I expect you to believe the person who killed him."

"What? Who killed Makenna?"

"His name is Aalim Hussien. He has a wife Nasreen and a young son Masud. Aalim was to be the fall guy for the attack on Manchester United. A few hours after the bombs exploded, police detained Aalim and his family at Manchester airport when they checked in for a flight to Egypt. I don't have all the facts yet, but I can give you the basics."

~

Wilson's coffee had long cooled by the time Wycombe finished Aalim's story: So had Wilson.

"My god Wycombe, Aalim is a hero. He risked his own family to save thousands."

"Yes I think everyone agrees, but let's not forget you were almost a hero as well. Your analysis was correct and…"

"Too late Wycombe, I was too late. I didn't push hard enough with Priest. Christ, if it hadn't been for Aalim, thousands would have died while I let Priest stall and do nothing."

"You did your best Craig. You got everything right. You just didn't have enough time."

After a long silence, Wilson faced Wycombe.

"It's still not good enough. I understand the 'bigger picture' as you put it and of course the need to protect Aalim and his family. That only addresses one set of problems. We have a systemic problem with our analysis capacity and a bureaucrat like Priest will not fix it. No, we, I have to expose the problems if there is to be any hope of fixing them. I can't let this go and see it happen again. If it costs me my job, even my freedom, then it is price I am willing to pay."

"There is another way Craig."

"What do you mean?"

"David Priest is no longer the Director of ITAC. The NSA met Priest earlier and suggested that he might want to retire. I'm certain Priest will have taken the NSA's suggestion."

"Well that's a start I suppose. Although the situation will only be as good as the next Director the NSA appoints."

"That's up to you Craig."

"Eh?"

"The NSA is inclined to agree with you Craig. She believes ITAC needs a more concrete and practical analytical capacity that can respond to the ever changing nature and evolution of intelligence analysis and methodology. In short, Craig she wants you as the next Director of ITAC.

Don't worry Craig, you won't be expected to run the place. You will have sole responsibility for the analytical direction and subsequent reporting for all of ITAC's intelligence functions. The day-to-day management, administration, logistics, etc. will be handled by a professional administrator who will report to you."

"I thought you didn't come here to bribe me?"

"I didn't and I haven't. You can still make your own choice about the bigger picture. I am merely presenting an alternative that would of course only be possible on the basis of complete secrecy about the circumstances related to the event in Manchester."

"Well Craig, do you want the job?"

Wilson analyzed the situation. Reaching a 'point in time' conclusion Wilson said.

"Yes."

"That's good Craig, really good."

"Hm, you might not think so when I get going…"

"Oh, it's good Craig because while you figured the involvement of Anthony Mitton-Wells. Don't bother denying it Craig. If you found Simon Spencer then you found Mitton-Wells."

"Then why didn't you tell me?"

"I wanted to see what you would hold back. Anyway, Craig what I also didn't tell you is that while you and the UK authorities got Mitton-Wells, neither of you have been able to identify a third implicated person."

"What?"

"There is evidence to suggest a third party was somehow assisting Mitton-Wells; someone in the Five Eyes community."

"My god Wycombe you can't be serious. How do you know?"

"The UK authorities analysed Mitton-Wells' cell phone. Two minutes after 3 pm, the game kick-off time and the time set for the bombs to detonate, Mitton-Wells received a six second call."

"That doesn't mean anything. It could have been anyone."

"Yes, except we have a recording of the call.

"And?"

The caller said 'you have failed us'."

"My God, Wycombe."

"There is more Craig. The call originated in Canada: In Ottawa.

That's why the NSA wants you to head ITAC."

<<<<>>>>